ALL WE CAN DO IS WAIT

a novel

Richard Lawson

RAZORBILL®

An Imprint of Penguin Random House

RAZORBILL®

An Imprint of Penguin Random House LLC

Penguin.com

RAZORBILL & colophon is a registered trademark
of Penguin Random House LLC.

First published in the United States of America by Razorbill,
an imprint of Penguin Random House LLC, 2018

Copyright © 2018 Penguin Random House LLC

LIBRARY OF CONGRESS CATALOGING-IN-PUBLICATION DATA IS AVAILABLE

ISBN: 9780448494111

Printed in the United States of America

1 3 5 7 9 10 8 6 4 2

Interior design by Corina Lupp

For Nell

Prologue

The Bridge

IT WAS CLOUDY when the bridge gave way, about a hundred cars crossing the Mystic River on the Tobin. People who saw it said it just suddenly happened, but how sudden could something like this be? It must have been years of bad maintenance, years of some important part being worn away by rust or stress or time. Really, the only sudden part was the very end.

From far away, it seemed to go softly, one section dropping down, and then another, splashing into the river, dust falling like snow after it. Up close, of course, it was a different matter: a terrible, quick quaking and then the horror of plummeting. It was hard to say who was less lucky, the ones who fell into the water or the ones who fell onto Charlestown, debris tumbling on top of them. Was it better to be swiftly crushed or to slowly drown in your car?

1

It's easy to forget, seeing a stream of cars on the highway or stuck in city traffic, that each of them represents a person, or several people, all trying to get somewhere of their own, home or to a meeting or to a funeral or starting out a trip. When the police and rescue teams arrived on the scene of the Tobin Bridge collapse, one of their first jobs was to determine how many people were involved. They needed to know who to look for, how many cars had gone in the water, how many had crashed down onto land and been buried by metal and cement. They needed some idea of the lives involved, of all the people they were searching for.

Kate Vong was driving back from a morning shift at the restaurant where she worked, tired and stressed about school, racing to make an afternoon class, worried about finding parking, thinking she'd love to quit her job and be a full-time student like so many of her friends. She was on the phone with her younger sister, who was complaining about wanting to use the car, a fight they had often. Kate honked at a car that cut her off, and was almost across the bridge when it juddered and broke. The last thing she saw before her car tipped toward the ground and everything went black was a few spatters of rain on her windshield, and she wondered if she had an umbrella.

Theo and Linda Elsing were on the other side, heading to their daughter's school for a meeting. Theo was on the phone with his office, annoyed that he'd been pulled away in the middle of the day. His wife was reading e-mails on her phone, gently putting her hand on Theo's arm and telling him to slow down, that they weren't going to be late. They'd had to take a detour because of traffic, and weren't even sup-posed to be on the bridge. Theo slowed the car and told work he had to hang up. He gave his wife an apologetic look, and then the road cracked underneath them, the car sliding to the edge and toppling over the side, Linda saying, "Theo . . ." and grabbing the dash as the car fell.

Aimee Peck was a few cars ahead, out over the water, heading north to Salem on a sort of field trip with her friends, their favorite song blaring. They were laughing about something that had happened at play rehearsal the day before, Aimee's friend Taissa driving fast, saying she couldn't *believe* the show was going up in only a few weeks. Aimee was excited about the trip, and about the play, but she was distracted. She was staring out the passenger seat window when she felt the car shake, heard Taissa screaming as she twisted the wheel and the car went flipping down toward the river. Aimee closed her eyes.

There were many others, nearly two hundred in all. A mother taking her children to her parents' place in Portland. A lawyer headed home after a frustrating morning in court. A newlywed couple on their way to the airport, suitcases in the trunk packed with warm-weather clothes. There was a woman fighting on the phone with her daughter in Arizona, a man crying about the dog he'd just put to sleep. There were three babies, there was a taxi driver taking a long fare to Revere, there were truck drivers heading north, others heading into the city. There were more.

That's what they—the paramedics, the police—found when they went looking in the rubble of the bridge, once they'd determined it was safe enough to do so. A whole panorama of lives—people trapped or injured or killed together. They dug people out as carefully and as quickly as they could. They set up triage onsite; they put the direst cases in a phalanx of ambulances, sending them off to the closest hospitals. They sent divers into the water, afraid of what they would find. The attention of the city, the great eye of Boston, swooped down and watched with grief and concern, helicopters whirring overhead, news crews trying to get the best angles.

Slowly, all across Greater Boston, the phone calls began. Loved ones getting word, rushing out of offices and homes and classrooms to make their way to the hospitals, reeling with panic and fear, tearing through a city once again roiling with tragedy. They descended on emergency rooms, pleading for answers, but instead were forced to wait for word of parents and sisters and girlfriends. To find out who, exactly, had just been lost.

Chapter One

Jason

THOUGH HIS PARENTS could be dead, lost to him forever, there was only one voice Jason wanted to hear just then. As he stood outside the hospital, the day darkening and surreal around him, Jason reached for the familiar, comforting talisman of his phone and opened a voice mail.

"Hey, you. I'm driving to Laurie's, wanted to say hi. I know you hate voice mail, so I don't know why I'm leaving you one. But—" There was a little pause, the rumble of the car going over a pothole, a faint bit of melody from whatever song had been turned down to make the call. "This is corny, but I think about you all the time. And right now is part of 'all the time,' right? So, I'm thinking about you now. Does that make sense? I hope it does. Anyway, as Carly Rae says, I really like you. O.K.? O.K. This is embarrassing. Goodbye! I like you! Goodbye."

Jason took the phone from his ear, tempted to restart the message. But then an ambulance siren blared next to him, jolting him out of the warm world of the voice mail, and Jason remembered where he was: standing outside Boston General, five P.M. on a Monday in November, waiting to find out if his parents were still alive. Jason could, he realized for maybe the hundredth time in the last hour, be an eighteen-year-old orphan. His parents were missing, or unaccounted for, like so many other people. Surveillance cameras had captured their car inching up the bridge in midday traffic, and then it disappeared with everything else when first one section, and then another one, gave way. Jason had seen the footage, somehow already leaked online, small and black-and-white and fake-looking. His sister, Alexa, had found out first, of course—and now here they were, along with all the other clueless, crying loved ones, waiting to find out just how much the world had suddenly changed.

But Jason couldn't even really begin to think about his parents, about where they might be and in what condition, if they were just bodies in bags somewhere, if they were hurt and bleeding, if they'd asked for their children. That was all too much to comprehend, to even consider processing, so Jason found himself reaching back, not dwelling on tangled metal and crumbled concrete but instead on the ski slope of a boy's nose, his gravity-defying hair, the way his mouth drooped down just a little on one side, into a pout or a sneer depending on his mood. He missed him all the time, of course, but now that ache felt profound—physical, elemental, molecular. This was what it was to love someone, Jason figured, but there was nothing to be done about that now.

Except, maybe, to listen to the voice mail one more time. He tapped the arrow button and pressed the phone in close, losing himself again in the melodic, confident voice, twinged with that bit of giddy nerves, saying to Jason what Jason wanted so much to say back. The voice mail ended and Jason began to feel himself emptying out again. The high of the message was quick, lasting only a few seconds before the realities of the day came crashing, thudding, screaming back in.

Jason looked up and saw the beginnings of chaos. People on phones—or clutching spouses or children—were hurrying toward the emergency room doors. Nurses and doctors were waiting expectantly for the first wave of ambulances from the site.

I'm too young for this, Jason thought. Most of the time, Jason tried to assert a worldliness, a cultivated jadedness. It was a pose he struck at school. (Or rather, schools—he was on his third school in as many years.) It was probably how Alexa would say he treated her. Jason suddenly remembered a brief conversation he'd had—tense and a little sad—with his mother, a year or two before.

They were in the library, what Jason's mother called the sitting room or parlor at the front of the house. Jason was sitting there in some fog, fiddling on his phone, when his mother came in, saying goodbye on her way to some event or other. She looked at him with that half-concerned, half-bored look of hers for a moment and then turned to leave, before remembering that, oh right, this was her teenage son, being left home alone, and she should probably make sure he wouldn't burn the house down.

"You'll be all right?" she asked, fastening a tasteful gold earring to an earlobe.

Jason looked up at her, gave her one of his withering looks. "Will you?"

His mother seemed a little stung, and was certainly annoyed. "You know," she said, her eyes cold and piercing, or as much as they could be from behind their usual glassiness, "you're awfully *haughty* these days, aren't you?" She said it in such a way—that word, "haughty"—that Jason thought there was something behind it; he had a suspicion about what kind of boys, what kind of young men, Jason's mother found to be "haughty."

Jason's mother was right, though. About the haughtiness, about what that haughtiness might mean. Trying so hard—for reasons he couldn't quite articulate, even to himself—to cover up a fundamental part of himself led to Jason projecting this air of betterness, of knowing, talking to his parents like they weren't his parents at all. He liked how it felt: detached and mature and, despite all his messes, self-possessed.

Still, it hurt when his mother made her subtle implications about what she might know, in such a pointed and disapproving tone. Jason remembered feeling stung there in the library, listening to his mother's heels clack out of the house. All he wanted to do was chase after her and tell her the truth and have her hug him. But he didn't, and the haughtiness, his remove, eventually returned, as it always did.

But now all this . . . he was definitely not old enough for this. He felt small and panicky, a swell of fear rising up in his chest. He'd need another. Just one more, before he collected himself and went to deal with the present. He found a favorite message, a short one. The sound of a party, one voice breaking through, drunk and happy, yelling, "You should've come with me toniiiiiight! I love you! I mean, shit, I'm drunk! I'm drunk! I gotta go!" Then a laugh, a blare of music, and the click of the phone hanging up. *I love you.* It was one of the few times someone who wasn't his parents had ever said that to him.

His parents. The hospital. Here. He had to be here. It was beginning to rain, the sidewalk pavement getting darker in splotches. Jason knew he should go inside, find Alexa, stay with her as long as it took to make sure everything was going to be O.K. It had to be O.K., didn't it? How much bad stuff could happen to one kid in a year?

His voice mail ritual done, Jason put his phone back in his pocket and ran his hands through his hair. The rain was picking up quickly, and it was cold. The clocks had been set back an hour the day before, and this was the first really dark afternoon of the year. So it was dark, and cold, and raining, and yet Jason still felt rooted in place, unable to turn around and go find his sister. Because he didn't know what was left of his life inside. Though, to be fair, he didn't know what was left of his life out there, either, standing on a street corner, listening to year-old voice mails.

"The whole summer?"

Jason was sitting at the dining room table with his parents and Alexa. May of the year before. Jason's face felt hot, indignant, like he'd just been slapped while being told he was going to jail.

"We think it would be good. For all of us," Jason's father, Theo, said, giving a hopeful little glance toward Jason's mother, Linda. "To get away, as a family. And you kids love it out there."

"For a weekend, I guess, when we were kids," Jason whined. He could hear the brattiness in his voice, could feel childish tears of frustration stinging in his eyes. Normally he would never show that much emotion in front of his parents, but right then he didn't care. They had just told Jason and his sister that they'd be spending the entire summer, the whole three-month expanse of it, at the family's vacation home in Wellfleet, on Cape Cod. Just the four of them. Together. Alone. All summer.

"You're *still* kids," Linda said, a little chiding, a little wistful.

"Alexa?" Jason turned to his sister. "Are you going to say anything about this?"

Before she even did it, Jason knew that Alexa was going to take their side. Even though Jason was sure Alexa didn't really want to go, that there was no way she was thrilled about being shipped off to the Cape with her fucked-up family until Labor Day, Jason knew his sister would say and do the right thing, the good thing, the responsible thing. Sure enough, she did.

"I don't mind," Alexa said. "I mean, I'll get a job. I dunno. It could be fun."

Fun. There were many things a summer in the beach house with Theo, Linda, Jason, and Alexa and no escape could be, but fun was not one of them. Jason rolled his eyes at his sister and turned back to his parents. They barely had any control over him then, and frankly barely monitored what he did. But this, here, this seemed serious. Like maybe Jason couldn't wriggle out of it. They were going, and there was no way they were going to leave him at home. Maybe he could run away. But where would he go?

Jason lived in the Back Bay, a beautiful old section of Boston full of well-appointed town houses, home to many of the city's wealthy and well-connected. It being Boston, the wealth there wasn't ostentatious, but it was certainly *there*. Jason and Alexa grew up in the thick of it, their mother the descendant of a long family line that could trace its roots back to the *Mayflower*. Not needing to work for money, Linda spent most of her time organizing and hosting benefits, for the Parks Department, for the Gardner Museum, for the Huntington Theatre. Everyone knew Linda Elsing. Jason's father, Theo, worked as a consultant or something, making lots of money by making even more money for other people.

So, in the material ways, Jason's life was comfortable. He'd gone to fancy private schools. Spent winter weekends at friends' parents' ski houses in Waterville Valley, or Killington, or Sunday River. Summer weekends in Wellfleet. They drove German and Swedish cars, had a show-quality yellow lab named Charles, who died when Jason was fifteen. Anyone peering in on the Elsings' lives from the outside would see something ideal—well-to-do New England WASPs at their finest, hale and smart and modest. (Jason's mother would tut-tut disapprovingly whenever she saw some gaudy new house being built out on the Cape, preferring the more reasonable Shingle-style home she'd inherited from her parents when they died.)

But, as is true of many homes, the Elsings' houses contained little darknesses, secrets and struggles that, as Jason and Alexa became teenagers, began to strain the seams of the family's bond. Linda was never without a glass of champagne at her many events, which turned into glasses of wine at home, descending her into a melancholy blurriness that Jason tried his best to avoid. As this happened, Theo grew distant, consumed by his squash games and business trips and, for a time, long walks along the Charles with Charles. Alexa, a year younger than Jason, was a tense and worried teenager. Their relationship, once close, had begun to fray, as Alexa worked herself into knots and Jason tested out his new role as the black sheep of the family.

There was also the gay thing, in the beginning a quiet, scary suspicion that Jason could mostly ignore when he first noticed it, a little bud in him not yet in bloom, but that had, over the last year or so, grown into something too big to turn away from or deny. Jason's parents weren't conservative people, not politically anyway, but theirs was not the kind of household where you talked about feelings and crushes and stuff like that, let alone sex.

Jason's friends, if you could call them friends, were all jockish, preppy boys from big houses out in the wealthy suburbs. They weren't the kind of guys who would tolerate a gay friend. Or rather, they *would* tolerate it, but nothing further. Jason had imagined one of these conversations playing out many times, always ending the same way. He and Carter Chapman, maybe, stoned or drunk in Killington, sitting on the carpeting in the downstairs rec room, snow falling outside. (There was always something a little sexy about this image, Jason had to admit to himself.) Jason, feeling warm and bold, would say, "You know, man . . . I'm gay," and Carter would bristle. Jason could see Carter thinking nervously for a second and then nodding his head, like you're supposed to do. Saying, "That's cool, that's cool," like you're supposed to. But then the night would end abruptly, and the rest of the weekend would be weird. And when they got back to Boston—Carter's parents dropping Jason off downtown before heading back to Concord—the city would feel lonely.

Maybe it would be better, Jason often wondered, to be alone. But then he'd get frightened at the thought of having no one, even people he didn't like all that much, and decide to bottle himself up, to not tell Carter or anyone, until he graduated and could leave.

Graduation would be hard-won. Jason was kicked out of his first school, a boarding school in New Hampshire he'd begged his parents to send him to when he was in eighth grade, for stealing a case of champagne from the headmaster's office—it was left over from some fundraiser, the headmaster explained—and distributing bottles to the kids in his dorm. The truth was, he'd been looking for a way to get booted, not wanting to tell his parents that he'd made a mistake, that he hated this remote school and its stuffy traditions and wanted to come home. He'd also developed a furtive, dangerous crush on his roommate, Jamie, a kid from some insanely rich family in Colombia, who had shaggy brown hair, a beautiful accent, and a habit of telling Jason long, rambling stories about his sexual exploits back home. Jason had spent the better part of that year tormented in this frigid prison, and thus the case of Moët, just waiting to be nicked, had been a perfect out.

Then there was a school in town, or in a close suburb of the city, a progressive kind of place where students called teachers by their first names and the choir sang nondenominational, or omnidenominational, songs during "the holiday season." It wasn't such a bad place, generous and laid-back as it was. But that was the year when, at fifteen, almost sixteen, Jason got into partying, first trying weed with a junior named Chance Righton in the wood-smelling basement in Chance's dad's condo in Stowe. He'd moved on quickly to drinking. It was many nights of booze from parents' liquor cabinets, maybe some pills brought back from New York City, where Chance's brother, Reardon, was a freshman at NYU. (Yes, Reardon Righton. They called him Rearin' Right In, which Jason thought sounded kinda gay but was apparently a nickname given to Reardon after an encounter with an especially adventurous girl from Choate on Nantucket two summers previous.)

Jason spent the winter of his sophomore year bumming around Chance's dad's ski condo, or up till dawn at the loft apartment on Commercial Street where a girl named Ainsley Briggs lived, essentially alone, as her parents spent most of their time at their country house. If Jason's parents noticed any change in their son, his odd hours and frequent overnights at friends' houses, they didn't say anything. Linda was often busy helping to plan First Night in the lead-up to New Year's, and then Theo went on scuba diving trips to Martinique with clients all throughout January and February. So winter was not a very scrutinized time for the Elsing children. By the time anyone but Jason and his teachers noticed his grades slipping, it was too late. He was not "asked back" for his junior year at the progressive school, leaving his parents frustrated, but not so much that they sat him down and talked to him, really asked him what was wrong.

"You've got to fix this, Jason," his mother said, frowning at him in the kitchen a week after his glorified expulsion.

"Fix what?" Jason asked, head pounding, not fully aware if it was day or night. The Elsings' kitchen was in the basement of their town house, and there was no natural light.

"This . . . whatever it is you're doing," Linda said, already sounding bored with the conversation. "We can't just keep shifting you from place to place, Jason. You need some grounding; you need roots. You need a track record, a history in one place, so you can go somewhere decent." She was referring to college, of course, though college was so far off Jason's radar that she may as well have been talking about Mars.

Jason nodded, said, "I know, I know," and that was it. Linda returned to whatever work she was doing, and Jason dragged himself up to his third-floor bedroom to go to sleep.

Mostly Jason's parents seemed annoyed that they had to find him another school on such short notice. Alexa's school was out of the question, because it was all girls. And even if Jason had been a girl, his grades were shit, so he never would have gotten in. So, the family settled on Neiman Prep, a small school in a quiet part of downtown that was known to be a dumping ground for rich burnouts, problem kids who had to bang around somewhere until they graduated and exploited legacies to go to universities they had no reason being at. If Theo and Linda were concerned or embarrassed about this downshift in Jason's education, they didn't let on, and Jason didn't much care. By that fall, he'd grown sick of Chance and Ainsley and preferred to hole up in his room, taking pills, an Adderall or a Xanax, sometimes, ones he bought from a public school kid, meeting him in the Fens about once a week.

There was something sexy about meeting a guy in the Fens, a known gay cruising and hookup spot between Fenway Park and the MFA, but Jason never dared try anything with the amateur dealer, whose name was Sean and who had the ratty, malnourished look of many a Dorchester or Charlestown boy. (He wore it well, though.) In fact, Jason didn't try anything with anyone. Potent and horny-making as getting wasted could be, it also effectively removed him from normal socializing. If he wasn't doing it alone, whoever Jason got fuzzy and fucked-up with—a few kids from Neiman, occasionally one or two of his less square, less preppy childhood friends—they all blended into the same amorphous blob, names and faces smeared together in the haze of the night.

Things continued on like that for all of Jason's junior year, his grades improving a little, but only because Neiman basically gave you a B just for showing up. Then, in May, the announcement of the Wellfleet plan. This dreadful moment at the dining room table.

"When do we leave?" Jason asked.

"June!" Theo said brightly. "Early June. Soon as you kids are done with exams."

I'm already done with exams, Jason thought, laughing a little to himself.

"There's a smile," Theo said happily. "See? We're going to love it."

Linda bobbed her head in agreement. "It's going to be a wonderful summer."

Not convinced of the plan's wonderfulness, Jason had a freak-out. He texted Sean and asked how big an order he could place before he left, but Sean replied *tapped out sorry* and then *wanna meet anyway tho? :)* and

Jason panicked and never wrote back. Jason certainly didn't know any of the townie dealers on the Cape, and so he was potentially faced with a summer without any of the downers that mellowed him out and put him to bed. It would likely just be weed and alcohol, which didn't seem like enough.

But as much as Jason was freaking out, he was, he slowly came to realize as May drew to a close, also a little relieved to be leaving Boston for a whole summer, to get away from the vacant, bottomed-out Neiman kids, to maybe reconnect with Brandon and Connor and some of his other old friends who'd drifted off into healthier, more productive lives. They were boring but safe, relatively wholesome. If nothing else, they were easier to pretend with. (Over the year, Jason had a couple of too-close-for-comfort moments with an out Neiman boy named Seth, a troubled, artsy kid from Brookline. There'd been some near-misses at parties, Seth touching Jason's arm or brushing past him in a hallway, lingering as they pressed by each other, Jason running from the electric pull of it.) He and Brandon and Connor and maybe Fitz, if he was around, would get drunk, steal the golf cart from the club, hang out at the beach. Simple stuff. There were worse ways to spend a summer. Jason at least knew that.

And so in June they went, the Elsings, packing up the new Volvo and the old Saab, Theo letting Jason drive once they got off 495, the cool, blue early June wind blowing in the windows, the deep, satisfying greens of a Massachusetts summer welcoming them as they wended up the thin arm of the Cape. As they approached the house, gravel crunching under the tires, Jason felt a sudden jolt of excitement, maybe even hope. It seemed, that early evening, the sky behind the house purple and dreamy and big, like maybe something was about to change.

"What the hell, Jason?" Alexa planted herself in the center of the ER entrance, her eyes red from crying, her chin trembling.

"Sorry, sorry, I just had to get some air."

"You've been gone for twenty minutes. I didn't know where you were. I mean, don't you care what's happening right now? Do you even *know* what's happening right now?"

"Do you?"

"I—no. I mean, yes, I do. They said the first people from the accident are going to be here soon and that we just have to wait. Someone will tell us if they, if Mom and Dad, are brought in. But there's, like, a million other people waiting in there. I don't know how they're going to find us."

"Mom and Dad?"

"No, the lady, the hospital lady who will tell us if they're here."

"Oh. Well. I mean . . . we'll just . . . be there, right? So she'll find us."

"It would really help if we're both in there, just in case."

Jason took her meaning. "O.K. I won't leave again, I promise."

They walked toward the waiting room, which was full of harried, frenzied people, most of them crowded around the reception desk, pleading with a tired-looking nurse or secretary or someone, who threw up her hands and said, "I can only help one person at a time. Please let me do that."

"Are they all waiting on people from the bridge?" Jason asked, knowing it was a dumb question as soon as he asked it, but finding it hard to comprehend how all these people—there had to be fifty of them, maybe more—knew someone who'd happened to be crossing the Tobin Bridge, in the middle of the day on a Monday, at the exact moment of the collapse.

Alexa nodded, and then seemed to get annoyed. "It's really bad, Jason. Like, really bad. I don't know if . . . They said a lot of people drowned."

"Who said?"

"Twitter."

Jason rolled his eyes. There it was. *Haughtiness.* "No one on Twitter knows what they're talking about. Remember the Marathon? They were saying, like, a hundred people had died at first, and it was really like two."

"It was three."

"Whatever. It wasn't a hundred. It can't be that bad. People were in cars. This is just . . . People are just panicking."

"Aren't you panicking? Are you even worried about them?"

"Of course I am, Alexa. I just . . . We don't know anything, do we? So let's just assume everything's O.K. Because it probably is."

Alexa stared at him in disbelief and, then, disgust. "Are you high right now?"

"What?"

"Are you high?"

Jason ground his teeth, looked down at the floor. He wasn't. He hadn't taken anything that day, he was pretty sure. But he still felt high. Maybe from the night before. Which scared him, and made him feel like a loser. Haughtiness, gone. "No. I'm not high, Alexa."

"Because 'let's just assume everything's O.K.' when there's been a huge accident involving *our parents* and we have no idea what's going on sounds like high talk to me."

"Jesus, Alexa, I'm not high. But I am sick of you bitching at me. I'm here. I'm staying. I'm sorry I went outside. I'll find the lady and ask her if she knows anything, O.K.? What does she look like?"

"She's got blond hair."

"That's really helpful, Alexa, thanks."

Alexa looked like she'd been slapped. "Fuck you, Jason. Honestly, fuck you." She turned from him and stalked off into the crowd of people, disappearing around a corner by some chairs. Jason stood there, feeling dumb, his face hot from something like shame. His hand itched for his phone.

He wanted to hear his voice again. He wanted his voice to take him back, to last summer, to all that possibility. When his parents, his imperfect but good parents, were intact, accounted for. When he was just a seventeen-year-old fuckup, not whatever he was now. An orphan, maybe. Whose sister hated him. He knew that all he had to do was talk to Alexa, to tell her why things had been so tense and sad between them for the past year, why he'd gone down another rabbit hole after a short summer when things had cleared up, when he was bright and alert again. But he couldn't find the words. Not then, not ever.

Not since Labor Day a year ago. Jason closed his eyes and thought of the boy in the voice mail. The boy who loved him, and had first said so while calling from a party in Provincetown late one summer night. In the magical, lost time before everything in the world seemed to crumble and fall apart.

Chapter Two

Skyler

THE BUS FELT impossible. Though she took a city bus to school every day, and home from school too, in that moment, as Skyler struggled to hold her bag while cradling her phone with her chin and trying to get her CharlieCard out of her wallet, for a second all she could focus on was how impossible it was to just get on this bus so she could get to where she needed to be.

Where she needed to be. After miraculously not dropping anything, and finding a seat toward the front of the bus, the horrifying fact of where Skyler was going rushed back in like cold into a room. The phone, still cradled on her shoulder, was making a weird purring, chirping sound, telling her that the call she was trying to make wasn't going to go through. Or no one was answering. What time was it there, anyway? She was trying to call her grandparents in Phnom Penh, where they were spending a month. But as she did the math she realized that it was four in the morning in Cambodia, and though her grandparents were light sleepers, they would, on principle, refuse to answer the phone that early. Because they didn't like to be bothered, but also, Skyler suspected, because they knew, more than most people, how bad the news on the other end of the line could be.

As the bus lurched down Summer Street, Skyler listened to the *brrrp-brrrp, brrrp brrrp* a few more times before hanging up and throwing the phone in her bag. She sighed, tried to calm herself down, leaning her head back against the cool glass of the bus window and closing her eyes. What good would calling her grandparents really have done, anyway? They were thousands of miles away and realistically couldn't just up and rush back. They were old and slow, and changing their flight would cost too much money. They weren't due home for weeks. Skyler was alone. She knew that.

Skyler had been on the phone with her sister, Kate, when everything went wrong. They were talking—well, they were arguing, really, about the stupid car and who was going to use it on Saturday—when Kate said, "Wait, something's happening. Oh my God, I have to—" There was a clattering, an awful crunching sound, and then the phone went dead. Then there were Skyler's few seconds of blind panic, then the frantic calling of 911, then the waiting, and now this, heading on a bus to the hospital to wait some more. To find out if her sister was crushed inside that stupid car on her way home from a job she hated. Or if she'd drowned. Or if she was alive and things would go back to being . . . if not perfect, at least not this.

Traffic was bad, a combination of rush hour and the broader madness of the accident tangling up the city. Horns were blaring, and Skyler thought about her grandparents, about the streets of Phnom Penh, choked with mopeds and scooters and tuk-tuks. She'd hated visiting there as a kid, the place her grandparents had fled years before so strange and foreign and inhospitable, too noisy and bright, nothing like their quiet enough street in plain old Jamaica Plain, where nothing much ever seemed to happen.

Skyler wished her grandparents were back, but she also knew that she'd hate to see them distraught, dealing with all this horror, real and potential. What if what Skyler was convinced she knew was actually true? What if Kate was dead, swallowed up by a random accident—it *was* an accident, wasn't it? Do terrorists blow up bridges?—and that was it? What the hell was Skyler going to do? The only person in the world who she could really *talk* to, who understood what Skyler had been through in the past two years, was her sister, her calm and resourceful and usually reasonable sister. It didn't make any sense that this could happen to Kate. This kind of calamity was supposed to befall Skyler—she was the messy one, the fragile one, the one who always needed scooping up after some disaster. Kate, solid, good, boring Kate, she was the rock. Kate was the one who would inevitably hold their small family together after their grandparents were gone. But now it was entirely possible that she had been ripped out of the world and that Skyler would have to sort out her life on her own.

Which was not the point, of course. The point was Kate. The point was whether or not she was O.K. It didn't matter then, maybe it wouldn't ever, if Skyler could manage her life on her own. What a selfish thing to even think. Skyler chided herself and bit a nail, the bus lurching as it stopped and started, stopped and started. She felt nauseated. She hadn't eaten much of anything that day, really, a yogurt before school and then nothing else. Not because she was too busy—Skyler was not exactly a model student—but because she'd been feeling unsettled all day, since the night before, when she'd gotten a text message from a number she didn't know. All it said was *Hey*, but it filled her with dread, knowing that it was probably him.

She'd gone to Kate's room to tell her about it, but she was studying and had just said, "Ignore it," which Skyler knew she wouldn't be able to do. And Kate should have known that too. Skyler stood in Kate's doorway, waiting for more advice, until Kate sighed and turned to her sister, sitting up on her bed. "Just do your thing. Don't respond, delete the message, and do your breathing thing. It's fine. You don't have to respond to a text message, no matter who it's from."

Skyler nodded. "I know, I know. Yeah. You're right. It's just . . . What if it *is* him?"

Kate sighed again. She looked tired. She was a full-time student at Lesley and working a job way across the city. She barely had any time to sleep, let alone counsel her little sister every time she had an anxiety attack. Or whatever this was. Things had been better for a little while at that point, but still, standing there in Kate's doorway, Skyler wanted more from her sister, some reassurance, some magic cure-all.

Kate probably sensed that. "Skyler. You're O.K. It's over. It is. I promise," she had said, before turning back to her textbook. Skyler wandered back to her room, the cramped little alcove in the corner of the second floor, clothes spilling off her raised bed, papers and blue books and other school ephemera littering nearly every surface. She tried her breathing thing, closing her eyes and inhaling deeply as she thought to herself, over and over again, *Waves on the ocean, waves on the ocean. It's just waves on the ocean.*

It was a little mantra Skyler had learned to repeat to herself when she was younger and scared of flying. They took a long flight to Cambodia every June when school got out, and Skyler had hated the turbulence as the plane rumbled along, flying north, over the Pole, down into Asia. Kate, always seeming so serene and practical on those endless flights, had told her that the bumps might feel big, but they were actually pretty small. "Think about being on a boat. You bounce a little, but not much. It's just little waves. That's all it is." And it helped. Like pretty much everything Kate said to her, did for her, this had calmed Skyler down.

Now, as the bus approached Fort Point Channel, another bridge looming, Skyler felt tetherless. She tried to focus on what she knew. The news had told her what? Cars that weren't over the water yet had fallen into Charlestown. Cars that were had landed in the Mystic. Some people had managed to get out of their cars before they fell, but they still may not have made it off the bridge. The direction Kate was coming from, chances were she'd gone into the water, that she hadn't made it to the Charlestown side yet. Skyler pictured the car, that familiar old Camry, bubbling and sinking.

Waves on the river.

Kate was a strong swimmer. Wasn't she? Skyler couldn't remember the last time they'd gone swimming. Maybe Buzzards Bay the Fourth of July before last. Maybe in their cousin George's pool, in Philadelphia.

But this water was cold. It was November, and dark. It had begun to rain. The bus's windshield wipers made low, mournful squeaks as they worked, and the night suddenly felt unbeatable, like there was no way anything good could come out of it, like the only thing waiting for Skyler when she got to the hospital was very bad news. She began to feel that familiar panic and worry rise up in her, curdling in her stomach and then pressing on her chest. She reached for her phone in her bag. It was now . . . 4:22 in the morning in Phnom Penh. Skyler's thumb hovered over the green "Call" button, but a new feeling of resolve stopped her. If she was going to be alone now, if she was going to have to help herself from here on out, this is where it would start.

She would ride the bus until the last stop, then walk the remaining few blocks to the hospital, in the rain if need be. She would wait as long as she needed to, she would ask as many questions as she could. She would keep herself composed, she would not cry or break down or worse. She would not text the mysterious number back, both fearing and sickly hoping that it was him. She would not try to call her mother, wherever she was. She would not bother her old, tired, sweet, and stern grandparents, who'd already seen a lifetime of death and horror before Skyler had even been born. She would handle this herself, whatever this was.

The bus hissed to a stop, and Skyler gathered her things. She stepped out into the cool rain falling on Cambridge Street in a thin veil. There was the world again, immediate and loud, car tires sloshing through water, sirens wailing both toward and away from her. Boston was a jumble, dark and disorienting, and Skyler felt herself standing very much in the middle of it. Not the center of it, not the focus of all this chaos, but caught in its tightest, fastest winds, circling around her, whipping past and jostling her like turbulence. She steadied herself, took a few deep breaths, and then turned toward the hospital, running down Cambridge Street until she saw the fluorescent glow of the emergency room sign cutting through the dark and rain.

As expected, the scene at the hospital was overwhelming. People were pushing and yelling, a crowd of them by the reception desk. Skyler immediately felt helpless. How was she ever going to get past all these people to ask whomever she needed to ask about her sister? She considered turning and leaving—flight, ironically, coming so much more easily to her than fight. But she closed her eyes and planted her feet. *Waves waves waves waves.* She felt her panic dip down a little, relieving the pressure in her chest, her head not tingling quite so much. When she opened her eyes she felt surprisingly clear, as if everything had snapped into focus. She knew she had to take advantage of this likely brief moment, before her brain reminded her of the dire gravity of the situation she was in and she was once again knocked off course.

She shouldered her bag and walked toward the crowd of people, a mix of ages and faces, some angry, some teary, others ghost-white with worry. As she got closer, she was able to plot a course through the crowd. She was small and slight, only about five-foot-three and skinny, so she could slip between people without much trouble. She scooted past a few people, saying a quiet "Excuse me," a turn here and a pivot there, and then she was through, past the scrum to where it was, somehow, quieter, like she'd passed through the wall of a hurricane and now here was the eye. Eerie and ominous and tingling with dread, but still.

Skyler looked around and saw an official-looking woman, tall and pale, talking in hushed, serious tones to a few people by some swinging doors. There were two women with babies, both miraculously asleep for the moment. Not many people were sitting, but Skyler saw a girl about her age, looking regal and sad. Something about the way the girl was dressed, the way her blond hair was somehow still shiny even in this drab lighting, in this terrible place, made Skyler think that she was rich, that she probably lived in some big house somewhere and was waiting to hear if her butler had died or something.

Skyler realized she was staring—something about seeing someone her age, also alone, in this very grown-up and real-life place was transfixing—and turned away, back toward the tall, pale woman. She seemed to be finishing her conversation with the couple, putting a bony hand lightly on the man's shoulder, so Skyler quickly strode up to her, not wanting to lose her chance to ask the official-looking woman what she knew.

"Excuse me?" Skyler croaked, barely any sound coming out. She suddenly realized she hadn't said anything out loud in probably two hours. She cleared her throat, thought about grabbing the woman's sleeve but didn't want to seem like a child. "Excuse me?" she said, louder this time, more confident.

The woman turned and Skyler caught a glimpse of her nametag. It said "Mary Oakes," and then "Patient Relations." The woman looked down at Skyler, regarding her with a cold curiosity.

"Where are your parents?"

Skyler was thrown. "Uh. I don't know."

"Were they in the accident?"

"What? No. My sister. My sister was."

"I'm sorry to hear that."

"Kate Vong? Do you know anything about her? Do you know if they're bringing her here?"

The woman's face softened a little. But just a little. "The patients most in need of care will be brought here, but extraction at the scene is taking longer than anticipated. It's a safety concern. I can only tell you what I've told everyone else: You are very likely in the right place, there is a high probability that your sister will be brought here, but I cannot guarantee anything. Of course, we will update all of you as often as we are able."

Skyler felt stuck, and oddly disappointed. She didn't know anything now that she hadn't an hour ago. "So I should just wait?"

"I'm afraid so," Mary Oakes said, turning to talk to the other people who were queuing up to ask her the same question. "If you would all just please wait as calmly as possible, we will know more soon."

Skyler stood still, not sure what to do now. She looked up at the wall clock: 4:52 in the morning in Phnom Penh. Her grandmother would be awake in an hour or so. She always woke up early and went to bed late. She had trouble sleeping, had had trouble sleeping since she left Cambodia in the 1970s. "I don't know why you go back there, *how* you can go back there," Skyler's mother had once said to her grandmother. "After everything they did to you." Skyler's grandmother had just pursed her lips and stayed silent, as she often did when her daughter, Leap— called Lucy in America—started in on her.

Skyler watched as Mary Oakes surveyed the room and then, with a prim little nod, turned and walked through the swinging doors, disappearing into some inner sanctum of the hospital, which was presumably being prepared for the first rush of victims. Skyler felt the flutter of helplessness rise in her again. Was knowing nothing better than knowing the worst? She wasn't sure.

She reached for her phone and swiped it open. Her heart sank when she saw that the mysterious number, with an 857 area code, had texted her again. *You O.K.?* For a crazy second Skyler thought maybe it was Kate, trying to reach her somehow, with someone else's phone. Impulsively, Skyler began to type back but then stopped herself. Why wouldn't Kate just call? She was one of the few people Skyler knew who actually remembered people's phone numbers.

And why would she be asking Skyler if she was O.K., when it was Kate who'd been in the accident? Skyler's grandfather—who was really her step-grandfather, her actual grandfather having gone missing before the family fled Cambodia—had once told her a story about the ghosts of people tortured and killed by the Khmer Rouge. They haunted an infamous prison, and even years later, guards would set food out for these ghosts, thinking they must be hungry. Skyler found herself wondering, insanely, if maybe Kate was already a ghost and was trying to contact her through the phone.

Which was dumb. The number had texted her last night, before any of this had happened. It was him. She knew it was. The broken, shameful part of herself wanted desperately to write back, to tell him that no, she was not O.K., that her sister was probably dead, that despite everything, she wanted to see him, to have him hold her and tell her that she was going to be fine. But knowing how angry her sister would be if she did that, Skyler didn't. She put her phone away, hoping he hadn't seen the little bubbles that indicated someone typing on the other end.

Her phone buzzed again, and Skyler thought about the turbulence on those plane rides to Cambodia, the little dips and sudden jolts, the steady drone of the engines sometimes interrupted by piercing whines or roars. "The plane's just readjusting," Kate would say when Skyler tensed in her seat. "That's all that's happening. Nothing's wrong, nothing's wrong."

Skyler would nod and try to believe what Kate was telling her. But then the plane would bump again and she would instinctively reach for her sister's hand, knowing then, at least, that she still had that to hold on to.

Chapter Three

Alexa

LONELY IN A *crowded room*. That phrase—something the school counselor, Ms. Reeve, had said a few times during their meetings over the last year—was running through Alexa's head as she stood in the ER waiting area, huddles of distraught people talking nervously, frantically typing on phones, pacing back and forth as much as they could in the cramped, fluorescent-lit room. Alexa was alone, and she felt it, a familiar empty feeling, a confusion and a resignation. Jason would be no help, it seemed. Which shouldn't have been a surprise, not when he'd been so distant, so caught up in his own moodiness, for over a year.

Wasn't it supposed to be the older sibling who took care of things? Wasn't Alexa, the younger sister, the one who should be freaking out and bratty, not left to handle all the heavy, practical worry? This seemed unfair. Which Alexa knew was childish, to think that anything on a day like this should have any sense of fairness about it, but there she was, standing by herself in a mass of strangers, wishing that just this once, things would work the way they were supposed to.

Looking around, Alexa assessed that she was probably the youngest person in the waiting room, save for two babies who were being clutched close by their wild-eyed mothers, maybe waiting on news of husbands or wives or, Alexa realized with a jolt of dread, maybe other children. Noise seemed to come in waves, no phones at the reception desk ringing and then, all of a sudden, all of them going off at once. That's when the talk in the room would swell back up to a din and the crowd would start moving its way toward the desk and the doors to the outside, looking to see if someone was being brought in from the scene of the accident. But then nothing would change.

Alexa got close enough to a blond woman to see that she was wearing a nametag. "Mary Oakes," it read. And beneath that, "Patient Relations." So she wasn't a doctor, just some sort of spokeswoman or something. Still, when Alexa looked at her sharp nose and little line of a mouth, it looked like she knew more than she was letting on, like there was a crucial bit of information she was calculatingly keeping from all these panicked people.

Alexa stood near Mary Oakes, tall and pale with hair the color of the white corn you could buy at farm stands on the Cape in the summer, as a timid, tired-looking woman walked away from Mary and toward a man who had just arrived. They were older than Alexa's parents, the parents of someone in college, or grad school, maybe. The man looked panicked as he asked his wife what was happening.

"He was on the bridge," she told him. "He was driving on the bridge."

"Where?" the man asked.

"On the bridge, the Tobin Bridge, when—" the woman stammered.

"I meant on what side, Eveyln. Northbound? Southbound?"

The woman looked annoyed suddenly, less tired from grief and more from years of frustration, maybe. "North, Howard. He was driving to see you . . ."

"I didn't know," the man, Howard, said quietly.

"Yeah, well . . ." Evelyn trailed off.

"Is north good?" the man asked after a small, freighted pause.

"I don't know! I don't know!" the woman yelped, bursting into tears. Her husband—or maybe ex-husband, from the sound of it—awkwardly put his arms around her.

The couple seemed so tiny and scared in the middle of the hospital's frenzy. Alexa pulled herself away, feeling nosy and intrusive.

It went on like this. Mary Oakes would disappear for a minute or two behind some swinging doors but then return, standing on the edge of the room with her arms crossed, making herself available for questions but never really answering anything. Eventually the room would ebb back into nervous quiet, which made Alexa feel restless and even more alone, like a little girl in a place full of grown-ups where she wasn't supposed to be. She found a seat—most people seemed too anxious to sit down—and tried to calm herself. She wanted Jason there with her, but also suspected that he'd just frustrate her if he was, as he had been doing pretty steadily since the summer before.

Like her brother, Alexa was wary of her parents' plan for a family bonding summer. But the truth was that a summer in Boston didn't really seem much better. Alexa had a few friends, girls she ate lunch with and would occasionally see on the weekends, but they always seemed like best friends with each other and not with her. She did a number of extracurriculars—she ran on the cross-country team in the fall, worked as the copy editor for the school paper, painted scenery for the theater club's productions—but she never found the community that others seemed to. A lot of what she did was lonely by design, solitary work that Alexa could focus on without the interference—welcome or otherwise—of other people.

"Why do you think that is?" Ms. Reeve, the school counselor, had asked Alexa once during one of their regular meetings. "That you seem to gravitate toward things where you're alone?"

Alexa hadn't really thought about it before. "I don't know. I guess . . . I guess it's just easier to do what I need to do when I'm the only person I need to rely on."

"But don't you think you might be able to do more things, or at least different things, if you teamed up with other kids?"

"Probably. But it just always seems easier not to."

"Are you lonely, Alexa?" Ms. Reeve asked, sitting forward in her chair, a concerned, imperious look on her face.

Alexa shifted awkwardly. Was she lonely? She hadn't thought of herself that way, but maybe it was true. Sitting there in Ms. Reeve's tiny office—filled with books and stacks of papers, a miniature jungle of potted plants on the windowsill giving the room an earthy, slightly rotting smell—Alexa thought back on all the dances and parties she'd skipped or didn't even know about in the first place. She thought about Simon, a shy and nerdy boy from Northrup's brother school who'd gently pursued her on Facebook after they met at a track meet the previous fall. She'd basically ignored his advances, if you could even call a few messages like "Hey" and "Up to anything this wknd?" advances. Why had she done that? Simon was cute enough, nice enough. But it had just seemed so complicated, when staying inside herself, streamlined and unbothered, was easier, involved so much less risk.

"I don't know" was all Alexa could say in response to Ms. Reeve that day, but the question stayed with her, made Alexa look at her life in a new and frankly depressing way. So when her parents announced this insane plan, this very un-Elsing idea of stillness and togetherness, something about it excited Alexa. It presented a radical change, something that Alexa thought she could maybe take advantage of, to become someone else. Or at least some different, more outgoing, less intense version of herself.

The Grey's idea—that she could get a job at the miniature golf course/snack bar/ice cream shop/arcade in Eastham that became the focal point of her summer, and meet kids her age—came to her in a flash. She'd always liked going there as a kid, and remembered there being a bunch of cool-seeming teenagers who worked there, scooping ice cream and working the mini-golf and various other jobs that had seemed exotic and mature to child Alexa. So she called them up, talked to a manager named Nate, and she basically got the job on the spot.

"It's not glamorous," Nate said on the phone. "And it can be hard work. But we have fun. I think you're my last hire of the season, so you called just in time."

Serving ice cream wasn't all that much fun, but everything around it was. After a few nervous days of training, she was welcomed as a full-time employee, ready to begin her summer, her *entire* summer, as one of the crew.

It was a job her parents didn't understand. "We give you plenty of money," her mother had said when Alexa told her about the job. They did give her enough, more than enough, but it wasn't about money. Alexa just wanted an excuse to get out of her head, doing something few of the other girls at school ever did. Mostly she wanted to get to know some local kids, many of whom had maybe never heard of Grinnell or Middlebury or the Sorbonne, or wherever girls from her school were already, not even in their junior year yet, talking about applying to. (Really, they talked about these schools as if they'd already been accepted, which many of them essentially had been.)

On Alexa's first day of training she met Laurie Gomes, whose parents, Portuguese immigrants, lived all the way in Fall River. Laurie was asked, or, really, had volunteered, to give Alexa a tour of the place, pointing out, *Clueless* or *Mean Girls*–style, who everyone was, starting with herself.

"I have a cousin who works at one of the resorts all summer," Laurie explained. "So we rented a place together. Just us. It's amazing." Laurie was seventeen, Jason's age, and wore lots of bracelets and sometimes smoked Parliament Lights in the little outside area behind the kitchen, near the tubs of fryer grease. (This seemed dangerous, and Boston Alexa would definitely have said something. But Cape Alexa just went with the flow.)

Laurie, who had a sharp accent to complement a pleasingly raspy voice, led Alexa back to a hot, barely air-conditioned break room located just past the bathrooms. She said, "Knock knock!" and then walked in, Alexa timidly following her into the stuffy room. Laurie pointed at a boy and a girl, the only people in there at the moment. They looked oddly similar, the same dirty-blond hair, the same slightly flushed cheeks and upturned noses.

"That's Davey and Courtney Price—say hi, Davey!" Laurie said. Davey looked up and gave a little wave, while Courtney remained glued to her phone. "They're twins, from Yarmouth. Davey's sweet," Laurie explained with a little conspiratorial smile. "He's usually on mini-golf duty, because he's good with the little kids."

Which was true. Throughout the summer, Davey proved gentle with the younger customers. But, doofy and affable as he often was, he was also not afraid to act like a bouncer with the drunk teenagers who sometimes showed up.

"Davey's gonna be in the navy," Laurie told Alexa, sounding maybe a little sad about it. "He already joined up. 'Davey in the navy, Davey in the navy,'" Laurie sing-songed in his direction, then turned to Alexa. "Like in that song?"

Davey said, "You know it!" and flexed his biceps. This was all part of an elaborate flirting ritual between the two of them that Alexa would soon grow to know well. (A year later, Alexa sometimes found herself thinking about Davey, about how he was long gone by now, out on a boat in the middle of some faraway ocean somewhere. It made her sad. And a little jealous.)

Courtney, quite unlike her brother, seemed cool and just a tad scary, sitting there flicking around on her phone, barely paying attention to the new employee being introduced to everyone.

"Hi, Courtney," Laurie said, a little note of menace in her voice, a challenge, a needling.

Courtney looked up, gave a big fake smile. "Hiiiii, Laurie. I like your earrings," she said, pointing to the big silver hoops dangling from Laurie's ears. Alexa couldn't tell if the compliment was fake or genuine. It was something she'd always wonder about Courtney and Laurie's relationship, whether they were friends or frenemies or what.

"Thaaaaanks, Court," Laurie said back in a sickly sweet voice. (Clearly this was a routine they did.) "They're from Claire's." Both girls laughed. "Anyway," Laurie said, "this is Alexa. She's new." She lowered her voice and leaned in toward Courtney, as if telling a secret about Alexa, even though Alexa was standing right there. "Her parents have a house in Wellfleet."

Courtney raised her eyebrows and gave Alexa a look up and down. "Fancy. Well, welcome to hell." She raised her phone to Alexa as if to toast, while Davey chimed in, "Yeah, welcome!"

As Alexa got to know Courtney, she saw that she had an edge about her that was probably the result of something bad in her past—there were rumors about a father in prison for murder—but which also gave her an aura of maturity that all the other Grey's kids gravitated toward. She was the group's de facto ringleader, her cute, slightly oafish brother her genial henchman. Courtney talked about moving to New York City to become a fashion designer, but the last Alexa had looked on Facebook, Courtney was waiting tables at one of the old seafood restaurants in Newport, Rhode Island. It was closer to New York than Eastham was, at least.

And then there was Kyle, sweet and fey, who would become Alexa's closest friend that summer, and probably the best friend she'd had since she was a little kid.

The first time she met Kyle, Alexa wasn't quite sure what to make of him. It was her second day of training—he'd been off the day she met most of the other employees. Alexa was at the counter, stabbing at the cash register with a finger, trying to make it do what she wanted it to do, practicing before the midday rush. Courtney was supposed to be training Alexa, but she'd wandered off to go flirt with some customer, an older guy, in college maybe, in salmon-colored shorts with sunglasses hanging around his neck on Croakies. Alexa was feeling desperate and frustrated, like she was already screwing up, when she heard a voice behind her.

"You have to press 'pound six' then 'enter.'"

"Huh?" Alexa said, turning around and seeing Kyle. He had an immediate softness about him, and she felt instantly relaxed in his presence.

She did what he said, and with a ring, the cash register drawer opened.

"Awesome, thank you. I'm new here."

Kyle laughed. "Yeah, I know. Laurie told me about you. You're Alexa, right?"

Alexa nodded, put out her hand and shook his.

Kyle looked up at the clock by the door. "Hey, we should take our break before it gets crazy in here. Courtney can watch the register. Court!" he called out. Courtney turned from flirting with the guy wearing Chubbies, and her face brightened when she saw Kyle. (He had that effect, Alexa would come to learn.) "Hey, baby," she cooed, striding over to give him a hug, suddenly seeming warm and kind.

"Have you met Alexa?" she said, again like Alexa wasn't even there.

"Yeah, I just showed her how to steal money from the cash register."

"Fabulous," Courtney said. "Oh my God, did you see who I was talking to?" She pointed to the preppy bro, now looking a little annoyed to be kept waiting.

Kyle's eyes widened. "Oh my God, is that . . ."

Courtney let out a loud laugh, throwing her head back and clapping once. "*Yes!* Can you believe it? He got kinda fat?"

Kyle looked over at the guy, thin tank top hanging over somewhat bloated muscles, skin deeply tanned already, from lacrosse or sailing or something. "I dunno, he still looks pretty good to me."

Courtney rolled her eyes. "You're so gross." She turned to Alexa. "He's so gross."

"We're gonna go on break," Kyle said. "I'm training her for the rest of the day, Nate said."

Courtney shrugged her shoulders. "Cool. Sounds good."

Alexa turned and headed for the break room, but Kyle motioned to her to follow him. "The break room's miserable; let's sit outside." He poured himself an iced tea from the huge dispenser next to the even bigger tub of iced coffee, and then they went out the back door by the kitchen, out to a ratty picnic table. Kyle sat down, draped himself over the table, took a long, contemplative sip of his iced tea. An eyebrow raised above his sunglasses. "So you're from Boston?"

Alexa sat down across from him. "Um, yeah. Yeah."

"What part?"

"Uh, the Back Bay?" Alexa said, a little sheepishly, knowing that "Back Bay" is near-universal Massachusetts code for "rich."

Kyle didn't seem fazed, though. Maybe he already knew—Laurie seemed like the kind of person who would tell everyone everything the minute she could—or maybe he didn't care. "Nice" was all he said.

"Where are you from?"

He smiled ruefully, looked down at the table. "Technically, here. Or, I mean, not *here* here, but near here, I guess. My mom lives in Bourne. By the bridge. So I'm from there. Like, during the winter and stuff. But

I'm out here all summer. I stay with Davey and Courtney sometimes. Or Laurie lets me sleep on her couch. It's cool. It works out most of the time."

Alexa suddenly found herself blurting out, "You're welcome to stay with us, we have extra bedrooms," before realizing how weird and bad that sounded. Not only a stranger inviting some boy to stay at her house five minutes after meeting him, but bragging about how many bedrooms her parents' house had.

But again, Kyle didn't seem bothered by it. He smiled and said, "Sounds good. Yeah, I mean, that would be amazing, thank you." He smiled again, and Alexa felt an ease wash over her. Who was this magical person?

"Courtney's kind of intense, huh?" she said, trusting that Kyle wouldn't report this back to Courtney.

Kyle laughed, nodded his head. "Yeah. She's cool, though. She's just a big-town bitch in a small town. She'll be fine once she gets to New York. That's more her speed or whatever. I think we're gonna move there together, actually. Or, well, I mean, I'm hoping to."

Alexa felt immediately envious of Courtney and her exciting new life in New York with Kyle. "That's awesome. When are you guys moving?"

Kyle shrugged. "I don't know. Soon, I hope. When I turn eighteen. I mean, it's not like my mom would call the police if I left now or whatever, but you know. It's just easier to wait until then. Plus we gotta work here and save some money, right?" He did a little *ta-da* with his hands, as if to gesture toward the splendor of the place. It was funny to see

Courtney and Kyle so down, jokingly or not, on a job that Alexa was so happy to have.

And that had been the start of it. Not that night, or the night after, but pretty soon Kyle began spending many nights at Alexa's house. There were two guest bedrooms that no one was using, and when they eventually met him, Theo and Linda seemed to find Kyle charming, or at least a diverting novelty. Even Jason, who was always so weird and aloof with kids he didn't know, quickly warmed to Kyle, Alexa and the two boys winding up spending many nights, after Theo and Linda had gone to bed, out on the porch, talking and laughing and sneaking Sam Summers.

As Alexa grew closer to Kyle, she told him things she hadn't told anyone else. About her brother's troubles, about her social stresses, about how she sometimes felt like an accessory in her parents' lives, rather than their daughter. In turn, he told her about his nervous, grand hopes for the future, about the troubled home life he longed to put in the rearview.

Kyle began to seem less magic, but not less good. He was caring and smart. Sure, he was a little moody and occasionally flaky, but other than that he seemed reliable, like Alexa could depend on him like she couldn't depend on her parents or her brother or, really, anyone at school. That was important, wasn't it? To find someone solid.

Plus, they had fun together. A week or two after their first meeting, the two happened to be in the break room together when Laurie's charging phone buzzed, and there, right on the break room table for all to see, was a particularly graphic sext from Davey—had he and Laurie already started hooking up by then? Alexa wasn't sure.

Kyle's eyes grew wide and he looked at Alexa, his mouth agape in delighted shock. Alexa had seen a penis before, of course, but not the penis of a guy she knew.

"Oh my God," she murmured.

Kyle nodded. "I know. I had no idea he had it in him. Or, I mean, *on* him."

Which was just about the funniest thing Alexa had ever heard. She and Kyle laughed about that on occasion for the rest of the summer.

They laughed a lot, and made fun of basically everything. But Alexa also felt safe being entirely earnest around Kyle. So much so that one quiet Tuesday night, Alexa found herself telling Kyle something she hadn't told anyone else.

"I don't think I want to go to college."

Kyle stopped counting the money in the register and turned to her. "Really?"

Alexa shrugged, sighed. "Yeah. I mean, at least not right away. I want some time to, like, figure life out before I just go off and do the next thing that's, like, expected of me. You know?"

"I guess," Kyle said, giving her a smile. "But no one really expects much of me."

Alexa laughed, hoping it didn't sound mean. "Well, *I* expect big things from you."

"Bigger than Davey's d—"

"Kyle!" Alexa cut him off, looking around to make sure no one was listening to them.

Kyle leaned back on the counter. "So what will you do? Instead of college, I mean."

"I dunno. Maybe something like the Peace Corps? If that's not too cliché or whatever. Or Habitat for Humanity. It's not like I just want to do nothing. I want to do good things—and travel and stuff."

"So you should do it," Kyle said, like it was settled.

Alexa sighed again. "It's not that easy. My parents would *freeeeak* if I even vaguely mentioned the idea of not going right to college. It's just, y'know, what we do. Or what all their friends' kids have done."

"Someone has to have, like, joined the army or moved to Hollywood or something."

"Not that I can think of. All my parents' friends' kids are in Ivies or at these super-intense liberal arts colleges in the middle of the woods."

Kyle rolled his eyes. "Well, fuck your parents' friends' kids. Why should they tell you what to do?"

"I know, I know," Alexa replied, feeling an anxiety, but also a relief, for actually having this conversation with someone, finally. "It's not like it would be illegal for me to put off college for a while. But it'd be hard. Because who knows what the hell my brother is going to do, and one of us has to be the good one. If I didn't go to school, I don't even know if my parents would, like, support me."

"I'm sure they would eventually."

Alexa frowned at Kyle's misunderstanding. "I meant with money."

"Ohhh," Kyle said, nodding his head and turning back toward the register. "Well, then you'd be like the rest of us."

"I guess so."

Kyle started counting the bills in the drawer again, but then stopped. "Just come to New York," he said. "There are poor people in New York you can help. You can help me. Build me a habitat! I'm humanity!"

Alexa smiled. "O.K. Sounds good."

"And I need a little *piece* in my *core*, if you know what I mean . . ." Kyle continued, another of his awful and wonderful jokes—dirty without being gross, somehow.

"Oh Jesus," Alexa groaned, and then they were both laughing.

This college thing was a relatively new and unformed thought, but it was a big, exciting, almost dangerous one. One Alexa relished in her mind the second she said it. She was, she knew, at least partly inspired by Kyle's enviable rootlessness.

He was interesting, and people were interested in him. Because of his dewy good looks, yes, but also because there was something arrestingly knowing about him, like he'd lived many past lives. No, he wasn't magic, but he seemed different from literally all the kids Alexa knew in her little world back home. "An old soul," Alexa's mother had called Kyle one night.

It was one of many nights when Kyle had dinner with the Elsings—he and Alexa having worked the early shift, blessed with an entire evening to enjoy themselves. During dinner, Kyle told a particularly funny, charming story, a comedy of errors about trying to score tickets to *Hamilton* on a New York visit the past spring. Alexa was laughing, as she always did, when she caught, out of the corner of her eye, her mother giving her a strange look—condescending, concerned, pitying. It snatched the laugh right out of Alexa's throat, and she fell quiet for the rest of dinner.

Afterward, Alexa helped her mom with the dishes, Kyle and Jason off on "a walk" (this meant smoking a joint on the beach, and everyone, including Linda, probably, knew it). Alexa, feeling more emboldened that summer than she ever had before, asked her mother what that look had been about.

Linda feigned ignorance. "What was what about?"

"That look you gave me. While Kyle was talking about *Hamilton.*"

Linda sighed, rested the platter she was washing in the sink.

"It's just . . . He's a nice boy, Alexa. You know that. Your father and I think he's wonderful. I just hope you're not . . . investing too much in him," Linda said, a little pointedly, handing Alexa the platter to dry.

"What do you mean?" Alexa asked, thinking she knew exactly what her mother meant.

"I just wouldn't want to see you wasting your time on something that isn't going to go anywhere."

"What, should I be studying all summer instead of having fun? Did you have this same conversation with Jason?"

Linda flinched. "That's not what I'm saying and you know it, Alexandra. It's just that Kyle, he's—"

"He's my friend, Mom. That's what Kyle is."

Linda shrugged. Returned to the dishes. "I'm just trying to talk to you, Alexa. You don't have to bite my head off."

Kyle had told Alexa that he was gay shortly after they met, though Alexa had already guessed. There was, well, the way he was. But also, the younger employees at Grey's talked, and someone there knew Kyle's ex-boyfriend, Donnie, who went to UMass Dartmouth. From what Alexa could gather, and what little Kyle told her about him, Donnie was a bad guy, mean and manipulative. Alexa, of course, didn't care that Kyle was gay. What bothered her was her mother's assumption, and maybe other people's assumption, that she was some sad girl pining after her gay bestie, like one of those girls who dated famous gay YouTubers before they came out, and then just had to try to gracefully step aside while the gay guys basked in all the attention. Alexa didn't see herself as one of those girls. She didn't like Kyle that way.

She liked him because they had fun together. Because Alexa could imagine herself visiting Kyle in New York in the future. On trips back from Africa or Indonesia or wherever she was living, building houses or digging wells. Alexa knew that however long it had been since they'd seen each other, she and Kyle would find their old rapport in an instant, that they'd share stories and ideas, and the same easy warmth of that summer would fill whatever room they were in.

But then a hospital phone rang and Alexa was jolted back into the present.

When she'd heard about the accident just a few hours earlier, she hadn't gotten a call. She'd been at school, waiting in the guidance office with Ms. Reeve and the head of the upper school, Ms. Cline. Alexa's parents were due there at 2:00 to talk about Alexa's "uncharacteristic" (Ms. Cline's word) grade slippage over the last term. When the meeting had been scheduled, Linda was exasperated, saying to Alexa, "Don't we have enough of this with your brother?" This was different, though. Alexa was pulling A minuses and B pluses, instead of straight As. She wasn't flunking or fucking up, she'd just lost focus, she'd lost some drive. She'd also opted not to run cross-country that fall, to everyone's disappointment.

They knew she'd had a hard year. They said that taking some time to process was natural, healthy. But maybe now it was time for Alexa to reapply herself, to get her junior year started right, so she could confidently apply to her long list of supposed dream schools. (At the top of the list: Amherst, Penn, Princeton, Georgetown. Bowdoin was her safety.)

Something in Alexa was fundamentally different, though. All the idle talk with Kyle that summer, about leaving after graduation, going off to do something that mattered in the world, had solidified into a determination, just not one she'd shared with her parents yet. And so this meeting was to be Alexa's grand reveal, a coming out of her own, when her parents, and Ms. Cline, and Ms. Reeve, would see that she wasn't screwing up. That she was in fact pursuing something even nobler than college. She was going to help people. They'd understand that, once she told them.

But tunnel traffic was bad, so Alexa's parents decided to go a little out of the way and take the Tobin Bridge to get to Alexa's school. Linda texted her that they would still be on time, they were almost at the bridge.

In the cramped guidance office, twenty awkward minutes went by. Alexa smiled at Ms. Cline and Ms. Reeve as they made small talk about some trip to Maine that Ms. Cline had taken that August.

"It's a beautiful island, Vinalhaven. Alexa, have you ever been?"

Alexa shook her head no. "We go to the Cape in the summer. Or we used to. I didn't go much this past summer."

Ms. Reeve nodded knowingly, frowning with concern. "No, of course not. Of course not."

Ms. Cline, choosing to breeze through this darker moment, said, "Well, you really should go. It's very peaceful. Not much to do there, and really too cold for swimming, but I got a lot of reading done, and we made wonderful food every night."

"It sounds nice," Alexa said weakly.

Ms. Cline beamed. "It is. It really is. There's this one—"

She was interrupted by her phone making a little trill, and then Ms. Reeve's phone went off too. Then Alexa's. She wasn't sure if she should answer her phone in front of faculty, but it could be from her mother, so she reached for her phone, but was stopped by a gasp.

"Oh! Oh my goodness," Ms. Reeve yelped. "There's been an accident. The Tobin Bridge. The news is saying there's been a collapse? That it collapsed?"

Alexa felt a plunge in her throat, stretching down to her stomach.

Ms. Cline and Ms. Reeve seemed to realize what this might mean at the same time, both turning to Alexa with looks of wild, uncomprehending worry on their faces.

"What do you mean, it collapsed?" Alexa stammered. "The whole bridge?"

Ms. Reeve looked back at her phone, adjusting her glasses as if that might make the news change.

"When?" Alexa implored, reaching for her phone in her pocket.

"Just now, I think . . ." Ms. Cline murmured. "Just now."

"I don't understand," Alexa said. But, somehow, she did. Alexa knew then, with some kind of supernatural sureness, that her parents' car had been one of the ones caught in the collapse, buried under a pile of concrete or, worse, twirling down to the bottom of the Mystic River. Alexa abruptly stood up and bolted out of the office. She heard Ms. Reeve and Ms. Cline both call out to her, but she didn't care. She tore down the hallway toward her locker. She needed to get her things and leave.

But leave for where? She stopped in the hallway, frantic and running on some strange energy, and opened Twitter on her phone. Her feed was mostly breaking news and speculation about the collapse, pictures of the Tobin Bridge, or what used to be the Tobin Bridge, making her stomach churn. She saw one tweet, from Channel 7, that mentioned "victims" and "Boston General." That was all she needed. Boston General wasn't all that far.

She ran the rest of the way to her locker, calling Jason as she went. He finally answered on about the millionth ring, sounding tired and out-of-it as ever, and certainly surprised to see his sister calling him in the middle of a school day. Or, really, calling him at all.

What she didn't tell Jason when she finally got him on the phone, what she couldn't tell him, now at the hospital, because he was Jason being Jason, and because he had stormed off, was that this was her fault. That her parents never would have been on that bridge if she hadn't been messing up at school, if she had just been the dutiful daughter for one more year, if she had just waited to figure her life out until it really belonged to her. But now she'd probably gotten two people—not just two people, her *parents*—killed, and she had no one to turn to.

The night before they left for the Cape that summer, Alexa knocked on Jason's bedroom door. He grunted an "It's open," and Alexa walked in, finding her brother standing in a sea of clutter, a mostly empty bag sitting on his bed.

"How's the packing going?"

Jason gestured to everything around him. "Great."

"Cool." There was a strained pause, not uncommon in interactions Alexa had with her brother. "So . . . I can't believe we're actually going. I mean, the whole summer."

He shrugged, threw up his hands. "Yup. Pretty much sucks."

"What are you going to do?" Alexa asked, leaning on the door frame, arms crossed over her chest.

Jason sighed. "I don't know, Alexa. Nothing? Sit around. Go to the beach. Whatever."

"Maybe it'll be good for you," Alexa offered tentatively.

His head jerked up and he glared at her. "What is that supposed to mean?"

Here we go, Alexa thought. "Nothing! Just that, like, I dunno. You seem so miserable here all the time."

"Well, so do you."

Alexa was surprised. Most days she wasn't sure Jason even noticed that she existed, let alone had any insight into her emotional state. "I'm not miserable," she said, more meekly than she meant it to come out. There was another pause while her brother stuffed some seemingly random items of clothing into his bag. Alexa hesitantly continued, "Maybe we could, I dunno, hang out or something. When we're there."

Jason looked up at his sister again, a hint of surprise in his eyes that quickly dimmed into another hard stare. "Yeah. Maybe."

Which wasn't a no, exactly, but Alexa knew that, barring some miracle, it was unlikely she and Jason would have some kind of bonding time on the Cape together.

"You're gonna have to hang out with somebody, Jason. We're there for three months."

"Alexa, why not worry about your little job or whatever and let me figure my shit out myself, O.K.?"

"Do you even have the first idea how to figure your shit out, Jason? What even *is* your shit?" Alexa snapped back, not wanting to get in another fight with her brother but also so frustrated with his moodiness, his dismissiveness, the way he was always cutting through her hope and optimism with snideness and ridicule. This time, though, Jason didn't take the bait. He just sighed again, looked around his room, and said, "I can't find any shorts."

Alexa stayed leaning against the doorway until she was sure the conversation was over. Jason was back to ignoring her, caught up again in his own gloom and fog.

In the hospital, Alexa longed for the Jason who had emerged so soon after that little spat, something about the Cape that summer turning Jason into someone so sharp and fun and *brotherly* for a few months. He had been so present. It really was something like a miracle.

The two of them even went for evening swims together on a few days when Alexa had worked a morning shift. Most of the other swimmers already gone home for the day. They had the water to themselves, and they swam out further than they might have if the other wasn't there. The water was bracing, but Alexa liked it, feeling her body cool down after a hot day, just as the sun was beginning to set. Jason would lie on his back, staring up at the sky, bobbing along like a bit of seaweed. There was something dreamy and childlike about it, her brother floating on the waves. Alexa watched him and wondered what he was thinking.

After their swim, they'd often sit up in the high dunes to dry off, like they used to when they were little. Most times Alexa would just babble on about work, joking about how Amelia, a kind, scrawny fifteen-year-old who manned the prize booth at the arcade, had a big crush on Jason. Amelia had seen Alexa's brother all of once, when he picked up Alexa, begrudgingly, to drive her home. But Alexa had heard whispers since, and she and Kyle would laugh, imagining Amelia trying, in vain, to find

Jason on Instagram or Facebook or anything so she could stalk him. She wouldn't have any luck; Jason wasn't on any of them.

But one evening, after a particularly invigorating swim in chilly, post-rainstorm water, Alexa leaned back on her towel and turned toward her brother, who was poking at the sand with a stick.

"Are you O.K.?" she asked him.

He seemed startled out of some deep thought. "Huh?" he said, dropping the stick. "Oh, I was just . . . digging, I guess."

Alexa laughed. "No, I don't mean with the stick. I mean, like, in life. Are you O.K.?"

Jason held her gaze for a moment, something he hadn't done in some time, before looking away. "Uh, yeah. I mean, the new school's good. It's better than the other ones."

She nodded. "Right, right. But I mean, otherwise? Beyond school? I don't even know what you're doing half the time. Like, if you're with friends, or if you're dating someone, or . . ."

Jason let her trail off. He shrugged. "I'm with friends sometimes. I don't know. Everyone's so boring, you know?"

Boston Alexa would agree with him. But Cape Alexa, quietly having the summer of her life, didn't agree. "I guess. But not all of them. Kyle's not boring."

"That's true."

"But you'd tell me, right?" Alexa asked, trying to get her brother to look at her again. "If something was wrong?"

Jason looked her in the eye, gave her the faintest smile. "Sure thing, *little* sister." This was meant to nudge her back into place, into her role.

Alexa figured they were done talking—probably the most, and most sincerely, they'd spoken uninterrupted for three years. But then Jason surprised her.

"Are *you* O.K.?"

The question took her aback. "How do you mean?"

"Like, school and shit. Is getting As stressful?"

"Of course it's stressful."

"But do you like it? Is it good stressful?"

Alexa realized she wasn't sure how to answer that. Or maybe she was, it was just hard to say out loud. So instead of saying "Yes, I hate it, I'm going crazy, I never want to take an exam ever again and I mean it," she aped her brother and gave a little shrug. "I dunno."

Jason nodded sagely. "Yeah. Yeah." He fell silent then, and it was clear that they were done talking. Which Alexa was fine with. It had been some time—in fact, had it ever happened?—since someone hadn't just assumed she was on top of the world. Of course, her mother gave her shit about studying *more* and practicing *more*, but it was never about whether the studying and the practicing were inherently good things for Alexa. And the thing with Kyle, the subtle hints about him, and about Alexa's perceived naivety—that wasn't really Alexa's mother being concerned for Alexa. It was more of a worry about a potential future embarrassment, an unpleasantness that could disrupt Linda's carefully ordered existence.

But Jason really seemed to be asking, to have seen past the goody-two-shoes airs he often sniped at her about and recognized some change in her, some restlessness. She felt connected to Jason then, there in the dunes. Maybe they were joined in that restlessness. Maybe that is what bonded the Elsing children together.

Alexa leaned back on her elbows and took in the breeze and the sound of the ocean. Jason laid out his towel and leaned back too. Alexa began recounting, once again, all she'd heard about Amelia's undying love for Jason, while they watched the sky turn orange, then deep blue, the wind hissing through the beach grass, the crickets chirping awake.

Now it was all beeps and rings and tense voices. Alexa looked around the waiting room, didn't see Jason anywhere. Mary Oakes was still in her corner, looking perturbed. Alexa watched as a teenage boy in a hoodie and sweats—she hadn't noticed him before—tentatively walked up to Mary Oakes to ask her something. She shook her head and the boy looked deflated. He nodded, turned, and walked off. Alexa stood up, walked quickly to intercept him. Up close he looked tired too, his brown eyes watery, dark hair mussed at odd angles.

"Hey, sorry to bother you, did she tell you anything new?"

The boy looked surprised that someone was talking to him.

"Huh? Oh—no. No, she just said that things are taking longer than they thought because, I dunno, it's dangerous for the rescue workers or something. There are still pieces falling. . . like, from the bridge? So it's taking time."

"O.K. Thanks."

The boy went to sit down and, impulsively, Alexa sat down next to him.

"Can I ask who you're waiting to hear about?"

The boy nodded. "Yeah, of course. Um, my girlfriend, Aimee. She was going to Salem, so they were . . ."

"Right. My parents were there too."

"Your *parents*? Oh man. I'm sorry."

"Thanks. It's O.K. They're going to be O.K."

The boy looked at her like he wanted very much to believe her but didn't. He sighed. They sat in silence for a moment before he spoke again.

"Where do you go? To school, I mean."

"Northrup?"

"Oh. Wow. Cool. Yeah. That's a really good school."

"It's all right. Where do you go?"

"North. Newton North. In, um, Newton. Obviously."

Alexa laughed, and immediately hoped it didn't sound mean.

"That's a really good school too."

The boy shrugged his shoulders. "It's fine. It's really big. I always thought it would be nice to go to a school like Northrup. But, like, a boys' one. Or one that allows boys. Y'know."

He sat back and was looking at her now, a kind and worried face. Alexa realized he might be there alone too. "I'm Alexa," she said, putting her hand up as if to wave. He smiled, a little crinkle. "Scott," he said, waving too.

They both leaned back in their chairs, falling into silence. Scott pulled his phone out of his pocket, Alexa figuring that he was checking his messages, probably his girlfriend's parents telling him they were on their way. But then he turned to Alexa and held his phone out.

"That's her," he said. "Aimee."

Alexa took the phone from him and looked at a picture, one of those outside-the-house-before-a-school-dance pictures, probably a semiformal, judging from the length of the girl's dress. Scott was in a blue blazer and wrinkled khakis, like a boarding school uniform, Alexa thought. Aimee, dyed blond and perky looking, was standing in front of him, his arms around her waist. The house behind them was small and simple, half aluminum siding, half brick. It didn't look like the proud, rambling Victorians or big brick colonials that girls Alexa knew from Newton lived in.

"She's really pretty," Alexa said.

Scott nodded. "Yeah. This was her sophomore semi. Last year. It was awesome."

"My school doesn't really do dances," Alexa said, handing the phone back to Scott. He looked surprised.

"Why, because there are no guys?"

Alexa shrugged. "I don't know. I guess they think they're dated or something. A tool of the patriarchy."

Scott frowned. "Wow."

There was a small pause. Not quite awkward, but not quite comfortable either.

"What year are you?" he asked.

"Junior."

"Oh, cool. Me too."

"Are you here alone?"

"Uhh, yeah. Right now."

"What about Aimee's parents?"

Scott seemed to flinch. He dropped his shoulders, leaned forward to rest his arms on his knees, ran a hand through his thick hair. "Yeah, yeah, they'll be here soon, I'm sure. So. That's good. That's good."

Alexa watched him for a moment. They were about the same age, but he seemed very young just then. Scared and confused, out of his depth. She could relate. "I'm here with my brother, technically, but I might as well be alone."

Scott bobbed his head, which was now hanging between his knees. "Yeah, yeah," he said, sounding distracted.

A moment passed, and the air in the room seemed to change. Alexa sat still, unsure what to do. Clearly this boy was upset, and she wanted to comfort him, but she felt too ragged to be much help. She looked at her phone and realized that thirty minutes had passed since she'd last seen Jason, who could be anywhere by now. Had he left the hospital entirely?

Alexa opened Twitter and scrolled through her feed—she followed mostly news outlets like the *Globe* and WBZ 4—to see if there were any updates from the outside world. But it was more of the same. The horrible photos, of billows of dust occluding twisted metal, of the bridge in bent tatters. Her friends from school were tweeting out blanket condolences, some saying they were praying "for all the victims," but none of them had gotten in touch with Alexa directly. They probably didn't know. They probably figured that Alexa had just left early for the day, because she'd been weird lately. Odd, changed, more mature, a little lost.

The guilty thing was, Alexa had slowly come to like the part of herself that had changed. She did feel older and more mature. She was ready to tell her parents that she wasn't the good daughter they thought she was, that she couldn't do everything they wanted just to offset the failures of their son. She was maybe done with anger and grief and was prepared to just move on. To let selfish Jason be selfish Jason, to let her parents be disappointed, to let old friends be gone. But then the bridge collapsed and the phones pinged and all of Alexa's impending independence suddenly seemed reckless, careless, like she'd unpinned something that was holding her world up and it had all come tumbling down.

What would Jason say if he knew? That Theo and Linda were on that bridge because of Alexa. That Alexa's stupid, childish dreams had probably killed their parents. Maybe Jason had the right idea. Better to disengage and self-destruct and be a callous jerk than to try to involve anyone else, to tether your expectations to other people. And what would Jason say if he found out that the meeting with Ms. Reeve and Ms. Cline had been Alexa's idea, that it really was all annoying, type A, goody-goody Alexa's fault? She had rebelled wrong. She'd insisted on getting her parents to officially sign off on her plans, and now they'd suffered for it. Jason hadn't even thought to ask why his parents were on the Tobin that afternoon, but Alexa nonetheless felt like she was lying. She felt like a sneak, like a criminal.

Still, she wanted Jason next to her, helping her. Even if a big, terrible secret was hovering between them, she needed her brother, whatever comfort he could provide. But they'd barely spoken since that Labor Day weekend a year ago. He'd reverted into the same bad, jaded, hazy Jason from before. And as much as Alexa knew Jason might never forgive her for what she'd done to their parents, she wasn't sure she could ever forgive Jason for his distance, his coldness. Alexa was indeed very much alone as she sat in the waiting room, looking at Scott, who was now rocking back and forth, one knee bouncing up and down, the laces on his beat-up sneaker thwacking away.

She wasn't sure why, but she reached a hand out and placed it on Scott's shoulder, gave it a little reassuring rub. He stopped rocking and looked up at her, gave her that same weary, sheepish crinkle of a smile.

Alexa smiled back and Scott sat up, rubbed his eyes. "Should we see if Dolores Umbridge over there can tell us anything new?" he asked, gesturing toward Mary Oakes. Alexa was about to say yes, but then Mary Oakes turned and disappeared once again behind the swinging doors. "Great," he said with a sigh.

Scott pulled his hood up and leaned his head back against the wall. Alexa sat back too, staring up at the stained white ceiling. They sat there like that in silence, the panic of the scene around them fading just for the moment.

After a minute or two, Scott sat up and turned to Alexa. "So wait, like, not even a prom?"

And they both laughed, together.

Chapter Four

Scott

SCOTT AND AIMEE had been dating for about a year when Aimee started seriously talking about colleges. It was the beginning of her junior year and Scott's sophomore year, and though Scott had always known this was coming, that Aimee would eventually start to make plans for leaving Boston—and him—behind, it still shocked him how sad and scared it made him feel when the day actually arrived. The thud of what he always knew would someday happen: that people were going to leave and he'd be stuck in Newton, with his parents, just like they had been stuck in Newton with their parents. But he tried not to show it, listening to Aimee as she listed dream schools and safeties, maybe nodding a little more enthusiastically when she mentioned schools that were closer to home.

"I guess Amherst could be good," Aimee said once over a weekend lunch at Johnny's in Newton Centre. It was a favorite place of theirs, where they'd been on their first official date, Scott attempting to pay for the meal with a wad of crumpled bills before Aimee insisted they split it. "Though I feel like their theater department is kinda small?"

Aimee tended to get the lead, or at least a big part, in most of the school plays. She was talented and pretty, in "an interesting way," as Scott's mom put it. "Doesn't BU have a good theater major?" Scott asked, trying to sound nonchalant, but of course wishing beyond wish that Aimee would end up at a school just down Comm Ave, instead of all the way at the other end of the state, or even worse, in a different state altogether.

"True," Aimee said, chewing thoughtfully on a french fry. "But I dunno . . . it'd be fun to be somewhere else, y'know?" She looked at Scott, maybe suddenly realizing the implications of what she was saying. "But not too far. I mean, obviously somewhere you can come visit a lot."

"Right," Scott said, giving her a smile and taking a sip of his Coke. He had a helpless feeling churning in his stomach, a gnawing certainty that he'd already lost Aimee, had been losing her since the day they got together, making out at a soccer party back when Scott was just a freshman on the JV team.

He'd since made varsity—one of the few sophomores at Newton North, a strong soccer school, to do so. So it wasn't like Scott didn't have his own stuff going on, his own things to be excited about. But beyond high school, his future didn't look anything like Aimee's. He wasn't quite good enough at soccer to get a scholarship, so he'd probably stay in town, maybe go to UMass Boston or Suffolk or something, somewhere that wasn't too expensive. He'd probably still work weekends at his parents' store, a pizza shop in Newton Centre that had gradually grown to offer a larger menu and also half-functioned as a kind of specialty foods grocery. The business did well enough, but it was small and local, and Scott's parents were never quite secure in their finances.

Newton was a rich town, with only a few scattered poorer families to give the place character or something. Scott was from one of those families, all of whom lived in houses in Nonantum or Newton Corner, near Watertown, where the terrorist kid was hiding in that boat after the Marathon bombing. Scott was often keenly aware of the differences between him and Aimee, whose parents lived in a big house on Farlow Hill and who had never once mentioned student loans or financial aid or anything.

After lunch, Scott and Aimee walked, hand in hand, to the T stop, taking the D train down to Fenway, where they saw a movie and cuddled and made out and ate popcorn, Scott letting things feel normal again, like this wasn't all going to end in a year and a half.

Things progressed regularly enough throughout that fall and into the winter, with soccer and plays and all the immediate stuff of high school taking precedence over Aimee's future plans. But when February vacation rolled around, Aimee announced that she was going to spend the week looking at colleges with her dad. Scott had assumed that they'd spend the break together, like they had the year before, watching Netflix and doing some discreet, quiet fooling around in Aimee's attic-like third-floor bedroom. He was crushed—and angry—when she told him just a few days before the vacation was set to start.

"Well, what am I gonna do for a week now?" he asked her, sitting on

Aimee's bed while she sat at her desk, half paying attention to the physics book on her lap.

She sighed, looked up at him. "I don't know! I thought you'd be working at the store most days anyway."

She was right, of course. Scott's parents put him to work during almost all of his vacation time, but he would have a few nights free at least, nights when he thought he and Aimee would be cozy together at her house, which was really the only place he ever wanted to be those days. He told her that and she rolled her eyes. "We can make up for lost sex time when I'm back," she said, returning to her book.

Scott didn't hate the sound of that, but he did hate the idea of Aimee exploring her potential new life without him, of her falling in love with some school and returning at the end of the week convinced she just had to move halfway across the country to go to Northwestern. (This trip was Aimee's Midwest tour of schools. The East Coast ones would be visited on weekends.) It made Scott feel bratty and hot in the face, like he was a kid wanting to throw a really big and cathartic tantrum. But he restrained himself. He didn't want Aimee to see him being so immature, so uncol- legiate, even though that was exactly what he felt, desperately wanting them to stay teenagers in love forever, not wanting time to move on, not wanting anyone to grow up any more than they already had.

Despite all of Scott's useless petulance, Aimee went on the trip, and Scott remained in town, working long days at the store and then mostly bumming around at night. One evening, he went over to Pete del Vecchio's house, a friend from the team who lived nearby. They played FIFA and Pete talked about girls, specifically Pete's longtime crush,

Taissa Groff, Aimee's hot and kind of strange best friend, who lived in a sprawling, ghostly old mansion that had an elevator in it. Scott was trying not to text Aimee too much, not wanting to seem too needy. But sitting there in Pete's dingy basement rec room while Pete droned on about how Taissa had provocatively brushed past him at a party back during Christmas break, Scott felt lonely and cramped and dejected. So he sent Aimee a text, asking how things were going. He was pretty sure she was in Ohio at the moment, looking at Oberlin and Kenyon.

Scott saw the "read" receipt pop up and waited for the little bubbles indicating that Aimee was writing back. But they never showed up. Aimee had seen the text and decided not to respond. Scott waited what he felt was a reasonable amount of time, and then wrote another message: *hangin at delvecchios. hes still in luv w taissa lmao. what r u doin.* This time, the message didn't switch to "read," and Scott became immediately convinced that Aimee was at some college party, making out with some pretentious theater guy, deliberately ignoring her buzzing phone, knowing that it was just a dumb text from her stupid high school boyfriend.

He told Pete he had to leave, Pete protesting that Scott was only leaving because he was losing at FIFA. Scott walked the few frigid blocks home and retreated up to his room, torturing himself by looking at old Instagrams of him and Aimee in what now seemed like happier times. Him and Aimee at Six Flags New England at the end of the school year last year, a sunny and exhausting and entirely thrilling day that had culminated with, back in Newton, Scott losing his virginity to Aimee.

In another photo, Scott and Aimee were at a table at J.P. Licks with Taissa and Cara and some of Aimee's other theater friends after the spring musical, *Pippin*, most of their faces still pancaked with stage makeup. Scrolling through Aimee's feed (Scott never posted much on Instagram, though he loved being tagged), Scott realized he had his arm tightly around Aimee in a lot of the photos, like he was always trying to keep her close to him. It hadn't worked, though, and now Scott was convinced Aimee would return from her trip and promptly break up with him. He checked his phone one last time—still nothing—and drifted off into a restless, unhappy sleep.

The next morning, he was cheered to wake up to a bunch of texts from Aimee, who was apologetic about not writing back. *my dad got mad at me for looking @ my phone @ dinner. said i had to turn it off. then i forgot. ilu.* Scott felt an immense amount of relief, though he wasn't entirely sure how Aimee—as frequently glued to her phone as anyone else— would have forgotten to turn the thing back on. Still, she sent him a cute picture of herself, looking coy in a drab hotel bed, and they had a little back-and-forth about mundane stuff, and Scott felt better.

When they finally met up after her trip, though, things seemed different. Scott went over to Aimee's house, saying hi to her parents as they cleaned up dinner. "Aimee's upstairs, sweetie," Aimee's mom said, and Scott climbed the stairs, excited and expectant, hoping Aimee would say she hated the Midwest, that it was too cold, even colder than Boston, and that she'd decided to stay put.

To his great dismay, he instead found her cheery and gushing, talking about how beautiful all the theater facilities had been at the schools, how talented everyone seemed. She'd seen two plays, one weird avant-garde thing at Oberlin and *Picasso at the Lapin Agile* at Northwestern.

"Oh my God, they were like real actors, Scott. And the sets were so cool. It was so professional. It was amazing."

"That's . . . great," Scott said, not doing much to mask his disappointment. "That's really cool."

Aimee turned from her unpacking and looked him, hurt or annoyed or both. "Gee, don't sound so excited."

"I am excited!" Scott replied weakly. "It's just . . . Ohio and Illinois are really far away."

"I know," Aimee said, walking over to give Scott a hug. She kissed him, running a hand through his hair and smiling. "But they're not *that* far. Plus, we're talking about a year and a half from now."

She continued to go on at length about how incredible everything and everyone had been, how the professors had these lengthy résumés and how intense the classes were. Scott sat glumly on her bed while Aimee flitted around the room, putting clothes away and chattering. He had thought that maybe they'd just have a quiet night in together—Aimee's parents usually let Scott stay until midnight, largely unbothered—but now he wasn't so sure he wanted to just sit there while Aimee waxed rhapsodic about how perfect and dynamic her life was going to be when she finally left Newton.

"There's a party at Sam Stein's house tonight," Scott interrupted.

Aimee wrinkled her nose in disgust. "Sam Stein?" Sam was a senior on the soccer team, a known asshole who barely gave Scott the time of day, except to yell at him when Scott screwed something up at practice or, worse, during a game. "Why would you want to go to a party at Sam Stein's house?"

Scott was irritable. "Because he's on the team with me. I don't know. I was invited. We were invited."

Aimee let out a little scoff. "Everyone on the team is invited to those parties. Isn't it, like, a bylaw?"

"Why are you being a bitch about this, Aims?" Scott spat out, immediately regretting it.

Her eyes darkened and she stopped unpacking. "Uh. Whoa. What the fuck, Scotty?"

"Sorry, it's just, like, I haven't seen you in a week and I just want to do something with you. Why do you have to make fun of me for that?"

"I wasn't making fun of you, Scott! I just didn't think you liked Sam freaking Stein. I mean, you don't care about soccer parties all year and then suddenly you're, like, dying to hang out with the *worst* soccer guys?"

"We met at a soccer party!" Scott said indignantly.

"Scott, that really doesn't count. That was Maddy Cohen's birthday party, there were just some soccer guys there. JV ones."

"I'm just trying to have a life too, Aimee."

"Oh! O.K. Sorry. Didn't realize you didn't have a life before. Or that going to basically a serial date rapist's big party was going to give you one."

"Whatever," Scott said, once again feeling like a bratty child. "I just want to go. If you don't want to come with me, fine."

"Oh," Aimee replied. "I guess I thought we were gonna hang out tonight no matter what. I wanted to tell you more about the trip."

"There's more? Good God."

"You know, you're being a real jerk right now, Scott." She was right, of course. He was being a jerk, or worse. "Maybe you should go to Sam's party. We can talk tomorrow."

Tomorrow was Sunday, and Scott had work all day. Aimee no doubt knew that. He'd worked practically every Sunday since they'd met.

"No, I'll stay." Scott sighed.

"Honestly, I don't know if I want you to. Not if you're gonna just shit all over me for being happy about my trip."

"I won't, I won't," Scott protested. "I'm sorry. I didn't mean to be a dick."

Aimee looked at him, hard. "I kinda think you did?"

Scott didn't know what to say. He'd clearly fucked this whole thing up, this grand reunion when all his fears about Aimee—and about how he'd been reacting to her lately—were supposed to be allayed, the strength of their relationship reaffirmed. "I didn't" was all he could come up with, probably pouting as he said it.

"Well, whatever." Aimee sighed. "I'm actually pretty tired from the plane and stuff. So maybe we should just, like, rain check on tonight or whatever."

Scott wanted to keep talking, wanted to stay and make things better. But he was worried he might mess things up even more. So he just said, "O.K.," and got up and walked out, not kissing her goodbye or anything. "Scott!" she called out after him, a pleading annoyance in her voice, but only calling for him once. Scott walked downstairs and out the front door, Aimee's parents looking surprised to see him leaving so early.

Scott didn't really want to go to Sam Stein's party, especially not alone, but he didn't want to just sit at home either. He could have a night out without texting too, just like Aimee had in Ohio or wherever the hell she'd been. So he texted Pete, *yo you wanna go to steins party.* Pete wrote back quickly, *aimee bringing taissa?* Scott's stomach did a little plunge. He wanted to go back and apologize to Aimee. That's where he belonged. But instead he texted, *no Aimee. boyz nite bruhhh.* Pete wrote back *LIT,* and Scott zipped up his jacket and started walking toward Pete's house— a long walk, but he didn't really care. He pressed on into the cold, leaving Aimee behind.

At the hospital, months and months later, Scott sat at a table with the grave but funny girl he'd just met. Alexa occasionally looked up and out through the crowd of people, waiting, hoping to spot her brother maybe, but otherwise they kept each other calm by talking. She went to a private school, lived downtown, so they didn't know any of the same kids. But there was enough else to talk about. Really, anything but the accident and the fate of their loved ones would do. They talked about soccer, about movies, about Cape Cod.

Scott had gone a few times with his parents, packing up the dented SUV and staying in a little bungalow in Barnstable for a few days. Alexa's experience seemed to have been, well, a little different, out there for whole summers at a time in some big house by the water, way out in Wellfleet. He could almost picture it, all those sunny days and breezy nights, the kind of summer the girls were always having in the books Aimee liked to read, by Judy Blume or whoever else. The perfect kind of summer when magical things happened. Of course, bad things happened too. Alexa mentioned something about a friend of hers, making it seem like something dire had happened, but then she caught herself, looking up once again and scanning the room for her brother, frowning a little when she didn't find him.

Was it terrible to notice that she was pretty? His thoughts should be on Aimee. Of course they should be. But what was he going to do, blind himself? She was pretty, feathery and pale like something out of a painting at the MFA, one of the portraits Scott's art teacher, Ms. Li, had droned on and on about during a field trip in ninth grade. All the great families in Boston—great families like Alexa's, just a hundred years ago—sat for portraits, she explained. It was a sign of status and, of course, a way to preserve the memory of a person in a time when photography was rare. All the people in the paintings looked sad, Scott had thought, or at least distracted. Like there was something just past the frame that was bothering them, some secret or heartbreak or something. Alexa looked that way, like there was a lot happening past where Scott could see. She was worried about her parents, obviously, but there was something else too.

She looked older than she was. More precisely, Scott realized with a sinking feeling, she looked older than Aimee, with her high ponytails and theater-kid fizziness. Alexa was something else. "Still waters run deep," Scott's dad would say sometimes, whenever Scott's mom would chide Scott for being too quiet at the dinner table, or she'd catch him at work at the store, staring off into space. "He's thinking things through, Inez," Scott's dad would say.

Scott liked that idea, that he was some deep, pensive person. Truth was, he wasn't. Not really. Usually if he was daydreaming he was thinking about sex—with Aimee, yeah, but also with Victoria Justice, or Danielle Hughes from physics class. Or, more recently, he was thinking about Aimee leaving, about what his last year at school would be like after she was gone. He'd entertain fantasies about her forgoing some faraway school, about visiting her at BU or somewhere, just up the Green Line, not so far away at all.

Now maybe none of that would happen. Maybe Aimee was dead. Jesus. No. That couldn't be true. That couldn't *actually* be true.

These thoughts ran through his head and then he'd ask Alexa something else about herself, where she wanted to apply next year ("Not sure, maybe nowhere"), what music she listened to ("Taylor. I'm boring."), and his mind would settle a little again. She had a calming effect, Alexa, the adultish rich girl with tired but piercing eyes.

Those eyes darted up suddenly, and Alexa made a little sound. Scott followed her gaze and saw a tall kid, broad-shouldered but skinny, making his way toward the table. The brother, he figured. Jason. He was wearing tight jeans and a dirty-looking sweater, longish hair swept back in a messy bird's nest on top of his head.

"Glad you decided to come back," Alexa said to him, the annoyance in her voice not really masking the relief that was in there too. Jason sighed and sat down across from her, slumping over the table and rubbing his eyes. "I was just outside again. I didn't really go anywhere."

"You see anything?" Scott asked, figuring what the fuck, they may as well all act like they knew each other. Jason turned to him, looking a little confused. "Where?"

"Outside," Scott pressed. "Did you see anything?"

Jason, eyes a little glassy, still looked lost. "Um . . ."

"He means, like, ambulances or anything, Jason," Alexa said, leaning in toward her brother.

Jason nodded. "Oh right, no. I mean, nothing new. I tried to find that lady, but I couldn't."

"Mary Oakes," Alexa explained to Scott.

He nodded his head. "Ah."

"Jason, this is Scott. He goes to Newton North. He's waiting to hear about his girlfriend, Aimee."

Scott extended his hand to Jason, who tentatively took it in his own, gave it a thin little shake. "Nice to meet you," Jason said. "Sorry about your girlfriend."

Scott nodded, said thanks. "Sorry about your parents, man."

Jason nodded too. "Yeah," he mumbled. "They'll be fine."

Which, of course, Jason had no way of knowing. None of them did. Mary Oakes had disappeared behind her swinging doors, and everyone in the waiting room was standing around aimlessly. Scott, Alexa, and Jason were among the few people sitting down. Scott felt a quick pang of guilt, like maybe he should be up and doing something, trying to get an update on Aimee. But what could he really do? He wasn't family. Aimee's parents would be on their way. They were both doctors. They'd know what to do, and Scott would just . . . be there.

"Hey," Scott heard, and looked up to find Alexa giving a friendly little wave to a girl perched on an end table a few seats down from them.

"Hey," the girl replied, quiet, shaky.

Alexa waved her over to the group, and as the girl approached, Alexa sat up straighter in her chair. "Are you here alone?"

"Oh. Um. Yeah," the girl answered. "Waiting to hear about my sister."

"What's her name?" Alexa asked.

"Kate Vong. I asked the woman at the desk about her, but no one really seems to know anything."

Scott could sense the girl's frustration; he felt it too. "Yeah, we're getting that sense too. I'm Scott, by the way. This is Alexa."

"Skyler," the girl said, giving another small wave. "Hi."

"This is my brother, Jason," Alexa said, but Jason just crossed his arms and gave a quick nod to Skyler.

Was this guy an asshole or what, Scott found himself thinking. Jason came off like he thought he was better than everyone else, even though he was obviously a total mess. Scott could see why Alexa seemed so annoyed with him, this hipster prick who didn't even seem to notice where he was, let alone why he was there. Scott wasn't really the aggressive, get-in-a-fight type, but he thought, sitting at the table and looking at Jason draped in his chair, that he would absolutely punch him in the face if Alexa asked him to.

Skyler sat down next to them, but kept furtively checking her phone and then putting it back in her bag, and it made Scott anxious, like something was about to happen. He turned to Alexa, who was staring hard at Jason as he picked at his nails. "You think we should go try to find Umbridge? See if she knows anything?"

Jason looked up. "I thought her name was Mary."

"Yeah, it is. I was just . . . It was a joke. Like Dolores Umbridge."

Jason looked at Scott blankly.

"From *Harry Potter*?"

Skyler laughed, but Jason's expression didn't change.

"Oh. Right. I didn't see it."

Alexa rolled her eyes. "My brother isn't into Harry Potter. Or anything else that involves joy of any kind."

Jason glared at her.

A tension settled over the table and then, surprising everyone, Skyler said, "I hate Harry Potter."

Scott laughed, bigger and louder than he expected. "How can you hate Harry Potter? Who hates Harry Potter?"

Jason raised his hand. *Asshole.*

Skyler thought for a second. "I don't know. It's just, like, I hate those stories where a kid has some shitty life but then he finds out he's special and his life gets really cool and exciting. Like he's saved. What about the kids with shitty lives who *aren't* special, who don't find out they're magic or whatever? Shouldn't there be books about those kids? Why does the story have to be about, like, wizard Jesus?"

"Totally," Jason muttered.

Alexa pursed her lips. She had nice lips. "I guess I hadn't really thought about it that way."

"Me neither," Scott said, wondering which one he was, the special kid or the nobody, but also sort of already knowing. He wasn't going to be whisked away to anywhere magical, probably not. The only good thing, like really good thing, in his life might be dead or dying as they spoke. Crushed in her car, with Taissa and Cara.

"She was driving to Salem," Scott said. The group turned to look at him. "Aimee, my girlfriend. She and two of her friends, Taissa and Cara. They're in *The Crucible*? The play? So the cast was driving up there to, like, I dunno, do research about witches or something."

Scott swore he heard Jason snicker a little. He looked up, gave him a hard stare, but Jason didn't even seem to notice.

"Anyway, that's why they were there. On the bridge, I mean."

There was a silence. People shifted in their chairs.

"My sister was just driving back from work," Skyler offered after a moment. "She drives that way, like, every day, I think, each way. I was . . . I was on the phone with her when . . ."

"Jesus . . ." Alexa muttered. "My parents—our parents—they were . . ." She trailed off. The others waited for her to continue, but all she said was "I don't know. They were just there." The group fell quiet again.

Scott sat back in his chair. It was so bizarre to think about. That they could all be gone. To think of how scary it must have been to be on the bridge. *I should have been with Aimee*, Scott thought. Maybe he would have skipped class and he and Aimee would have driven up together, stopping at Aimee's house for a quickie or something, and then they would have missed it, they wouldn't have been on the bridge when it happened. There were so many things that could have been different, that could have prevented it all from happening. To Aimee, at least.

Skyler's phone started buzzing in her pocket, snapping Scott out of his fantasy, the hazy vision of an entirely different November afternoon disappearing. Suddenly the Mary Oakes doors swung open and there she was, striding through alongside a girl with streaks of purple in her hair, wearing a black hoodie stuck through with safety pins. The girl's eyes were sunken and red from crying, and she was wiping her nose with her sleeve. Mary Oakes had a tentative hand on her shoulder and murmured something to her before turning away and walking back through the doors.

The girl, tall and tough looking, collected herself and then, standing there alone in the middle of the room, seemed not sure what to do next. She stood there, fiddling with her safety pins, shifting her weight from one boot to another. Scott, feeling some wave of charity, or just wanting even more distraction from the realities of the moment, called over to her.

"Hey!"

The girl turned, eyeing him a little suspiciously. "Yeah?"

"Did she tell you anything? Mary Oakes?"

Something flashed across the girl's face, then disappeared. She nodded. "Yeah. Uh. My dad. I was finding out about my dad."

Alexa frowned. "Is he O.K.?"

The girl shook her head. "Um . . . I don't know? I don't know. He's just . . ."

Scott was confused. "He was at the accident? They already brought him in? I thought none of the, uh, the victims were here yet."

The girl walked closer to the table, her messenger bag making a jangling sound—keys or something. "Yeah, no, he's still there, I guess. My mom used to work here, at the hospital, so I know Mary a little. She just wanted to make sure I was O.K. or whatever."

"Oh," Scott said, wondering what else Mary Oakes might have told this girl. He gestured toward the table. "Well, want to sit with us? While you wait for your dad?"

The girl pulled her sleeves over her hands, crossed her arms. "Uh, yeah. Sure. Cool, thanks."

She walked the rest of the way to the table and sat in the remaining chair, the five of them introducing themselves. "I'm Morgan," the girl said, giving everyone a wave.

"I like your pins," Jason said, leaning forward and giving one a little yank. To Scott's surprise, the compliment sounded sincere.

Morgan looked down at her sweatshirt, as if she'd forgotten the safety pins were there. "Oh, thanks. I put them on in, like, eighth grade. They're dumb."

"They're cool," Jason said, nodding with certainty, before turning his attention back to the surface of the table.

"You come here often?" Scott said to Morgan, for no other reason than to fill the silence.

Jason picked his head back up and shot him a withering look. Scott felt immediately embarrassed, but Morgan laughed. "Actually, yeah," she said, her face then falling into a darker expression.

"Sorry, I didn't—" Scott stammered, but Morgan waved it off.

"No, it's fine. It's fine. It was funny." Scott nodded appreciatively as Jason rolled his eyes and returned to his inspection of the table.

The other four smiled at each other nervously, but maybe hopefully too. If Morgan had heard something about her dad, had heard that he was alive and on his way, maybe that meant good things for the rest of them. For Skyler's sister and Alexa's parents. (And Jason's parents.) For Aimee.

Scott pictured Aimee doing her ponytail thing, one effortless motion pulling her hair tie off her wrist and then up into her hair, just a little idle thing that she did, Aimee whom he knew so well. Aimee, the first love of his life, the girl he'd lost his virginity to. The girl he wanted to follow into her new life and never look back. If she was O.K., Scott knew then that he'd say goodbye to his parents, goodbye to the store, and head off wherever Aimee was headed, if she would let him.

They just had to get through this. This shitty thing. This awful bit of life before they became special together.

Chapter Five

Skyler

SKYLER WONDERED IF she should clarify for Mary Oakes that her sister's real name, her Khmer name, was Kun Thea. What if news came in and no one knew to update Skyler because she had only inquired about "Kate"? But they had her last name, Skyler reminded herself. Which would probably be enough.

Everyone called her sister "Kate," just like everyone called Skyler "Skyler." Her real name, or her birth name anyway, was Srey-leak. But only her grandfather called her that, and even then not that often. Only when he was in one of his weird, misty moods, lost in the past. Skyler had two cousins who grew up in Cambodia, though they were both at university in France now. When they were younger, they'd cooed over Skyler's American name, calling her a "Valley girl" with jealousy and awe.

But to Skyler it was just Skyler, not terribly special, just her name, just who she was.

That all felt like a million years ago now, those hazy, humid summers with her cousins and Kate, the four girls gabbing about faraway things, about what they hoped to do with their lives once they were older.

Kate always said then that she wanted to be a veterinarian, but she was now getting an English degree. "Too much science," she'd said of vet school. She'd told Skyler about her big plan to not apply to veterinary school—a plan her grandparents fully endorsed—in the very same car that Kate might have just died in. They were driving somewhere, to the Fenway movie theater or maybe to Coolidge Corner; all Skyler remembered was they were off to see a movie. And Kate said, "Yeah, I don't want to do it, turns out. I think I just wanna, like, read books and write stuff. Maybe teach."

Skyler had no doubt she could do it, but it was surprising to see her sister, her steady, level sister, make such a big, sudden swerve in her life. School was only a few months away, and now there was this bombshell. Kate hadn't yet told their grandparents, and Skyler certainly wasn't going to blab. So for a while it was just their secret, one on top of a pile of many.

At the time, Skyler was holding back a big secret, a big fact of her life, from her sister. And she'd wanted to tell her that day in the car, now that her sister had divulged the truth about school. She almost did. But then she caught herself, knowing after she told her sister about Danny, about what was happening, that there would be no going back. Not once

Kate knew. She'd never let it go until it was done. So she said nothing, just let Kate ramble on about her big plan, the car zooming down the Jamaicaway, fast but safe.

When Skyler became a teenager, some innate presence in her, maybe some genetic rebelliousness inherited from her long-gone mother, kicked in. So when she met Danny, two grades above her, a not terribly close friend of Kate's friends, she felt an irresistible pull toward him.

"He's an asshole," Kate said when she first found out that Skyler and Danny had hooked up. "Seriously, Sky, he's, like, the worst. I don't think Owen and Ryan even want to be friends with him anymore."

They'd met at a party in Roslindale, Kate taking Skyler along after a week of begging. It was at some Xaverian boy's house, a shabby place that could have been nice with a little paint and attention. As it was, though, it had sallow shag carpeting and fading, smoke-stained wallpaper. The lighting was dim, and the downstairs—cramped living room and dining room, grim, dated little kitchen in the back—was crowded with kids, red cups strewn everywhere, a pulsing Zedd song blaring from unseen speakers.

Skyler quickly lost her sister in the crowd, near immediately regretting coming to this party full of strangers. She wished she was just hanging around Copley with her regular friends, joking about dumb things and taking turns on the one skateboard shared between them. But here she was, alone at a party of juniors and seniors who didn't even go to her school. Skyler was clinging to the wall by the staircase, the upstairs looking dark and ominous, save for one light coming out from under a closed door, when she felt a tap on her shoulder.

She turned around and there was a boy, rangy and red-haired with a pronounced Adam's apple, a little beery-eyed but still staring, intense and focused, right into her eyes.

"You alone?"

"Huh?" Skyler asked, stepping up a stair to get some distance from him.

"Sorry, sorry," the guy said. "That sounded really fuckin' creepy. I just meant, like, did your friends ditch you?" He smiled, his teeth surprisingly white and gleaming.

"Uh, no, not exactly. I'm here with my sister. Kate Vong? Do you know her?"

The boy thought for a second, then shook his head. "I do not remember."

"Well. That's my sister!"

The boy nodded. "And what's your name?"

"Skyler," she said, over the din of the party.

"Like Miley?" the boy asked, looking confused.

"No, not Cyrus, *Skyler*. Like, uh, Sky."

"Oh, Skyler!" the boy said. "Like in *Good Will Hunting*."

Skyler shrugged. "I haven't seen it."

The boy pretended to be taken aback and then leaned in, closer than before. "Well, I guess that'll have to be our first movie date then."

It was a bad line—was it really even a line?—but something about this boy's shiny white teeth, his freckles, and Skyler's utter aloneness at the party made her not care. So when he leaned in even closer and said, "Well, listen, my name is Danny, and I know this is kinda lame, and I swear I'm not trying anything, but would you want to talk upstairs? It's so loud down here," Skyler agreed to go with him.

They walked up the stairs and past the closed door with the light on. "I think that one's, uh, in use," Danny said with a little smile, keeping things feeling breezy, casual. They found another room, dark with the door open, and when Danny turned on the light it appeared to be a child's bedroom, full of little gold sports trophies, with bunk beds in a corner.

"A kid lives here?" Skyler said.

"Well, he did. But I'm not a kid anymore."

Skyler turned to him, mortified. "Oh my God, this is your house?"

Danny smiled, nodded. "Yeah. It's kinda busted, I know. But, hey, it's home. Half the time, anyway. I mostly live with my dad."

"I'm sorry," Skyler said. "I didn't know."

"Hey, it's O.K.," Danny said. "You didn't do anything wrong."

He seemed easygoing, which relaxed Skyler, and soon they were both sitting on the bottom bunk, leaning on their elbows, introducing more of themselves to each other.

"My mom left when I was a kid," Skyler told him at one point. "She was, like, this grunge girl in the '90s or whatever. She went to Seattle and then came back with the two of us. We were just babies, and she basically dumped us on my grandparents—well, my grandma and my stepgrandfather—and then a few years later she disappeared."

"That's rough." Danny sighed. "And I thought my parents' divorce was bad."

"I'm sure it was! I didn't mean . . ."

Danny turned to her, looking kind and handsome in the dim light of the bedroom. "I know you didn't. Man, you're so . . . polite."

Skyler grimaced. "Is that an Asian joke?"

Danny's eyes widened. "No! No, not at all."

She smiled. "Just kidding."

Danny laughed and leaned back onto his elbows, this time a little closer to Skyler.

"So you came here with your sister?"

"Yeah, Kate. I mean, she's my sister but she's kinda also like . . . an aunt or something. Maybe even a mom. She's only two years older than me, but she basically raised me. Back when my mom and my grandparents were fighting all the time, before my mom left. Kate, like, protected me from all that."

Danny nodded. "That's cool, that's cool."

Skyler felt dumb. Like she'd been talking too much, about way too much personal stuff. They were supposed to be talking about, like, school and music and Netflix shows. Not her family trauma. "Sorry, I—" she started, but before she could finish, Danny leaned over and kissed her. She was startled, and pulled back.

"Is this O.K.?" he asked, his brown eyes peering into hers. Skyler froze for a second but then nodded her head. "Yeah, yeah, it's O.K.," she whispered, and they were kissing again. And then Danny was getting up to turn off the light, and then, a little while later, they were having sex. It wasn't Skyler's first time, but it almost felt like it was, in the comfort of Danny's childhood bedroom, Danny seeming so kind and quiet, with just a little bit of mischievousness—or was it danger—about him.

Even though Kate insisted to Skyler that Danny was an asshole and best avoided, that he had a reputation for fucking with girls' heads and possibly worse, Skyler quickly started dating him, fooling around with him up in her cluttered room on many afternoons after school when Kate had practice or a club meeting or whatever it was she was always so busy doing.

At first, Danny had been sweet, and generous. He was the youngest of a big Irish Catholic family, and was very into his Irishness. He gave Skyler a Claddagh ring, told her to wear it with the heart facing toward her, so people would know she belonged to someone. That word, "belong," so chilling later, then seemed romantic and old-fashioned, like Skyler finally had a place in the world that had nothing to do with Kate, or her grandparents, or her mother, who they thought was maybe living in California somewhere. (They'd gotten a postcard at Christmas when Skyler was thirteen, a picture of the Golden Gate Bridge on it. Her mother had written, "You girls would love it here," but there was no invitation to come visit, or any indication that that was even where she lived.)

Danny made Skyler feel special and free and all those things it was hard to feel in her buttoned-up house. Maybe this was the feeling her mother had been chasing all these years, a sense of looseness and sexiness and excitement.

Skyler was fifteen when she and Danny started dating, and by the time she was sixteen, Skyler was in full, consuming love, most waking moments of the day taken up by Danny or thoughts of Danny. She loved the wiriness of his red hair, his skinny but muscled frame, the dumb shamrock tattoo he'd gotten on a trip to Montreal, the gold cross he wore around his neck, a gift for his confirmation.

She loved the way he always had her pulled close to him, whether they were wandering through the Prudential Center or at parties in the Arboretum, everyone drunk on Bud Light cans, all the other girls named Meghan or Ashley, the boys Tommy and Timmy and Mike. Danny always had an arm firmly around her waist, his hand often traveling down to give her butt a squeeze. She liked being Danny's girl, liked playing up whatever hint of a Boston accent she had.

And she liked, even though she knew it was wrong, that Danny was often jealous, that he had once knocked a tooth out of a Latin Academy kid's head for talking to her at a party. She liked his roughness, the way he almost devoured her during sex, pinning her arms above her head, that gold cross dangling above her. It all felt very grown-up, somehow, that Danny had such an obvious passion for her, that she felt so protected by him, provided for. Danny worked as a caddie at The Country Club in Brookline in the summers, and he must have gotten good tips, because he always had money, was always insisting that he pay when they went to see a movie, or got ice cream at J.P. Licks, or, on special occasions, dinner at Bertucci's.

Still, there was a small, nagging voice deep inside Skyler, which sounded a lot like her sister, telling her that this was all going to turn bad someday, that the dangerous flicker she saw in Danny's eyes sometimes—rarely at first, but then more and more as they became more intertwined, when he was drunk or was swerving between cars on Arborway—was eventually going to turn its dark, frightening glare onto her. She never told Kate about these worries, as Kate had mostly opted to let Skyler make her own mistakes, greeting Danny coolly whenever he came over and raising her eyebrows in skepticism whenever Skyler told her sister about a nice thing Danny had done. So Skyler let this fear, a little gray bead lodged somewhere in her, stay quiet, mostly unaddressed and ignored.

There was a sick kind of relief, then—the strange satisfaction of having a persistent fear finally manifest itself—when, on the night of Danny's senior prom, Skyler learned what it felt like to have Danny's anger pointed directly at her.

Skyler spent all afternoon getting ready, Kate helping her with her hair and makeup, wanting to make her sister look nice for the dance, if not for Danny.

"You know, you could always skip," she said to Skyler, the two of them in Kate's room, Skyler with her hair up as Kate did her makeup. "We could go get a fancy dinner somewhere instead."

Skyler sighed. "Come on, Kate. I'm going to the dance."

"I know. I know."

"He's really not like what people think he's like. He's sweet."

"Yeah, but aren't they always sweet in the beginning? Isn't that how they get you?"

Skyler laughed. Kate was being so dramatic. "What would you know about how 'they' always are, Kate? When's the last time you even dated someone?"

Unfazed by Skyler's teasing, Kate took a step back to examine her progress with Skyler's makeup. "You know fully well that I went on a date with Chris Chen last month."

"Chris Chen?" Skyler laughed again. "Chris Chen is gay."

"Yeah, but he doesn't know that yet. So it counts as a date."

"That is so sad."

Kate shrugged and gave her sister a goofy smile. "I think you're ready," she said, getting out of the way so her sister could see herself in the mirror. Skyler liked the job Kate had done—it was a subtle amount of makeup, but it still made her cheeks glow, her eyes sultry and inviting, her lips pouty and sophisticated.

"He's gonna love it . . ." she murmured appreciatively.

"The important thing is that *you* love it," Kate said, a pointedness in her voice.

"I do, I do. Thank you. What time is it? I should get dressed."

The dress Skyler had saved up for was a pale blue two-piece, satin and hugging with a thin layer of chiffon over the skirt. It was lovely and ethereal. When Skyler first tried it on she felt like some sort of ancient goddess, powerful and graceful. There was only the slightest hint of midriff showing. It was strapless, but nothing plunging or otherwise risqué. It was the kind of dress that Skyler wasn't afraid to wear in front of her grandmother, so she certainly didn't anticipate Danny taking any issue with it. She hoped he'd think she looked good, that he'd be proud to have her as his date. It was a good dress, and had cost her all the money she had saved from work, plus a little from her grandmother, who said, "For your party" when she gave Skyler the check.

Skyler unzipped the dress bag, laid out carefully on Kate's bed, and looked at the gown with admiration for a moment before slipping it on, Kate helping her with the zipper in back, then letting her sister's hair down—a kind of casual beach wave look that had taken hours to get right—and saying, "O.K. Take a look."

There in the mirror, Skyler saw someone elegant, someone ready for a beautiful night. "Wow! Not bad, huh?"

"Not bad at all," Kate said, fixing a stray strand of hair and hiking Skyler's top up just a bit. "We could also still just go have dinner, even with you dressed like that."

"Kate . . ."

"I know, I know. I just hope . . . I hope you'll be careful tonight. With him."

"Ew! Kate!"

"Not like that. Well, yes, like that. But just . . . Don't let him control the night, O.K.? I know it's his prom, but it's your night too. And you look too good to be told what to do."

"O.K."

Skyler heard a car pull up outside and then the doorbell ring, and she felt a shiver of excitement. She couldn't wait to see Danny's face when he saw how good she looked, some mix of awe and love and lust that would bode well for a magical, memorable night.

But when he walked in, Danny took one look at Skyler—posed expectantly and sort of embarrassingly, halfway up the stairs, waiting for him—and his face changed, becoming tense and angry.

ALL WE CAN DO IS WAIT

"Are you going to wear something over that?" he asked with a scary, strained tightness in his voice.

It was the end of May and seventy-five degrees outside, so Skyler had not thought about wearing a wrap or anything, and she certainly didn't have anything to match the dress. "No," she said cautiously, walking the rest of the way down the stairs. "I was just gonna go like this."

Danny laughed a little, incredulously, taking a step toward her. From the smell of him, Skyler could tell he'd already been drinking, probably with his friends in the limo, which was waiting outside. "Baby, what if it falls down or, like, rides up?"

Skyler put her hand on Danny's arm, trying to reassure him, to calm him down. "It's not going to, I promise. It's fine."

He pulled his arm away, a violent yank, and stepped in even closer. "You're not going to my prom to show your tits to everybody," he said in a low voice. The lewdness of that word, "tits," mingling with the sourness of Danny's breath, startled Skyler, and her stomach plunged. Danny put a hand around her arm, tight, and she was about to try to wriggle free when she heard Kate's voice at the top of the stairs.

"Hey," Kate said warily but loudly. Danny backed off, shooting his gaze up at Kate with a menacing look. Then Skyler's grandmother, either not picking up on the tension or wanting to defuse it somehow, said, "You look so handsome, Danny. And Skyler looks so pretty. I want a picture!"

She made them pose on the stairs, Skyler with her back to Danny, his arms around her waist. She could feel his heart beating; his breathing was deep. He was still worked up, but he didn't say anything else.

He posed for the pictures, put the white corsage he'd brought around Skyler's wrist, and took her hand and led her out to the limo, where the Meghans and the Ashleys and the Timmys and the Tommys were waiting. They all gave a little whoop when they saw Skyler, Ashley Costello saying, "You look fucking hot!" and Tommy Keegan passing Skyler a half-empty fifth of vodka as she settled into the car.

Danny was stony and silent the whole ride to the hotel in Natick where the prom was being held. When they got there, she quickly lost sight of him.

"Have you seen Danny?" she asked Meghan Murphy at one point. Meghan was one of the nicer girls in Danny's friend group, but she still had a hard edge to her, a chip-on-her-shoulder iciness.

Meghan gave Skyler a pitying look and said, "Drinking in the bathroom, probably."

"Oh," Skyler said, trying to hide her disappointment. "Right. Sure."

"It's what they always do at these things," Meghan yelled over the loud music. "It's not like they dance or nothing."

Of course they didn't dance. What had possessed Skyler to think that she and Danny might dance all night? Especially after the fight over the dress? She felt dumb, like a silly puppy dog who had eagerly followed Danny to the dance only to be ignored.

Meghan leaned in close, smelling like hair spray and sweat, and said, "Doesn't mean we can't have fun!" She waved to Skyler to follow her, and they went into the women's room, where Meghan produced another little bottle of vodka. She took a swig and handed it to Skyler, an eyebrow raised. "If they can do it, we can do it!" Skyler was already a little woozy from the couple of pulls she'd taken in the limo, but whatever. She felt newly indignant about the whole night. She was going to force herself to have fun. Meghan whooped and clapped as Skyler took a big swig then coughed, her throat burning.

They heard the beginnings of a favorite song, "We Found Love," coming on and tore out of the bathroom to join the mass of kids waiting to jump up and down at the drop. It was a different kind of fun than Skyler had expected, but it was fun nonetheless—reckless and messy.

She spent most of the evening dancing with Meghan and the girls, feeling warm and happy from the vodka, careful to adjust her dress whenever it seemed to slip just a little.

But toward the end of the night, when Danny had finally emerged from the bathroom, pretty far gone and seemingly forgetting to still be mad about the dress, Skyler convinced him to slow dance with her, resting her head on his chest as they swayed to "XO" by Beyoncé, that great, swelling song about deep, eternal, magical love. Danny had softened, kissing her forehead as they danced, holding her gently as they rocked back and forth.

Skyler figured they were past it now, that it had just been an isolated flare-up, because Danny had been a little buzzed, because he was graduating and emotions were running high. They all took the limo back to Timmy McDonagh's house, where there was a party since Timmy's parents were away on a Caribbean cruise. Danny didn't let Skyler out of his sight the rest of the night, but it felt like the good kind of Danny attention, the us-against-the-world kind, and when they'd gone up to an empty bedroom and had sex—almost like it was their first night together all over again—he said, "I love you, I love you, I love you" while they did it, the two of them falling asleep while spooning, Skyler feeling secure and reassured in Danny's arms.

Skyler felt her phone vibrate again, quick and sharp, in her bag. Another text. She wasn't going to look. She wasn't going to look. It was him. She wasn't going to look.

Suddenly, the emergency doors swooshed open, and with a cacophony of yells and siren blares and pounding feet, the first of the Tobin Bridge victims were rushed into the hospital on gurneys, the present moment suddenly so close and immediate and urgent that Skyler could feel it clamping her in place.

Here was the rest of her life, the rest of Kate's life, about to be decided.

Chapter Six

Alexa

SHE WASN'T SURE why, but Alexa found herself reaching for Scott's hand as she watched the emergency room explode into action, nurses and doctors appearing as if from nowhere, all streaming toward the wail of the ambulances outside. It felt strangely like the people of honor had just arrived at the party being hosted for them, Alexa and all the other guests relieved that they were finally here, so the real evening could begin.

Alexa caught herself before she found Scott's hand, instead turning toward her brother, who was looking at the flurry of activity with a dazed, open-mouthed expression. Jason turned toward Alexa, gave her a weak look, eyebrows raised. "This is good. Right? This is good. They're gonna be with this group, I bet." Alexa still wasn't sure where this optimism, manic and seeming forced, was coming from. That was not the

Jason she'd known for some time now, save for maybe the few peaceful, happy months they'd spent in Wellfleet a year ago. That time had been a mostly unexplained anomaly, and soon Jason was back to his sulking, his stormy moods.

When Alexa pictured her family, there was the brightness of those twelve weeks surrounded by a sad sort of emptiness. It was hard to picture her family as a family, instead of separate units all floating around the same house by chance. Still, that her parents might be hurt, or worse, threw Alexa off balance in a way that made her feel she might never right herself again. She was trying to think positively. But she couldn't help but already feel like an orphan, as if the last vestiges of her always distant parents had finally evaporated, disappeared, drifted off somewhere unreachable.

The crowd of people in the waiting room was surging toward where patients were being brought in, against the loud protestations of Mary Oakes, hair out of place now, and the nurses who worked the reception desk. "Please! Please! Everyone remain calm," they were all saying in near-unison, as people shouted demands for information. All of Alexa's tablemates were standing, but Skyler was the only one trying to push forward into the group, using her small size to squeeze between people. Morgan, the girl who had just sat down with them minutes ago, was hanging back, biting a thumbnail and looking lost. Scott had a determined look on his face, as if he was about to go into battle. But he stood still, as unsure what to do as nervous-looking Morgan, as Alexa.

A strange impulse shivered through Alexa, and she got out her phone. She selected her mom's cell phone number from her contacts and pressed "Call," wondering if maybe, now that people from the accident were in the same building as she was, she might hear it, her mom's familiar ringtone, the soothing classical cello piece calling to her out of all this pandemonium. But the phone went straight to voice mail, her mother's high, crisp voice instructing her to leave a message.

Alexa hung up and tried her father's phone, a number she rarely called, and it actually rang, giving Alexa a surge of hope before it too went to voice mail. Her father hadn't set up an outgoing message, so it was just the robot lady reciting his number, then the dull beep of the prompt to start talking. Alexa considered saying something, an "If you get this, call me." But she'd already left plenty of those for her mother hours ago, and it was really unlikely, even if he was in perfect shape, that her father would even check his messages. He was an e-mail man, glued to his BlackBerry at all times.

Except, of course, for that summer—that charmed June, July, and August when her whole family found some kind of harmony, a cruelly brief little miracle passing through their lives, binding them together before pulling them apart as it left. Her father had put down his phone sometimes then, looking out at the ocean from the porch, leaning back in his Adirondack chair, legs crossed, ice in his cocktail glass tinkling. "Pretty good," he would say, nodding in approval. And Alexa agreed. At least then, the view was remarkable.

What had it been, back then? What crept in and fixed them for a little while? It was several things, most likely. Chief among them, the fact that Jason was clear-headed and almost kind. Not every day was like that evening on the beach, when they'd actually *talked* to each other. But things were lighter, airier, full of jokes and little kindnesses. Jason didn't mind driving her to work, would even let her plug in her phone to listen to her music.

One day on the drive over, Jason had surprised her by asking, "So, are you, like, dating anyone?"

Alexa blushed. "Uh, no, why?"

"I dunno. You're always so eager to go to work. I figured you were, like, hooking up with someone in the pantry or whatever."

Alexa laughed. "Well, I'm not. I am definitely not."

"Well, you should," Jason said. There was an awkward pause. "I mean, you're, y'know, cool, and pretty."

Alexa laughed again. "Gee, thanks," she said. "Thank you for validating my prettiness. That's all I needed. Now I will go screw someone in the pantry."

"I didn't mean it like that." He turned to her, looking serious. "I didn't, honestly."

"I know."

They drove in silence for a moment, "Cake by the Ocean" blaring incongruously—or maybe perfectly aptly—on the stereo.

Alexa turned to her brother. "Are *you* screwing someone?"

"What, in the Grey's pantry?" he said, eyes on the road. "No."

"But you are screwing someone."

"None of your business."

"You asked me if *I* was!"

"Yeah, but I get to. I'm your protective older brother."

"Oh, *gross*," Alexa said, making a retching sound. "I think you are, though. Not at Grey's, but somewhere. I think that's why you brought it up. You want to tell me, don't you?"

"I do not," Jason said, the smallest of smiles creeping across his face.

Alexa let it drop, content that she and her brother were getting along, making jokes, dancing around details of their personal lives.

With her two kids coexisting in harmony, Linda seemed to calm down some. She drank less, for one. Sure, a cocktail with Theo before dinner, and some dry white wine during the meal, but nothing so excessive that she'd fall asleep on the sofa, like she did much of the time back in Boston, waking up the next morning testy and short with a hangover. There weren't any blurry reveries into the past, no painful, forced conversations about girls from Linda's college way back when. Theo seemed less distracted, less pinched about work. He and Linda both were back and forth from Boston, but far less than Alexa had expected them to be. They stayed for days at a time, falling into easy rhythms of morning and evening swims, tennis and lunch at the club in between. The trip was working.

And, of course, there was Kyle. Maybe he'd been the key to all of it. Kyle had warmed the house. Though staying with Laurie and her cousin held the promise of a fun night of getting drunk and listening to music too loud well into the night, Alexa suspected that Kyle liked staying at the Elsings' best, maybe because it offered some sense of family and normalcy that he didn't get at home. Kyle, of course, was seeing the magical Pollyanna version of Alexa's family—he'd likely have been shocked by how estranged they all were in Boston. But on the Cape, wrapped in the spell of those perfect summer winds, they'd put on a good show, and Kyle enjoyed it.

He fit right in, engaging with Jason about bands and books—it turned out that Jason liked Chvrches and thought the movie version of *The Perks of Being a Wallflower* didn't do justice to the book, who knew? Kyle made Linda laugh, a sound round like a bell, and she'd put her hand on his wrist and say, "Oh, you are funny. You really are funny," as she wiped an eye. Theo was fascinated by Kyle's scrappy, jerry-rigged existence, which Kyle was frank and forthcoming about. Alexa's dad thought it was noble somehow. Kyle was "a real bootstrapper."

Alexa didn't feel like she was losing him to her family, though. She felt like she was sharing him. She and Kyle still had plenty of time when it was just the two of them, at work and in the evenings after—and on some days off, though they didn't share many of those. Alone together, they could easily, pleasantly fall into long conversations about big things. Places to travel, lives they'd like to lead.

They played a game they called, simply, Five Houses, in which they had to name the five places in the world where they'd buy a house if money was no object.

"A flat in Paris," Kyle said one night, he and Alexa curled up on the love seat on the Elsings' porch.

"What about the town house in Notting Hill?" Alexa asked.

"Oh right. Um . . . can I do both?"

"You can do five houses anywhere you want. That's the point. But remember, there is the Chunnel."

"The Chunnel!" Kyle exclaimed. "How could I forget the fucking Chunnel. O.K. So forget London. I'm Brexiting or whatever. I can just take the train from Paris if I want to see something in the West End."

"And to stay at my house in Oxford."

"In Oxford, yes, of course."

"A tree house in Bali, too," Kyle murmured.

"That's four. Tokyo, New York, Paris, Bali. Where else?"

Kyle thought for a while. He looked out toward the water. "Here."

"Like, Wellfleet?" Alexa asked, a little surprised. She figured he'd want to get as far away from the Cape as possible.

"No, like, *here*. This house."

"My parents' house?"

Kyle turned toward her. She could only barely make him out in the dark, but he seemed to shrug a little. "Yeah. I'll buy it from them."

"I don't know if it's for sale. I don't know why you'd want it anyway. We're talking any five houses *in the world*."

"It's a good house," Kyle said. "Full of good people."

Alexa laughed bitterly. "Ha. Right."

"Absolutely right," Kyle said, grabbing Alexa's hand in the dark.

"I want to get out, though," Alexa whispered. "I want to leave."

"So, you will."

"Yeah."

"You will."

There was something funny about the Five Houses game, the ridiculousness of it. But they took it seriously too, as if they should treat it with respect on the very slim chance it would jinx it not to.

Kyle knew about all kinds of places, holding forth on streets in Rome and national parks in Africa, though, he confessed to Alexa, he'd never really been anywhere.

"Not even to see *Wicked*," he sighed to Alexa that night, sitting on the porch with a dreamy look on his face after getting back from smoking a joint with Jason. They laughed, *Wicked* being the kind of show that dumb tourists would go to New York to see. Not them, though. They'd go see weird plays and eat at ethnic restaurants in Brooklyn. "I can't wait," Kyle would say quietly, whenever they talked about New York, like the dream was just around the corner, coming fast—but also like it was very, very far away.

When he was around, which was surprisingly often for her brother, Jason indulged Alexa's idle fantasies more than he might have back in Boston. Sometimes he'd sit on the steps of the porch, listening to Alexa and Kyle prattle on. He'd chime in with some random comment, something like "I hear Budapest is cool," but mostly he seemed content to just sit and listen, a happy, stoned expression on his face, hair salty and knotty, a true beach bum.

Once Kyle had told Jason that the scruff he'd grown out—a barely there scraggle of blond beard—was cute, and Jason had blushed. Him! Alexa's brother, blushing. It was a whole new Jason.

The summer unfolded, endless and green, and Alexa felt herself changing. Passing thoughts about altering her own course, of taking a cue from Kyle and Courtney and, hell, even her brother, developed into a conviction. She was going to listen to all these ambitions inside her and do something about them. Not put them on hold for four years while she went to a socially acceptable school.

She was envious of Kyle, of his relative freedom, the fact that he could just pack up and go. And he, in his way, gently encouraged her to see that she could be free too.

"I mean, you'll go to school eventually," he said. "But why can't you, like, live a little first? British kids do it. A gap year. Before they go to *uni*."

He said that in a sing-song British accent, Anglophilia another of his interests, most of which seemed to take him away from his life in Bourne with his mother.

Another night, later in the summer, mid-August maybe, when they were closing up Grey's together, Kyle seemed in a particularly chipper mood, bopping around the store and singing Carly Rae Jepsen to himself.

"What are you so happy about?" Alexa asked him, washing the frappé cups and wiping all the dribbled ice cream from the stainless steel countertop.

Kyle smiled and said, "I don't know! I just think things are going to be good. When they come, the things. They're going to be good."

"The things," Alexa repeated.

"Yeah. You know, life or whatever. Stuff. Stuff that isn't this!"

Alexa always felt a little hurt when Kyle, or the Price twins, or even Courtney, alluded to how much they hated it there, in Eastham, at Grey's. "I like this stuff," she replied, quietly.

Kyle stopped restocking waffle cones and looked at her, hard. "I know you do. And so do I. You know I do. But like we've been saying:

We're both gonna get out at some point. And when we do, when the time comes, I'm just saying I think it's going to be good. I can *feel* it."

And for the first time in a long time, Alexa found that she really agreed with him. It did feel like that, there in the middle of August, hot but not sticky, the crickets outside like a chorus of assent, a million "yes yes yeses," telling Alexa, and Kyle, that this feeling was real, that they really were changing, that life was beginning, full of promise and possibility.

Now, of course, she realized that she'd been wrong, that Kyle had been wrong, terribly so. Here she was in the hospital waiting room a year and change later, in the middle of all this mess, all these endings. A few families who seemed to have gotten some bad news were crying in corners of the waiting room. A lone woman, looking silly and out of place in her gym clothes, was sobbing so loudly by the nurses' station that Alexa almost wanted to ask her to quiet down.

But other people, including one of the mothers with a baby, had seen their loved ones, husbands and wives and children and sisters and brothers, wheeled through, and now, at least, had some sense of hope. They'd caught a glimpse of their person, still alive, making Alexa feel mean and jealous.

Still no sight of her parents. Still no reassurance from Jason, who was craning his neck toward all the activity but not doing much else. She wanted to smack him, just then, to do something to get that dull look off his face. But then she thought about what he might do, what he probably would do, when he inevitably found out—whether her parents were alive or not—why they'd been on the bridge that day.

Perhaps sensing Alexa's unsteadiness, Scott took a few steps toward her, gave her a sympathetic sigh.

"All this and still nothing. I mean—not *nothing*," he caught himself, looking off at one of the weeping families.

Was it good news, or bad? Were they crying from joy and relief—this big couple and their little wild-haired beanpole of a kid—or had some other child been crushed to death and they'd just found out? "This is so confusing . . ." Alexa heard herself muttering, feeling stupid the second she said it.

Scott reached out a hand, sort of swiped at her shoulder, a clumsy offer of comfort, but still appreciated.

"Yeah. It is. It really fucking is." He laughed, the swear surprising him maybe, and ran his hands through his hair, which looked a little unwashed.

Alexa looked at Scott, his broad nose and dimpled chin, and she couldn't help finding him attractive, droopy and worried as he looked just then. A sharp pang of guilt stabbed through her. How dare she be thinking about a boy right now, let alone a boy who was waiting to hear if his girlfriend, whom he really seemed to really love, was alive or dead?

Scott, maybe oblivious to Alexa's staring, maybe not, took another step toward her, so they were standing shoulder to shoulder, watching the hospital roil in front of them. Scott nudged her with his elbow and nodded at Jason, who was looking into the middle distance, expression blank and eyes unblinking.

"So, uh, what's his deal, your brother?"

Alexa laughed, a dark little sound that she didn't like. "If I knew what Jason's deal was, my life would be a lot easier right now. In general, it would be easier."

"Is he stoned or something?"

"I don't know. I asked, he said no."

"Is that, like, a problem for him?"

A sudden flood of tears filled Alexa's eyes. She was so tired of talking about her brother, of worrying about her brother, of trying to build the world around his anger and sullenness. She was tired of all of it. Especially now, when she considered the possibility that it might just be the two of them from here on out.

Would Jason ever do the same for her, try to shape his life around her, around her whims, her needs, her moodiness and self-absorption? No, probably not. Certainly not when he found out that she was the reason her parents were on the bridge. He'd blame her. It would finally be the excuse he needed to disappear from her life altogether. He'd finish school, maybe, and then he'd be gone. And Alexa would be stuck wishing he'd come back, maybe even begging him to come back to her, for the rest of her sad, guilty life.

"A lot of things are a problem for Jason," she said, wiping her eyes and taking a deep breath to calm herself, to tamp down her emotions so she could focus.

"Sucks," Scott said. "I mean, it's so selfish. To be like that."

Alexa flinched, recoiled a little from Scott. "I mean, you don't know my brother," she snapped.

Scott's face paled a shade. "No, no, I know, of course not, I'm sorry, of course not."

"It's just . . ." Alexa trailed off. She turned to look at her brother, skinny and floppy haired, looking half like a kid, half like someone about to be a man, and she felt a longing for him, or for some old version of him, him on the Cape. She saw a flash of her brother, sitting on the porch, framed by purple sky, arms wrapped around his knees, laughing at something she or Kyle had said. He was still in there somewhere, that Jason. He had to be.

"It was my fault," she said quietly. To Scott, to herself. It was the first time she'd said it out loud. "My parents. Today. It was my fault."

Scott started to speak, probably to say something about how of course it wasn't her fault, but before he could, Alexa turned and walked away, finding a chair to sit in, crumpling up, feeling entirely alone, wanting to disappear into whatever hole the bridge had left, the one that had swallowed up her whole future in one hungry gulp. She wanted to dive in and chase after it, even if all it led to was blackness and nothing.

Chapter Seven

Jason

THE FIRST TIME he kissed Kyle, Jason had felt like he was both lifting off the earth and sinking into it. It happened quickly and slowly, unexpected and yet like all of life, or at least all those first early days of the summer, had been leading toward it.

Maybe it had been there, this inevitability, since they first met. Jason had gone to pick his sister up at Grey's, since Linda didn't like Alexa riding her bike home alone at night, and Alexa hadn't yet started getting rides from her coworkers. Jason got there early, or Alexa was running late, he couldn't remember which. What he remembered is that he'd been standing by the car, fiddling on his phone, when he heard a soft and friendly "Hey."

Jason looked up from his phone and there was a boy about his age, tall and willowy, with a fount of loose curls. Jason had been attracted to guys before, of course, usually from a distance, but this was something different. He was immediately, intensely drawn to this boy, whoever he was. "Uh, hey" was all he could stammer back.

"You're the brother? Jason?" the boy asked, giving him a sideways smile.

"Um. Yes. Yeah. Jason. Hey. Who . . ."

"I'm Kyle," the boy said, extending his hand for Jason to shake. Insanely, Jason had a quick mental flash of him kissing Kyle's hand like they did in olden days. But he instead gave it a perhaps overly enthusiastic shake and burbled out something about how it was nice to meet him.

"How come you don't work here too?" Kyle asked. "We have a few sibling duos, you know."

Jason wasn't sure how to answer politely. How did you say "Because scooping ice cream all summer sounds like abject hell" in a way that isn't offensive to someone who was spending all summer scooping ice cream? So instead he said something dumb, "Uhh . . . I don't know. I guess I didn't even, um, think about it?"

"Ah," Kyle said, that sideways grin getting bigger. "So what *are* you doing then?"

Nothing. That was the truth, wasn't it? Jason really wasn't doing much of anything, besides lying around, watching TV, jerking off, complaining. But he couldn't say any of that, of course. So he just said, "Oh, you know, lotsa random stuff. I might, uh, teach myself to sail again?" He just made that up on the spot, but it actually didn't sound so bad.

Kyle laughed a little—but not meanly. "Sounds nice. I'd love to learn how to sail. Get in a boat and get the hell out of here . . ."

"I mean, I could—" Jason started to say, but then he saw his sister striding across the little parking lot toward them.

"Hey!" Alexa said. "Jason, don't bother Kyle."

Kyle shook his head. "I think *I* was bothering *him*. Anyway, I gotta run. I forgot to feed Laurie's cat and have to do it before she gets back or she'll kill me. Or I'll kill the cat. But I'll see you tomorrow. And Jason," Kyle said, turning to him and giving him another mysterious smile, "happy sailing!"

Jason drove all the way home in a daze, Kyle's lilting way of speaking—the music in his voice, its slight girlishness—echoing in Jason's ears.

A week or so passed, and the feeling mostly abated. Jason almost forgot about it. But then Alexa texted him to say that she was bringing Kyle over to hang out.

Though he didn't usually spend much time with his sister, Jason was determined that night to be near Kyle, to figure out who he was. Kyle wasn't exactly the type of guy that Jason had been furtively attracted to before—he wasn't some jock closet case, in other words. But something about him, like he was from another time, maybe the past or maybe the future, was entrancing to Jason.

So when Kyle came over, a simple "Oh, hey, Jason" when he walked into the kitchen, Jason stayed, listening to Kyle and Alexa talk about all these places they wanted to go, wishing he could participate but realizing he'd never really actually let himself think about the future, or where he wanted to travel, or what he wanted to do. The more he spent time with them, that night and many others that summer, the more Jason felt limited around Kyle—and around his sister, he realized.

She suddenly seemed so cool, so grown-up and worldly. When had that happened? Maybe she'd always been like that. Seeing Alexa like that on those evenings, often out on the porch in the perfect nighttime air, made the magic of Kyle—surely he was magic—somehow more potent. He'd cast some spell on Alexa, and on Jason, and now suddenly they liked each other, they got along, they had fun together.

On their fifth night of hanging out, Jason said he was going to go smoke a joint, and Kyle raised his eyebrows. "Would you mind if I joined you?"

Jason's insides did acrobatics, but he tried to play it as cool as possible. "Sure, that's cool. Alexa, you wanna come?" *Please say no, please say no, please say no.*

"No thanks, it'll just make me go to sleep."

Jason shrugged, knees knocking a little. "K."

He and Kyle walked down to the beach, passing the joint between them.

"Your sister's the best," Kyle said.

Jason nodded. "Yeah, I guess so. I mean, yeah, she is."

"She's my favorite person at work."

They sat on the sand by the big white lifeguard chair, one person walking a dog off in the distance.

"It's fucking beautiful here," Kyle said quietly, looking out over the beach.

It felt stupid to admit to himself, but Jason realized he maybe hadn't ever noticed that before. But Kyle was right. It was beautiful. Both the crispness and the wistful haze of it, the warmth and the wind. Or maybe he was just stoned. Or maybe he was just in love with Kyle.

A week like that passed, the three kids hanging out most nights on the porch, Kyle and Jason going for little walks to get stoned, not saying much of anything, but always taking a moment to appreciate being on the beach. Usually it was dark, and they'd silently look up at the stars, gleaming and flickering millions of miles away.

Things changed eventually. One early evening in mid-June, Alexa called from work and asked Linda if it was O.K. if Kyle—who tended to come by after Linda had gone to sleep or was back in Boston for some function—came over for dinner. Linda, perhaps thinking Alexa had a boyfriend, said yes, curious to see what proud summer son of Wellfleet her daughter had been spending so much time with.

If Linda was disappointed when Kyle showed up, in his rolled cut-offs and billowy shirt ("It's a blouse," Jason had joked to him, a month or so later, the two of them whispering in Jason's bedroom), she didn't show it, welcoming him in with her trained society warmth.

Theo was back in Boston—"a big meeting with the Hong Kong people," Linda said—so it was just the four of them. "Why don't you sit at the head of the table, Kyle," Linda suggested. "You can be the man of the house tonight."

Kyle laughed, genuinely comfortable wherever he was, and seeming to see something, some charm or wit or elegance, in Linda that her own children had long been blind to. "I'd be delighted," he said, and Linda clucked contentedly.

Dinner was airy and fun. They ate corn salad and grilled swordfish, good Massachusetts food, as Theo often said. Kyle kept Linda occupied, asking her questions about her days at Barnard.

"Though I'd probably rather live downtown instead of uptown when I move."

Linda waved a hand at him in agreement. "Well, that's where the young people go. And there are so many fabulous galleries down there." She took a sip of wine. "Do you like art, Kyle?" she asked.

Instead of giving Linda a simple yes, the easy, accommodating answer many guests Kyle's age, or any age, would have offered, Kyle actually thought about it for a second.

"You know," he said. "I don't really know art all that well? But I think I will like it, when I learn more about it."

This just about sent Linda over the moon, as much as she ever went over the moon. "Well, I'd be happy to lend you whatever art books I have lying around here," she said, referring to the huge, very expensive volumes she had littered on the coffee table and on the bookshelves in the living room. "So long as you take good care of them, and return them by Labor Day."

"I'd love that, Mrs. Elsing," Kyle said, somehow not sounding like a brown-noser. Like he actually *meant* it.

"And then of course you'll have to visit Alexandra and us in Boston this fall," Linda declared. "I'll take you on a personal tour of the museum."

"That would be great, Mrs. Elsing. Thank you so much."

Linda sat back in her chair, beaming, pleased with herself, with everything.

After dinner, Linda was in an uncharacteristically generous mood, saying she'd wash and dry the dishes herself. "You kids go out and enjoy the night, it's so lovely out. Show Kyle the beach maybe."

Alexa rolled her eyes. "He's seen the beach, Mom."

Linda waved her away. "But not *our* beach." (Kyle had, of course.) She turned to the dishes, and the kids did what she asked, walking out to the porch, the nearby ocean roaring with all its mystery and allure.

Jason had sneaked two more than the usual one Linda-approved glass of wine at dinner, so he was feeling buzzed and loose. He pulled the joint he'd rolled before dinner from the breast pocket of his shirt—one of Theo's old blue striped oxfords—and held it up to Alexa and Kyle.

Alexa shook her head, said she just wanted to sit, that she was tired from standing all day at work. "My dogs are barking!" she moaned.

Kyle laughed—the best sound Jason had ever heard, he suddenly thought—and said, "O.K., but do you mind if I join your brother for a joint?"

Alexa shrugged. "I don't care. Wouldn't be the first time."

So the two boys walked down to the beach, the tide high, pulled toward the beach by the moon, beaming and perfectly round in the sky. Jason lit the joint, took a deep hit, passed it to Kyle and watched him put his lips on it. Jason's stomach felt knotty as Kyle exhaled then passed it back. Their feet were in the water, lapping at their ankles.

"Your mom's so fun," Kyle said, taking a step further into the water.

Jason shrugged, took a hit. "She certainly thinks so."

Kyle laughed again, a sharp pierce that melted into a little song. "You're funny, Jason," he said, turning to face him. Jason held the joint out for Kyle and he approached and took it, their fingers brushing, a million shivers of electricity traveling up Jason's arm. Something was different tonight.

Kyle looked at him and smiled, and then, very simply, put one hand on Jason's cheek, leaned in, and kissed him. Jason hesitated for a second and then kissed Kyle back, his hand on Kyle's shoulder, his knees knocking, the whole world gone spinning and tingling around him.

After a moment, Kyle pulled back. He smiled again, took a drag from the joint, almost burned down to the end. "I've been wanting to do that since the first night we met."

Jason was surprised. "Yeah, me too, I guess."

Kyle raised an eyebrow. "You *guess?*" he said, splashing some water in Jason's direction.

"I mean," Jason stammered, "no, I know. I know. I just didn't, like . . . *know* know. Until now."

Kyle leaned in close, gave Jason a peck. "Well, now you *know* know." He turned and started walking up the beach, then looked back at Jason. "Come on, your sister is waiting."

Jason could see Kyle receding up the beach, toward the glow of the house, could feel the riot of elation and stonedness and horniness that had flooded over him after that first kiss. Kyle disappearing in the tall grass, the waves rushing in and seeping away. Jason blinked, the light of the hospital pinging back into focus. *Your sister is waiting.* Jason turned around, toward the table, but didn't see Alexa, only that Morgan girl, hands hidden in her sleeves, arms crossed tightly over her chest. "Hey," Jason croaked at her, his voice sounding scratchy and tired. Morgan looked up, as if to say *Me?*

"Have you seen my sister? The girl with the—"

Morgan turned and pointed at a corner of the room, and Jason saw Alexa, curled up in a chair, face buried in her knees. She looked so small, so lost in this ugly, harshly lit place. Jason hated seeing her here, hated places like this. He knew it was a dumb thing to wonder, but why did it all have to look so *clinical?* All the inoffensive off-white walls, the sallow fluorescent lighting, the blond wood of the railings that were everywhere, for people too weak to stand on their own. Couldn't a place like this be cheery and optimistic? Or, maybe more honestly, dark and stern and serious? Wouldn't that be more truthful—a hospital painted in black, or a worried gray, dim lamplight in the hallways, somewhere entirely ready to be filled with ghosts, night after night after night?

Jason felt a sudden protectiveness over his sister. He wasn't used to seeing her like this, retreated and scared. Maybe this was an opportunity, for Jason to make up for all the times when he should have stepped up, should have been there for his sister. He could do something.

The woman. The hospital woman. How long had it been since they'd brought in the first patients? Twenty, thirty minutes? She must know something. Jason was going to be useful.

"Hey," he said again to the tall girl, Morgan. "What's the lady's name again, the hospital lady?"

Morgan took a few timid steps toward him. "Um, it's Mary. She's Patient Services."

Jason nodded. "Yeah, yeah. Can you come talk to her with me? I need to ask her about my parents, but I'm not really sure what to ask her. You know, like, specifically."

Morgan seemed to think this over for a second before giving a quick nod. "Yeah. She's over there. You just have to . . . I'll tell her I know you. She knows me."

They walked over to Mary Oakes, who was cradling a phone under her chin. She saw Morgan, looked a little surprised, then held up a finger, asking her to wait.

"Uh huh, uh huh, it's looking like forty to fifty, yes, that's the latest we've heard, I don't know, Dan, it's not like—Yes, I understand, we're already almost at full—No, of course, I understand. O.K., thank you, Dan."

She hung up the phone. "Morgan. You're still here." *Still here?* Of course she was still here, Jason wanted to say. *We're all still here.*

Morgan nodded quickly, "Yeah, uh, this is . . ."

Jason realized he'd never told her his name. "I'm Jason, Jason Elsing. I think my sister, Alexa, asked you about my parents, Linda and Theo . . . uh, Theodore Elsing?"

Mary shot a look at Morgan, like it was her fault that this dumb kid was bothering her. She turned to Jason. "I'm sure she did, but unfortunately at this time there is only so much we're able to tell the families. If you speak with the nurses and give them your parents' names, they will update you as soon as they know something concrete. As you can see, right now we're really trying to focus all our energy and attention on the victims—on the patients."

She took off her glasses and rubbed the bridge of her nose. "In the meantime, I'm afraid you'll have to wait. I'm sorry there isn't more I can tell you. And Morgan, you should have someone come get you. Is there someone who can pick you up?"

Morgan shook her head. "No, I want to be here."

Mary Oakes sighed, nodded. "Well, do what you want, of course. But you'll have to excuse me now, I have about a hundred more phone calls to make." She picked the phone back up and turned away from them. Morgan looked at Jason and shrugged. They stood there for a second, not really sure what to do, Jason feeling like he'd already failed at his half-assed attempt to take some of the burden off his sister.

"Hey," Morgan said, sounding a little sheepish, maybe feeling bad that she couldn't help more. "Do you maybe want to, like, go outside, get some air?"

"Yeah. Sure," Jason said, feeling defeated.

Morgan smiled a little, a hint of crooked teeth, and nodded her head toward the door. They made their way through the crowd, not saying "Excuse me," just pushing through, and then finally they were outside, where the rain had let up and the air felt wonderfully crisp and bracing.

Morgan reached into her pocket and pulled out a small electronic cigarette. She took a drag off it, releasing out a cloud of vapor, which rose up and mingled with the rest of the wet air. Jason laughed, those things always looking so silly. But when Morgan held it out to Jason, he looked at it a little quizzically before taking a long drag himself, his lungs feeling cold and tingly. He handed it back to her, and they stood there for a moment in silence, Morgan taking another drag, the noise of the hospital wafting out in intervals as the doors slid open and shut.

"I'm sorry I couldn't help more," Morgan said after a while. "She's kind of a bitch, Mary. I mean, she's fine. She's helped out me and my dad a lot. But her, um, what's the thing, with doctors, like bed manners."

"Bedside manner."

"Yeah. She's not great at that."

A weird thought burbled up in Jason's mind. "She kinda reminds me of my mom, actually."

Morgan laughed, then, realizing who she was laughing about, abruptly halted herself. "Sorry."

"No, no, it's O.K. It's not a bad thing, not really."

Morgan nodded and they stood in silence for a while longer. Jason rubbed his eyes with the heels of his palms, let out a long, slow sigh. "Man. This blows."

Morgan laughed again, louder this time, a chortling bark of a sound. "It certainly fucking does." She had a thick Boston accent, but not the fake kind you'd see in bad movies about Southie. The real kind, the kind with melody, and grace. It reminded Jason of Kyle, the way he had said certain words: clipped, hushed, elided.

Before he could stop himself, Jason said, "You remind me of my boyfriend."

Morgan looked a little surprised, but absorbed this new information in stride. "He's tall too?"

Jason laughed, shook his head. "No. Just your accent and, I dunno, something else. He was . . ."

"Poor?"

Jason shifted uncomfortably.

"Kidding," Morgan said, giving Jason a meek smile. "I mean, about your boyfriend, not about—I mean, my dad always says we're gonna be the last poor family in Dorchester. You know, since you got all the rich people buying houses in Savin Hill. First it was the gays . . ." She looked at Jason. "Sorry."

"No, it's O.K. I am a gay, it's true. But, uh, don't tell anyone that."

"They don't know?"

"They might, but I've never told them. So."

"I get it."

"Your dad, is he going to be O.K.? Did she tell you?"

Morgan nodded, held the fake cigarette between her fingers, flicking it back and forth with her thumb, though there was no ash to flick off. "Yeah, yeah, he'll be fine. I don't know. Your parents are gonna be fine too."

"That's what I told my sister, and she freaked out. She said I was high."

"Are you?"

"Eh. Hard to tell at this point."

"Yeah. My mom used to take Oxy? Got hooked working at this hospital, ironically enough. She'd be fucked up for days. I hope you're not taking that shit."

"No, no, nothing like that. Did she quit, your mom?"

Morgan pulled up her hood, puffed on the e-cigarette. "Nope. She died."

"Oh man."

"I mean, I assume she died. You can't get Oxy after a while, so you go for heroin, 'cause it's easier to get, and cheaper. Which is pretty fucked up. So she was on that for a while, and then she left. My aunt said she came to stay with her in Nashua for a little while, but then she left there too, and that's the last time anyone saw her. In fucking New Hampshire."

There was a long pause, then finally Morgan broke the silence.

"So, tell me about your boyfriend," she said, offering him the cigarette again. He took it, pulled on it, thought for a second. Jason felt a sudden closeness to Morgan, the way she set him at ease, talked to him like a person instead of a collection of disappointments.

He wanted to tell her about everything that happened after that first kiss on the beach. About the next kiss, on the porch after Alexa had gone to bed.

And the next one.

And the next one, and the next one. In places he couldn't remember anymore.

He wanted to tell her about how he had said "I love you" while he and Kyle were driving to Provincetown, their first and only time going there together. The way Kyle had said nothing at first, only reached out his hand, the other hand loosely on the steering wheel, and ran it through Jason's hair. How Jason had felt so seen and known and safe and alive just then.

He wanted to tell Morgan about the first time he and Kyle had sex, awkward and giggling in Jason's bed one night after drinking a bottle and a half of Linda's wine. He wanted to tell her about how Kyle fell asleep first afterward, and Jason lay there listening to him breathing, running a finger along Kyle's freckled back, wanting to eat him alive, to absorb him through his skin, to bury himself under Kyle's armpit or behind his knee.

He wanted to tell Morgan about all the bad things too. About how melodramatic and petty Kyle could be, about how much he lied about trivial things. About how he sometimes treated his and Jason's secret like a weapon or a threat, to get something he wanted or to guilt Jason into indulging his fantasies for a little while longer.

Jason would sometimes get annoyed hearing about all the wonderful things Kyle was going to do in New York—because as much as they were consumed with each other then, those future plans never quite seemed to involve Jason. He would tell Kyle that, and Kyle would frown, his eyes darkening a little bit, and then, with a sinister breeziness in his voice, he would say, "Well, if I can't talk to you about that, maybe I should talk to Alexa about us, or to your *parents* about us," and Jason would give him a little shove and say, "Fuck off."

Jason wanted to tell Morgan about the fight that he and Kyle had, when the summer was fading and the real world loomed on the horizon. He wanted to tell Morgan how sorry he was. How he'd do things differently if he could. If he could, if he could, if he could.

He didn't tell her any of that, though. Instead, he just took another drag off Morgan's cigarette and said, "You would like him."

She smiled, friendly but lined with sadness, shivering in her sweatshirt, pale under the streetlights.

Chapter Eight

Skyler

SHE'D MADE HER way to the nurses' station, squeezing between what felt like an endless tangle of people, but whatever answers Skyler had hoped to find on the other side weren't there. Just more confusion, more questions, more worry. Yet another nurse asked her where her parents were, but as Skyler tried to explain who she was trying to find, the nurse was distracted by someone else's question and turned away from her. Skyler felt small and silly, yet again, so after a few frustrating minutes, she edged her way free from the reception desk and back into the emptier recesses of the waiting room, where she saw Scott, looking guilty. Alexa was curled up in a chair, looking like she'd given up.

"Hey," Skyler said to Scott, who gave her a halfhearted smile. Skyler gestured toward Alexa. "She O.K.?"

Scott shrugged. "I guess. O.K. as we all can be right now."

Skyler sighed. "Yeah." She and Scott stood there for a moment, not sure what to say to one another. Skyler, feeling nervous and wanting to sit down, said, "Maybe I'll go check on her."

She made her way to Alexa and sat next to her, Alexa acknowledging her by pulling her head up from her knees, letting her feet drop to the floor, and leaning back in her chair in a slump. After a short silence, Alexa, eyes on the ceiling, asked, "Did you find anything out? About your sister?"

Skyler shook her head. "No. Just . . . more waiting."

Her phone buzzed, again. Why hadn't she just turned it off? She ignored it, but Alexa had heard the vibrating. "Shouldn't you answer that? I mean, what if it's your parents?"

Skyler folded her hands over her bag, as if to muffle the sound of the phone. "It's not my parents." Alexa didn't press it any further.

"Where are you from again?" Alexa asked, her tone light and conversational, maybe trying to distract Skyler from whatever tenseness had seized her when the phone buzzed.

"JP," Skyler answered, a vision of the empty house, of Kate's pristine room, just across the hall from Skyler's messy one, darting into her head.

"Oh, cool. JP seems cool. Like, lots of old hippies, right?"

It was true. Parts of Jamaica Plain had long ago been taken over by crunchy vegetarian types who ran co-ops and held an annual Wake Up the Earth Festival every spring, and whose kids were white boys with dreadlocks and hyphenated last names. That generation of kids was mostly grown now, and so the neighborhood felt a little different, a newer, younger, less crunchy crowd of people moving in. But

Skyler's grandparents' house had sort of weathered it all untouched, tucked away on a quiet street off South Street, close to the Forest Hills T station.

"Yeah, lots of old hippies. And new yuppies. It smells less like pot all the time and more like . . . yoga mats."

Alexa laughed. "I thought hippies did yoga."

Skyler shook her head. "They're the ones who, like, introduced yoga to white people. But the yuppies have taken it to a whole 'nother level."

"I've only been there once," Alexa said. "Jamaica Plain. A girl from school lives there, and she had this party. It was pretty lame, but it was kind of funny because all these girls from my school were so, like, fascinated with the public school kids? They thought all the boys were so hot, with their accents."

Skyler wasn't sure if she should find that story funny, a bunch of rich girls doing public school kid tourism in JP, which was by no means poor, at least not the part of JP Alexa had probably visited. But there was something amusing about it, a bunch of girls ogling all the dumb, basic, same-y boys Skyler was surrounded by at school every day. Everyone was interesting to someone, she guessed. And, of course, those boys had been interesting to her once too.

Skyler fiddled with the ring on her finger, two hands clasping a heart.

"I love those," Alexa said. "They're so . . . Boston."

Skyler wasn't sure why she still wore it. It had once represented something good, something that made Skyler feel safe. Now, two years later, maybe it still kept her safe. Only now it was a talisman, used to ward off something bad.

In the weeks after prom, things had been good between Skyler and Danny. The euphoria of the about-to-graduate seniors was infectious. But then summer came, and shortly after the Fourth of July, Danny was fired from the golf course for vague reasons that, no matter how many times Skyler asked, Danny would not explain to her. He didn't even tell her that he got fired. She had to hear that, embarrassingly, from Meghan Ehlers, the two of them standing off to the side during an Arboretum party, Skyler wondering aloud why he was in such a mood.

"Oh, you didn't hear?" Meghan asked, seeming a little too excited to have information that Skyler didn't.

"No . . ." Skyler answered cautiously.

Meghan made a little gasping sound and said, "He got fired. I don't know. There was some fight or something."

No wonder he was thrashing around like crazy that night. But when Skyler asked him the next morning, knowing that asking him the night before would not have been a good idea, he shrugged it off. "I quit," he said, kicking out of bed and stomping to the bathroom, Skyler realizing that was the end of the discussion.

Skyler was in summer school, having failed physics that year. When she wasn't in class or trying, halfheartedly, to study, she was with Danny, helping him pack and get ready to move to the apartment in Roxbury he and two of his friends would be living in when they started at Suffolk in the fall. Without a job, Danny might not have enough money to cover rent, and his parents, stretched thin with so many kids, three in college, would not be able to help him. They suggested he live at home, he could choose his mom's or his dad's house, but Danny wouldn't hear it. He and

Tommy and Timmy had too many plans for their newfound freedom—parties, mostly.

So Danny was brooding and mean most of the summer, testy with Skyler and getting drunk pretty much every night. Sometimes he'd text her and demand that she come pick him up, seeming to forget that, though Skyler had her license, her grandparents wouldn't let her drive the car after dark, let alone to pick up Danny in the middle of the night.

Some nights, Skyler was able to convince Kate to do it, Kate looking frustrated as she drove to West Roxbury or Hyde Park or wherever it was that Danny was stranded. Other nights, Skyler would have to say no, and Danny would send angry texts, calling her a bitch and threatening her with the names of other girls, saying Ashley so and so or Meghan so-and-so would pick him up instead.

Skyler hoped that once the summer was over and Danny was back in school, things would calm down, he'd have his place and she would go over there as much as she could, as much as Kate was willing to cover for her with her grandparents, really. But the summer ended and Danny moved and things only got worse. There were some scary nights when Skyler and Danny were alone in the apartment and he'd start thrashing around, demanding to know what she was doing all day. "I was in school, I was in school," she would say, crying, but Danny would demand to see her phone, convinced she was cheating on him with someone.

The first time he pushed her against the wall and punched it, barely missing her head, he'd been immediately apologetic, saying, "Baby, baby, baby, I'm so sorry, I'm so sorry, I fucked up." By the end of his first semester, though, stuff like that had become routine. He threw a lamp, he cracked her cell phone while slamming it down on the night table after finding nothing incriminating on it. He was getting in fights with random guys at parties most weekends, heaving and bloody-nosed and wild-eyed, stomping around the apartment afterward while Skyler tried to calm him down.

She didn't tell Kate about most of this, but her sister could sense something was wrong. She'd started asking more pointed questions about Danny. She'd heard stuff too, of course, from the diffuse circle of friends who'd all known each other in high school. Kate had started at Lesley and was supposed to be living her own new, independent life, but she spent an increasing amount of her time checking in on Skyler, texting to make sure she was O.K., knocking on Skyler's bedroom door when she heard her having some tearful late-night argument on the phone with Danny.

"He's abusing you," Kate finally said, in February, the two sisters riding the 39 bus downtown to go shopping for a birthday gift for their grandmother. Kate couldn't see the deep purple bruises on Skyler's arms from when Danny had grabbed her the night before, furious about some imagined slight. (By then he'd all but dropped out of school, selling weed and, Skyler suspected, other things out of the apartment.) It was a sad kind of relief, hearing her sister say it out loud.

Skyler began to cry softly, turning toward the window of the bus, not wanting her sister to see how bad she'd let things get. How ashamed and afraid she was.

Kate turned toward her sister and then looked away. Skyler was scared it was out of disgust.

"You just have to end it," Kate said, matter-of-factly. The bus rumbled down Huntington Avenue, such a familiar route for such a strange conversation. But there it was. Skyler didn't say anything, hoping her sister would keep going. Kate being Kate, she did. "You know you can, right? You'll be O.K. We'll get a restraining order if we have to."

That sounded so harsh, though, so severe, so criminal. Danny was just . . . having a hard time, Skyler rationalized to herself.

"I don't think we need to do that," Skyler said quietly. "It isn't that bad."

Kate made a scoffing sound. "It isn't that bad? Pull up your sleeves then, Skyler. Show me your arms."

"Kate . . ." Skyler pled. But she wasn't sure what she was pleading for. She didn't want Kate to stop. It felt good to have someone finally say these things, even if it wasn't her saying them. "Things will get better. I'll talk to him. He's not a bad guy, Kate. He's not a bad guy."

Kate threw up her hands, sighed in resignation. "If I . . ." she started and then trailed off. They sat the rest of the bus ride in silence, stop requests pinging and the doors wheezing as passengers got on and off. By the time they got downtown, neither was much in the mood to shop, and they wandered Copley and the Pru aimlessly, finding nothing for their grandmother. With a cruel irony that almost made Skyler laugh, or maybe cry, all of the shops were decorated for Valentine's Day.

It was almost like Kate could sense the night coming. Just a few weeks from then, on a windy, wet March night that felt far more like winter than spring, when she got a frantic, panicked phone call from Skyler begging her sister to come to the Roxbury apartment.

Earlier in the night, Skyler was having a perfectly fine evening at Danny's. He was relatively placid, playing Xbox and drinking rum and Cokes. Skyler was doing homework—just staring at her books, really—trying to avoid another session of summer school. She heard her phone trill, a text message. She looked around for it, but it was nowhere on the little kitchen table where she'd set up her laptop.

"Who's Boli?" she heard, coming from the living room. She must have left her phone on the coffee table, while she and Danny were watching the Celtics. (They'd won, hence Danny's decent enough mood.)

"Huh?" Skyler replied, turning around in her chair. Of course she knew who Boli was, but Danny would seize on any little vibration of tension in the room, so she wanted to keep things as calm as possible for as long as she could.

"I said, who. Is. Boli," Danny said in his menacing, deliberate sing-song, the tone that meant he was probably about to lose his shit.

"Oh, *Boli*," Skyler said, still trying to play the casual game. "He's this kid from school I'm doing a dumb project with."

"What project?" Danny asked, sitting forward on the couch now, setting his drink on the coffee table.

"For American history. It's just this stupid thing. I don't even know why he's texting. It's not due for, like, another week."

"Is the project on 'Hey, what's up?' Because that's what the message says. It says, 'Hey, what's up?' What part of American history is 'Hey, what's up?'"

He was standing now, the phone clutched tightly in one hand.

"Danny," Skyler began, knowing he probably wouldn't let this go, but hoping, wishing, that just this once he might. But she didn't have time to finish saying that it was no big deal, that she really had no idea why Boli was texting her—Boli, a shy, nerdy, sweet boy whose name sounded so strange coming out of Danny's mouth, in that dim, drafty apartment—because Danny hurled the phone at her. She ducked out of the way, a grim reflex, while jumping out of her chair. The phone bounced off the wall, somehow not shattering, and skidded across the floor.

"Danny!" Skyler screamed, moving to a corner of the kitchen, instead of, she chided herself in her head, for the door.

Danny was advancing on her, face red, eyes dark but unfocused. "Who the fuck is Boli, and why the fuck is he calling you at eleven o'clock on a Sunday fucking night?!"

"He didn't call me, Danny!" Skyler yelped. "It was just a text!"

This was dumb. She knew it was dumb as she was saying it, before she even said it. Now was not the time to correct him. Sure enough, this seemed to make him angrier. He grabbed for her arm and caught a bit of her shirt as she wriggled out of his grasp and ran into the living room.

He chased after her, drunk and unbalanced. Skyler knew she was essentially trapped now, stuck in the interior of the apartment, Danny's roommates not home, not that they were ever much help when one of Danny's storms blew through.

"Danny, please," she pled, as he lunged toward her, grabbing again for her arm. He got a better grip this time, and as she tried to twist away he pushed her back, directly into the long, thin mirror affixed to the wall.

The back of Skyler's head hit the glass, and she heard a crunch. She couldn't tell if it was the glass or her skull. She stood there dazed for a second, her vision blurry, and then snapped back into focus.

Danny looked shocked, maybe even a little scared. "Jesus, Skyler," he said.

Skyler reached a hand back and touched her head. There was wetness, and she felt something, blood, dripping down her neck. "Danny . . ." she murmured, before a sudden surge of something—terror, will, whatever—had her bolting for the bathroom door, grabbing her phone up off the floor as she went.

Danny yelled, taking a few steps toward her, but she made it into the bathroom and locked the door behind her, sinking to the floor and letting herself cry while she dialed her sister's number, her phone badly cracked but still working. She felt the back of her head again and pulled her hand away. It was bloody, but not totally red. She would probably be O.K. She would be O.K.

Outside the bathroom, Danny was stomping around, making noise. He hadn't yet begun banging on the door, but Skyler knew he would. This wasn't the first time she'd locked herself in the bathroom, but it was the first time it felt this serious. Like something was going to break or end here, tonight.

Her sister picked up on the third ring.

"Skyler? What's going on? Are you O.K.?"

"Kate, Kate," Skyler said, barely able to get the words out between sobs. "Can you come get me, please? Please?"

Hearing Skyler on the phone, Danny began banging on the door.

"Skyler, what's that sound? What is going on?"

"Kate, can you please just come get me? Everything's fine. I just need you to come get me, please."

"I'm coming now," Kate said, and Skyler could already hear her leaving, the familiar whine of the front door. "Stay on the line, O.K.?"

And so Skyler did, she and Kate barely speaking, Skyler mostly hearing the sounds of the car, the jangle of Kate's keys as the wheels rumbled down Centre Street. Skyler waited.

Danny's banging had slowed to intermittent thuds, and he was whimpering, saying, "Skyler, please. Baby, please open the door. Please don't call the cops. Please, baby, please." Skyler realized that's what he was concerned about. Not her head, not the blood, not whether she was dead on the bathroom floor. He just didn't want to spend the night in jail.

Five minutes, ten minutes, fifteen. Then, a strange quiet, Danny either no longer at the door or having given up. Then, a banging, and another one, a clang.

Skyler heard Kate's voice, suddenly in the apartment. She was yelling at Danny, who was yelling back at her to get out, that she needed to mind her own fucking business. Their voices grew louder as they moved toward the bathroom. Skyler heard her sister yelling, "Back the fuck up, Danny! Back the fuck up right now!" and then she was knocking on the door. "Skyler, Skyler, it's me. Unlock the door. We're leaving, now. Back up, Danny!"

When Skyler opened the door, her sister was standing there, in her winter coat, jeans, and flip-flops, clutching the tire iron from the trunk of her car like a club. Danny was pacing furiously on the other side of the room, but not advancing on them. Kate looked hard at her sister and said, "Go to the car now," and Skyler obliged, noticing on her way out that it looked like Kate had broken the apartment door down, forcing her way in to get to her sister. Danny didn't say anything as Skyler left, but as she and Kate got in the car, he leaned out the window and yelled, "Bitch!"

Skyler cried the whole way home, apologizing over and over again to her sister, who just stared straight ahead, trembling a little, taking deep breaths. "It's O.K., it's O.K.," she said a few times, speeding all the way to the house.

Their grandparents were already asleep, so the girls quietly made their way up to Skyler's room, where she cried some more. Kate made Skyler show her her arms, the bruises and marks that Danny had made.

"Give me your phone," she said, and Skyler handed it to her. There were already texts from Danny, twelve of them, and Kate deleted each one. She then blocked his number and blocked him on Instagram and Facebook. "There," she said, handing the phone back to her sister. "You're done with him."

Skyler looked up at her sister, calm and tired looking, and wanted to believe her. That she really was done with Danny, even though some awful part of her still loved him, even though he was only a few miles away.

And of course, it wasn't done, not entirely. He showed up to Skyler's house, but only once. Kate stood on the porch and threatened to call the police, their grandmother watching quietly from the dining room, a solemn expression on her face. Kate's threats seemed to have scared Danny—he knew she was serious—and he didn't come around again. There were occasional texts and calls from unknown numbers, though—still, eight months later. The awful part of Skyler, the part that still wanted Danny back despite everything, itched to answer every one. But when Skyler was clearer headed, not lost in Danny's thrall for a day or a week, she knew she was ridding herself of him. Slowly and uncertainly, maybe, but she was. She knew that she couldn't make him go away, not entirely, and that was still scary, many months later. But she at least felt more sure of herself, bit by bit, day by day. Like she didn't have to tiptoe through the world quite so much.

In her bedroom that night, after they'd cleaned up the cut on her head and Skyler got into her pajamas, she threw her arms around her sister and said, "I'll pay you back, I promise. I'll do something for you, too." Kate just laughed and said it didn't work like that, and she and Skyler fell asleep together, like when they were little and their mom would be fighting with their grandparents downstairs, those bitter few months before she left for California, or wherever.

Their mom had left, their father remained an unknowable mystery. But Kate was always there, her warmth close to Skyler, enveloping and protecting her in ways Danny's arms never could.

And now this. Kate could be gone, before Skyler was able to repay her, like she said she would. The hospital was cold, and Skyler's clothes were still damp from running in the rain. She shivered. Alexa noticed and offered her the sweatshirt lying on her lap. "I took it off because I was hot. You can wear it if you want." Skyler said no thank you, she'd be fine. They sat in silence, the sound of Kate's voice, consoling and steady, echoing in Skyler's head.

"My sister saved my life, I think," Skyler said, to herself, to Alexa, not sure why she was sharing this fact with this stranger, but knowing that it felt good to say out loud.

Alexa nodded. If she wanted to know what Skyler meant, she didn't ask. "Yeah" was all she said. "She sounds great. You're lucky to have her." Skyler's eyes welled with tears. *Lucky to have her*. She couldn't lose Kate, she couldn't lose Kate.

She was repeating this mantra to herself, like she was back on the plane to Phnom Penh, when Alexa stirred and made a little sound. Skyler looked up and saw Mary Oakes, the Patient Services person, walking toward them with a serious-looking woman, short gray hair and little round glasses, beside her. Skyler and Alexa stood, Skyler fixing her hair for some reason, smoothing it down and collecting it all on one side.

"Skyler Vong?" Mary Oakes said, flat and grave. Skyler nodded. "This is Dr. Lobel. She'd like to speak with you about your sister, about Kate, if you could come with us, please." The doctor nodded, smiled tightly, and Skyler felt the plane dip down toward the earth. She was falling and there was nothing left to catch her.

Chapter Nine

Scott

ON THE FEW occasions that Scott had scored a goal during a soccer game—a few perfect fall afternoons when things had gone just right—there had been a moment when everything slowed. When the world distilled, and there was only Scott and the space of grass between him and the net, the movements of the goalie and the defenders becoming almost predictable, as if Scott had tapped into the Matrix and could see it all laid out so clearly in front of him, ones and zeroes streaming down in green. But weirdly they were also quick, these moments of excitement and frenzy, gone before they really had a chance to register.

Scott felt some version of that sensation—the world narrowing, both slowing down and flashing by—as he watched Mary Oakes and a woman who looked to be a doctor walk toward him. Was this it, the moment when he found out? That Aimee was dead, that Aimee was alive? He felt anxious, his insides tight. The doctor had spiky short gray hair and little glasses, and her mouth was tight with—what was it? Concern? Pity? Scott braced himself, stood up taller and clenched his jaw, as the doctor approached.

But then she and Mary Oakes walked past him and over toward Alexa and Skyler, both girls looking up, then standing up, a flutter of hesitation, of fear that they were about to hear the worst. The news wasn't for him. Scott felt a rush of relief quickly followed by another stab of fear. He still knew nothing, and now, from the looks of it, someone else was about to have their world cave in.

Scott assumed the doctor was there to speak to Alexa. He wasn't sure why, and it made him feel terrible to think it, but he had some dark intuition that Alexa and Jason's parents weren't going to be O.K. That they had been crushed or drowned or whatever else, and these two kids, so dark and worldly seeming, would be orphans. They could handle it, though. They'd figure it out. They had money, they had each other, even if Jason was an asshole. That meant something. They could bear the news somehow.

Mary Oakes, though, had turned to Skyler, was pointing at the doctor, who nodded and put her hand on Skyler's shoulder. Skyler flinched at her touch and looked, panicked, at Alexa, and then to Mary Oakes, and then back to the doctor. Slowed down, sped up, all of this happening in the tick of seconds, but seeming to take forever. Now the doctor was turning, walking back toward the swinging doors, and Skyler was following her, nervously, taking halting steps, eyes wide and teary.

Alexa trailed after her until she reached Scott, grabbing his arm and staring off toward the doors.

"What happened? What did they say?" Scott asked. Alexa shook her head.

"I—I don't know. They just said that they had to talk to her, about her sister, and they said that they wanted to talk somewhere quiet. That can't be good, right? That's got to be bad news . . ."

Scott heard something in Alexa's voice that he thought he recognized. Something he was feeling too. There was, in the meanest and shittiest of ways, a twisted kind of hope burbling up in Scott. If Skyler's news was bad, did that tip the scales somehow for the rest of them? What were the odds that they'd all get bad news that night? All their loved ones couldn't be dead, right? So wasn't there a kind of cruelly hopeful arithmetic in the fact that Kate was gone? If Kate died, then the odds were better that Aimee would be O.K., that Jason and Alexa's parents might be O.K. Scott looked down at Alexa and wondered if she was doing this same math in her head, this same wishful equation, one that, he knew deep down, wasn't really how these things work.

How did he get here? Wishing that some strange girl, who seemed nice enough and had been a comforting, calming presence all night, had lost her sister so that Aimee could be saved? It was so easy to suddenly feel like a bad person, Scott thought. It was so easy to *become* a bad person. To stand there and wish for something terrible for someone else.

He saw that Alexa was crying and, instinctively, he hugged her, pulled her in tight and thought of Aimee, the way she used to cry so easily—sometimes because she was practicing, to get better at her acting.

She'd go on YouTube and watch random videos and would pretty much instantly lose it. She'd be laughing soon after, and Scott had gotten used to just letting her cry.

Sometimes he'd cry too, around her, because she made it so easy. They watched *Toy Story 3* and cried together, not, like, big embarrassing sobs, but definitely tears. Definitely something he'd never do in front of his friends. It was almost fun, to be so nakedly *emotional* with Aimee, to feel like a kid again, when you could just cry any time you wanted.

"See, don't you feel better?" Aimee said once, after showing him some video of a dog being reunited with his owner, a soldier who had just come home from Afghanistan.

"I guess?" Scott said, tears streaming down his face, and laughed. Aimee laughed too. A good, weird day.

Alexa's crying was something else, though: deep and scared and meaningful. But it didn't make Scott want to do the same. It only made him want to disappear, to close his eyes really tight and have this all not be what it was, to not be here, to have the bridge uncollapsed, to not have anyone dead, anyone sisterless, anyone orphaned. He wanted Aimee in Salem with Taissa and everyone else, he wanted things the way they had been not that long ago.

When Scott was in third grade, his parents had spent the better part of the year fighting. Business at the store was bad, and money was tight. But there was something else happening too, some worse problem in his parents' relationship, that at eight or nine years old Scott couldn't understand, and certainly couldn't fix. But he tried, praying fervently every night that his parents would stop fighting, that they wouldn't get a divorce, that things would just go back to how they had been, when things were simpler and happier.

Scott's mom was always saying things like "What happened to my little baby?" So much so that Scott began to feel guilty for growing up. Of course, he knew now that his mother hadn't meant it, that she knew he couldn't actually go back to being a baby, and didn't really want him to. But back then it had wracked him. He felt sad and guilty all the time. A teacher at school noticed that his behavior had changed and spoke to his parents about it, and they stopped fighting in the house so much, and eventually things got better and everyone seemed to move on. Scott never forgot that feeling, though, that desperate wish that things could just be easier.

He felt it now, a yearning to go back to when life was less complicated, when it wasn't so difficult and frightening. But what could he do? He could only hope that Aimee was alive, that she'd be all right, and that things would eventually get better, like they were supposed to.

Alexa sniffled and pulled back from his hug a little. "Sorry, ugh, I'm sorry. I just feel so bad for her. I mean, I feel bad for all of us. But . . . I don't think that was good news. It didn't look like good news."

Scott nodded, then looked up and saw Jason and Morgan walking in from outside. They were laughing about something, but they quickly stopped as they caught sight of Scott and Alexa hugging, and Alexa's red and tear-streaked face. Jason quickened his pace, his eyes looking a little sharper now, more focused.

"What, what was it? What happened?" he asked, notes of panic rising in his voice. "Alexa? Are they here?"

Alexa shook her head, pulled away from Scott, smoothed her shirt. "No, no. It's Skyler. Skyler's sister . . . They took her back there." She pointed to the ominous doors. "I don't think it's good news."

Jason ran both hands through his hair, letting out a long exhale. "Oh. O.K. O.K. That's . . . O.K."

Scott thought he saw a quick brightening in Jason's eyes, some spasm of relief. It was oddly comforting to see Jason reacting externally the same way Scott was inside. Maybe Scott wasn't such a bad person after all. Maybe it was natural—unavoidable—to feel this way. Of course, tragic news could still be waiting for him, for all of them, but they weren't out of the game just yet. There was still hope, still a chance.

Morgan had been hanging back, but then she approached the group, gave them a timid wave. "They took Skyler back?" she asked, and Scott said yeah, that it probably meant nothing good. Morgan shook her head. "Not necessarily. I mean, they might just not want to, y'know, give her good news in front of other people. You know, out of, like, respect." Scott knew she was right, of course.

"Yeah, I guess that's true," Alexa said, nodding a bit too vigorously. "Yeah. I mean, maybe it is good news. They took you back there to tell you about your dad, right?" she asked Morgan, who looked down at her feet.

"Yeah, they did. But, like, I know them here, so . . . I don't know. I'm just guessing, really. I don't know how all this works."

Jason made a sound. "I mean, it doesn't seem like anyone does," he said, gesturing toward everyone else milling about the waiting room. Scott realized that the crowd had thinned. Other people must have gotten their news and Scott hadn't even noticed.

"This is a mess. It's all a mess," Jason muttered. Something caught in his voice as he said it, and Scott felt a sudden pang of sympathy for him. Maybe Jason was only just now realizing the gravity of the situation. "It all just fucking sucks," Jason murmured, and despite himself, Scott burst out laughing. Then Morgan did too, Jason even giving a little half-grin.

"It really does, man," Scott said with a sigh. "It really does." Alexa stayed quiet, only sniffling a little more and crossing her arms over her chest. Morgan cleared her throat.

"You know," she began timidly, "my mom used to work here, like right in the ER, right where we are. And when I was little, she wouldn't tell me about all the really bad stuff she'd seen. 'Cause she must have seen, like, the worst things—people who'd been shot or burned or whatever. She never talked about work, unless it was, like, about some annoying co-worker or something. I guess maybe she talked to my dad about it? But I never heard it, if she did. And one day I realized that maybe she didn't have to talk about it because, for all the bad things she saw, there was good stuff too, you know? They save people here. Like, all the time. Maybe . . . maybe most of the stories here actually have happy endings?"

She smiled wanly, and the others returned the gesture. Scott nodded. "That's a good way of looking at it, I guess."

"But it's probably bullshit . . ." Jason muttered. Scott was about to snap back at Jason, to stand up for Morgan's little pep talk, but Morgan laughed.

"Oh, it almost definitely is," she said. Jason laughed too, and then even Alexa was laughing, snapped out of her funk for a second.

"I mean, it's probably a fucking nightmare here all the time!" Jason said.

"All the time!" Morgan yelped, looking like she might cry—from laughter, from fear, from tiredness. It was a desperate moment, but it also felt good to feel a little giddy, a little punchy, Scott realized.

They stood like that, the four of them laughing to stave off the fear. Scott thought that it felt a little like a team huddle, like they were ending a time-out, catching their breath one last time before heading back into the game. He closed his eyes for a second and wished himself back to one of those thrilling afternoons playing soccer, lungs screaming, hair sweaty, muscles burning. Then he heard Alexa say "Oh my God," and opened his eyes in time to see Skyler walking through the double doors, Mary Oakes behind her, a hand on her shoulder. She said something to Skyler, who nodded and gave her a tentative, awkward hug. Mary Oakes pulled back, nodded quickly, and then disappeared once more behind the doors.

Skyler looked over to them. It was clear she'd been crying. "Oh my God . . ." Alexa whispered again, breaking the huddle to walk over to Skyler. Scott followed, as did Morgan and Jason. If nothing else, if Kate was dead, they were here for Skyler. Maybe that counted for some tiny something.

Alexa was the first to reach Skyler. She gave her a big hug, Skyler bursting into tears, Alexa saying, "I'm so sorry, I'm so sorry."

Skyler shook her head—seemingly unable to comprehend the loss she'd just suffered—and said, "No, no, no." Alexa kept hugging her, until Skyler gave her a light push back, said, "No, she's O.K. Kate's O.K. I was just with her. She's going to be fine."

Alexa blinked at her, then turned to Jason. "She's O.K.?" he stammered out.

Skyler, bleary and smiling now, blubbered, "Yeah. Yup. They said she's going to be fine. I mean, she broke her legs really bad and is gonna need a lot of physical therapy, but it's not life-or-death. She's O.K. She's O.K."

A sick feeling coursed through Scott, dread and envy swirling together. He was happy for Skyler, for Kate, of course. He wasn't a monster. But if Kate was O.K., then hadn't the odds shifted? Wasn't Aimee now firmly back in the bad column? Had he just somehow condemned Aimee to die, by thinking such terrible things about Kate? Alexa must have been feeling something similar, because she staggered back and grabbed for Scott's arm again.

They stood, smiling weakly as Skyler wept. Morgan kept her distance, watching quietly, a resigned look flickering across her face before she said, "That's great. That's so great, Skyler."

Skyler nodded. "I know. I know. I have to try to call my grandparents. It's . . . I don't know what time it is there, but I have to—I have to do that." She went to her chair and started gathering her things, bag and coat and phone, pulling her hair into a messy bun as she shouldered her bag and took a deep breath. She looked at all of them and then seemed to realize. That her good news, her good fortune, wasn't theirs too.

She let a little "Oh" escape before steeling herself and putting a hand on Alexa's shoulder. "I'm not leaving, O.K.? I'm not leaving until you guys all know. I'm just gonna . . . I'm just gonna go call my grandparents and my family and . . . just not be in here for a second. But I'll be back, I'm not leaving." She smiled at them and then said, "O.K.," before striding out of the room, already dialing her phone.

And then there were four, Scott dipping his head and letting out a long breath, Alexa retreating to her chair, Jason standing, looking stunned and confused, as the sounds of the room returned. Morgan seemed to sense all of their worry. "If she's O.K., that could mean everyone else is too. I mean, people are surviving this, right? People are alive."

Scott wasn't sure what to say, what to do. He felt as helpless as ever, maybe even more helpless than before, somehow. He realized that, until then, he'd been quietly convinced that everything really was going to be fine, that things couldn't actually be as bad as they seemed. But somehow Skyler's news—her great, happy, miraculous news—made him doubt all that, made him convinced that everything was only going to get worse for him now.

He heard Alexa crying again, a despairing sound. Jason stayed rooted in place as Morgan walked quietly over to Alexa and sat down next to her, not touching her, not saying anything, just sitting. Of course, Morgan had had good news too, hadn't she? She didn't seem to know a lot, but at least she knew her dad was alive. Scott felt a flash of anger toward her, and then guilt again, and then panic. Things were back to that strange, dreamlike pace, Alexa's crying the only sound Scott heard. And then, he realized, he was crying too, a sudden rush of tears, a choking in his throat. He turned from the others and closed his eyes and tried to make it stop.

He thought about Aimee, in her sunny third-floor bedroom, practicing some monologue from some play, crying on her bed with a funny smile on her face, turning it on and off with ease.

"How the hell do you do that?" Scott asked, amazed.

Aimee smiled, casting him a serene gaze. "My natural ability!"

Scott laughed. "No, seriously. How? Do you just, like, think of sad things?"

"Sorta. I think about Google ads."

"Wait, what?"

"Yeah. You know the Google ad with the guy who moves to Paris?"

Scott had no idea what she was talking about. "I do not."

"Oh my God!" Aimee yelped, jumping up from her bed to grab her computer from her desk. Scott grabbed at her, wanting to pull her in for a kiss, but she swatted him away. "Not now, this is serious."

She got her laptop and brought it over, sitting next to Scott on the bed, Scott taking in the smell of her, soap and fruit and a little of the incense she liked to burn in her room when she was trying to set a sexy mood. (She didn't really need to try, Scott always thought.) "O.K. So there are a few really good Google ads, like the 'It Gets Better' one. But the Paris one is the absolute best. Oscar-winning. It should win Oscars."

Scott was skeptical as Aimee searched YouTube for the video. He wasn't a terribly sentimental or emotional guy—very few of the guys he knew were—and he doubted a commercial for a search engine would do much to move him. Aimee found the ad and let out a little "Aha!" and pressed "Play."

Visually, the ad was very simple. Just a search text bar. But it nonetheless told a story, about a kid studying abroad in Paris, searching for ways to woo a French girl, then going on a date, then getting a job in Paris and moving there, then getting married, and then, at the end, searching for how to build a crib. A whole romance, a whole life, told in a little ad set to wistful music. It was really something, and Scott's eyes were welling up with tears by the time the guy was searching for a job in Paris.

Aimee, tears streaming down her cheeks, looked at him and burst out laughing. "See? *See?* It's unreal! Every time I watch it!" She looked at him again, ran her thumbs under his eyes to wipe away the tears that were, yes, now falling. "I knew you would get it," she said, cupping his face and kissing him. "I knew you would. That's why I love you."

It was the first time she'd ever said that, and Scott instinctively, but meaning it, said it back. "I love you too. I love you, Aimee." And then they were kissing again, the day tumbling along as they fell into each other.

Scott closed his eyes and wondered if he would ever see Aimee again. He wondered if Skyler would actually come back. He wondered if he prayed then, harder than he ever had—even as a little kid when his parents were fighting and the whole world seemed to be crashing down around him, if he somehow prayed harder than that—if he could open his eyes and be somewhere else entirely.

Chapter Ten

Jason

IT KEPT REPEATING. The cycle of thinking that maybe some news was coming, and then nothing—then the worry and the daze rushing back in. They were spinning in place, all of them. Except, of course, for Skyler, whose life could, after a few hard weeks or months of her sister's therapy, return to normal, almost like all of this had never happened. Jason was bitter and angry, so tired of this feeling that nothing in his life could get better.

Then came the numbness. A strange sensation of calm muffling the sound of Alexa crying, dulling the sting of Skyler's happy news. Still, he wanted a pill, or a drink, or something that would hasten his retreat from the world.

The taste Jason had had—of a life that felt real and present and good—had been so short. Just a few months. The joy of that first kiss, followed by many other wonderful things. Kyle didn't mind the occasional joint, the occasional drunk and bleary night spent wild and laughing together. But the other stuff, and the constancy of Jason's stonedness, had bothered Kyle. And before too long, to make Kyle happy—and, he slowly realized, to make himself happy too—Jason eased up. It wasn't like he was some crackhead dying for a fix. There was no withdrawal or anything. He mostly just felt clearer and sharper and brighter, not waking up every morning flattened and headachey and grouchy. He actually felt, well, *happy* some mornings.

He and Kyle could only have a very few mornings in bed together, theirs being a secret kind of a thing, but at least the memory of Kyle, the knowledge of him, was in Jason's head every morning when he woke up, for nearly that whole summer. Some nice or funny or comforting thing Kyle had said echoing in his ear, some smell of him, some tingle somewhere on Jason's body where Kyle had touched him. He woke up eager to explore the day. To see Kyle, yes, but also to see where else this new feeling could take him.

He went sailing. Theo had a boat, a little Beetle Cat that was easy enough for one person to handle, and Jason spent most mornings out on the bay, everything blue around him, the wind whipping. He'd taken lessons as a kid and was surprised at how quickly the muscle memory returned to him. Pretty soon he was confidently sailing out far enough that he could barely see the beach anymore, alone on the water, the day laid out before him, shimmering with possibility. He hadn't felt so calm in his own skin in a long time, and he quickly grew to cherish those mornings, loving the expanse of the ocean rolling out in front of him as he raced across it, and loving watching the land get closer and closer as he turned and headed for home, knowing that things back there were pretty good too, for the time being anyway.

Jason couldn't really remember how he'd spent most of his days after sailing. There was just a handful of persistent memories. The day he got caught in a little storm, trying to manage his mounting fear as he desperately made his way back to shore, texting Kyle when he got home, *I almost died!*

Kyle wrote back *omg* and then, sending a shirtless pic of himself, *will this revive u?*

Jason replied, *no now im really dead.*

There was the day Jason rode his bike—another skill reclaimed from childhood—all the way to Orleans and back, forty miles or so, probably the most exercise he'd gotten in years. He'd just done it to do it, getting back home right before dinner, his mother asking him where he'd been all day. Jason told her he'd just been around, not doing much, and Linda smiled and said, "That's nice. It was such a nice day, wasn't it," chopping tomatoes for dinner, Garrison Keillor droning away softly on the radio.

And of course there had been days with Kyle, when he wasn't working. After they'd "broken the seal," as Kyle (a little grossly) called it, and had sex for the first time, a lot of their hours together were devoted to finding discreet, available places to do it. Usually that meant Laurie's when she was at work, or Jason's house when his parents were in Boston or at the club. But they found other places: Kyle's car a lot, a motel once, one time even doing it in the walk-in fridge at Grey's, a cold, sorta scary, entirely thrilling experience.

Of course they had to be careful not to be seen together, in any capacity really, so a lot of their precious, too-rare alone time was spent in Kyle's car, driving further west, toward the rest of Massachusetts. Everyone figured that Kyle was visiting his mom in Bourne, and they assumed Jason was . . . well, off being Jason somewhere.

But they were together instead. Eating lunch or early dinners at places by the water in Dennis and Yarmouth, hanging around on the beach, swimming. One afternoon they drove to Corporation Beach in Dennis, wide and crowded with swimmers and sunbathers, even on a late Tuesday morning. They'd fooled around in Jason's bed earlier—Alexa off at an early shift, his parents playing golf at the club with another couple—and Jason still felt hot and flushed as they drove, giddy and sexy and, he was beginning to realize, in love.

They found a place, a little ways away from the bulk of the crowd, and laid out their towels, Jason lying on his back while Kyle got out a book to read, a dog-eared paperback with a drawing of San Francisco on the cover.

"What's it about?" Jason asked.

"*Tales of the City*? It's, like, a bunch of people living in San Francisco. It's pretty old and pretty gay. I found it on Amazon."

"Oh, cool. What do you mean, 'pretty gay'?"

"I don't know. I mean, there are gay guys in it, and a gay guy wrote it. But it more just, like . . . *feels gay*."

"What does that mean?"

"You know. It's just got a gay vibe."

"Aha."

Kyle put the book down and leaned in closer to Jason. He reached out a hand and fixed Jason's bangs. Jason flinched for a second, scared that someone might see them. But then he thought about the morning, all that nakedness and intimacy, and he thought about what it meant to *feel gay*, and he let Kyle touch him, there in public.

"You should read it."

Jason closed his eyes, reveling in Kyle's touch. "Maybe I will."

"And we should go."

"Like, leave?" Jason asked, surprised. "We just got here."

"No, idiot." Kyle laughed. "To San Francisco. Someday. It sounds amazing."

"O.K.," Jason murmured. He would have agreed to anything just then, if it meant feeling more of the peace and contentedness he felt at that moment. "I like you," Jason said, eyes open now, looking directly into Kyle's. "I like you." Then, rather brazenly for him, he kissed Kyle, not a quick peck, but a long and lingering one. Making out on a beach, in the middle of the day! How about that.

When Jason eventually pulled away, Kyle smiled and said, "I like you too. A lot. But I kinda wish we didn't have to, y'know, drive all the way to Dennis just to hang out."

"We hung out this morning, at my house . . ." Jason said.

"Yeah, when your whole family was safely not home."

"What, you wanna hook up while they're home?"

Kyle sighed. "No, obviously not. I just . . . I wish you would tell them."

This conversation again. Jason rolled over, onto his back, the sky a pure and jewel-tone blue. "I can't."

"Why not?"

"Because . . . I just can't. We don't talk about stuff like that."

"Like what? Like dating?"

"Yeah, like dating. Like sex."

Kyle laughed, maybe a little annoyed. "Well, you don't have to tell them that we have sex."

"But they'll know . . ." Jason trailed off, hoping they could be done with this particular conversation for the day, for the summer even.

Kyle sat up and then there was his face, looming above Jason with a weird, serious expression. "Maybe I should tell Alexa."

Jason reared back, sat up too. "What?"

Kyle shrugged. "Maybe I should tell Alexa. Wouldn't that make it easier? Like ripping off a Band-Aid, only you don't even have to do the ripping. I'll do it for you."

"Kyle, no, please don't. That would be really shitty. Please don't do that."

"She's my friend too! She's one of my best friends. I can't tell my best friend about the great guy I'm dating?" He was trying to soften the moment with affection there at the end, but it wasn't going to work on Jason, not then.

"Please, Kyle. I'm serious. Do not tell my sister anything."

Kyle frowned, looked off at the water. "I wish you weren't so ashamed of me."

"What? Oh, come on. Don't be dramatic. I'm not ashamed of you."

"You sure act like it sometimes."

Jason put a hand on Kyle's shoulder, gave it a squeeze. "I'm not. I promise. And I will tell them. When it's the right time. I will."

Kyle leaned into Jason's touch and Jason felt him relax, the tension gone. "O.K.," Kyle said quietly. Impulsively, Jason scooted forward and wrapped both arms around him, his hands on Kyle's bare chest—as much physical contact as they'd ever had in public. He rested his chin on Kyle's shoulder.

"I will. I promise. I will." And Kyle seemed to relent.

The rest of the day was easy and relaxed, Kyle reading and Jason watching him, sometimes dozing off, the sounds of seagulls cawing and kids laughing in the surf creating a soothing kind of lullaby.

The coming out thing was not the only issue that Kyle pressed that summer. He was always pushing to go to Provincetown, but something about that place, about its supposedly unbridled gayness, scared Jason. He had refused all of Kyle's pleas that they drive out and spend one of his days off there, but then, at the end of August, the Friday of Labor Day weekend, Kyle announced that it was his birthday (Jason wasn't sure he was telling the truth) and that he was demanding that they go. So, after making sure his sister and his parents and everyone he knew would be nowhere near Provincetown that day, Jason agreed. Kyle yelped and jumped and gave Jason a kiss, saying, "You're going to loooove it. You'll be a total queen by the end of the day."

Kyle picked Jason up early, but not so early that Alexa wasn't at work and his parents weren't playing a game of doubles at the club. Jason fretted over outfits, not wanting to stand out either way—to be too gay or too straight. He settled on a pair of shortish shorts, rolling the legs up once to get them the right length, and a tank top. Feeling a little brave, maybe because it was the end of summer and there was a sense of *fuck it* and finality in the air, Jason got a pair of scissors from the kitchen and cut the sleeve holes open a bit more, not so low that it would qualify as a "skank tank," but low enough that, sure, he felt a little sexy.

He was turning in the mirror and just about to get second thoughts when he heard Kyle's run-down car putter up, then its sad little cat's moan of a horn. Jason braced himself and bounded out the door to meet Kyle.

"You look cute," Kyle said when he saw Jason. "You dressed the part! All you're missing is a little snapback hat."

Jason blushed, immediately regretting this daring (for him) outfit choice. "Whatever. And I don't own any hats."

Kyle, used to this routine from Jason, the push and pull of Jason coming into himself, said, "You look great," and put the car into drive, zooming them off toward the very end of Cape Cod.

The drive out was lovely, windy and green, full of excitement and romantic charge. Kyle was babbling on about some drag show in P-Town he'd talked his way into with a bad fake ID last summer. It was always so strange for Jason to imagine Kyle having a similar summer, working at Grey's and traveling around the Cape on days off, the year before they'd met, but Jason couldn't really focus on any of that. Not because he wasn't interested in what Kyle was saying, but because something that felt so much bigger and more urgent was pressing on his mind.

Kyle eventually realized he was rambling, or noticed that Jason was staring at him in a new and different way, and he turned to him, giving him an unsure little smile. "What? What is it?"

Jason smiled back, feeling hot in the face, his knees knocking like the first time he and Kyle had kissed, almost two months ago now, not that long, but also an eternity.

"What?" Kyle asked, his smile broadening. Maybe he knew what was coming.

Jason blinked. *Just say it.* "I love you," he said, and then, rather involuntarily, let out a huffy little laugh, like he was surprised he'd just said it. Which, really, he was.

Kyle raised his eyebrows, turned back toward the road. They drove in silence for a second or two before Kyle turned back to Jason. He reached out, affectionately ran a hand through Jason's hair, a little thing he liked to do. "Well," he finally said. "I guess I love you too."

A wave of relief passed over Jason, a sudden comfort. "You guess? I mean, you already said it in a voice mail, if you remember . . . Which, from the sound of it, you might not."

Kyle grimaced. "No, I know. But I didn't *know* know then. But now I do."

"You do what?"

"I do love you. I love you."

"I love you too," Jason said, giving Kyle a peck on the cheek and leaning back in his seat, a million little fireworks going off under his skin. They drove on, the sun dazzling above them, as if it was saying "Congratulations."

But by the time they got to Provincetown, clouds had rolled in, threatening rain, and the streets Kyle insisted were normally "packed with gays" weren't really any busier than any other tourist town on the Cape. And it was a lot of straight people, from the looks of it.

"How fabulous," Jason said at one point, immediately realizing it was the wrong thing to say, more haughty sarcasm at a moment that was supposed to be fun, was supposed to be big.

Kyle was disappointed, dejected, and, despite the excitement of the conversation in the car, he quickly slipped into one of his petulant bad moods. They ate lunch in a sulky quiet. Jason made a joke, something like "We can come back for your next birthday, in two weeks," but Kyle wasn't really having it.

"Maybe we should just go," he said dejectedly.

Jason was fine with that, fine to head back toward home and find a place to be alone together. But he didn't want Kyle to be disappointed. "We can stay," he said, grabbing for Kyle's hand.

Kyle shook his head. "No, it's fine. This was stupid. We should have checked the weather."

They probably should have, and Jason was actually a little surprised that Kyle hadn't. But it was too late now. Still, he wanted Kyle to have fun. The problem was, he'd never been to Provincetown before, so he had little in the way of suggestions. "Is there, like, a drag thing we could go to?" he asked lamely.

Kyle shot him a withering look, but it quickly dissolved into a little smile. "You're sweet. But no. It's the middle of the day, dummy."

"I thought there were drag shows twenty-four/seven in P-Town!"

Kyle rolled his eyes. "Nothing's twenty-four/seven in Massachusetts. Come on. It's O.K. We can go. I know you wanna go anyway."

As they made their way to the car, Jason felt bad that Kyle's big day hadn't gone as planned. But, he had to admit to himself, he was also deeply relieved to have gotten through the day without any real catastrophe. Then, just as Jason was thinking they'd made it, a voice behind them called out, "Kyle?" They both turned around—what could Jason do, really, just stand facing the other way while Kyle talked to whomever this was?—and there, to Jason's plunging horror, was Nate Carlsson from Grey's, one of the older workers there, a manager or something, in his mid-twenties.

"Heyyy," Kyle said, shooting a look to Jason, either scared to see Nate or scared that Jason was going to freak out.

"Crappy day, huh?" Nate said. It had started to drizzle, and people were scurrying toward their cars or houses.

"Yeah," Kyle said, nodding. "Yup."

Nate looked at Jason, and there was a slight flare of recognition in his eyes, a subtle change in his expression. "You're Lexa Elsing's brother, right? Jared?" Jason was dumbstruck, speechless. He'd just been spotted, with a known gay guy, alone together in Provincetown. They might as well have been caught in bed.

"Uh, Jason" was all Jason managed, feeling naked and exposed in his stupid tank top and shorts. Kyle let out a strange little laugh, and Nate smiled, nodded again, slowly, with a dawning comprehension. "Cool,

cool," he said. "Well, I'll let you two . . . get back to it. See you at work tomorrow, Kyle?" Kyle, stifling another laugh, said, "Yup, yeah, see you then. Bye, Nate!"

When they got to the car, Jason didn't say anything for a minute, wanting Kyle to focus on getting the hell out of there before anyone else saw them. When he was sure they were safely enough away, he turned to Kyle.

"Why the fuck were you laughing?"

Kyle shot him a glance, annoyed, maybe a little alarmed. "It was so awkward! What did you want me to do?"

Jason's face was hot, and he had a panicky tangle in his stomach. "Do you not understand that it is a big fucking deal that he saw us?"

Kyle didn't answer for a moment, eyes trained on the road as the rain splattered down on the windshield, the barely functional wipers whining. "I guess I *don't* understand that," he finally said, coolly.

They drove in silence almost all the way to the beach parking lot where Kyle usually dropped Jason off, so Jason could walk the rest of the way home alone. But before he got out of the car, Jason had to make sure that Kyle treated this as seriously as it was.

"Will he say anything? Nate? Is he friends with my sister?"

They reached the beach, and Kyle pulled into the little lot. He put the car in park and sighed. "I don't know, Jason. Why does it matter? Who really cares? The summer's almost over. It's not going to be so easy to sneak around once you're back in Boston and I'm . . . wherever I am."

Jason wasn't sure why it mattered, but it did. It was important that he and Kyle remain a secret. Not because he was so scared to tell his family that he was gay, but maybe because announcing it to the world, that he and Kyle were a thing, that they were, officially as of a few hours ago, in *love*, would invite so much shit into this perfect, contained, protected thing that they had. The rest of the world would find a way to ruin it, Jason was convinced. To pick it apart and sabotage it and pull them away from each other. And the thought of that . . . Jason couldn't think about that. He couldn't think about the end of the summer either, so close now. And he realized he was furious at Kyle for not understanding that, for thinking this was all some kind of joke.

So he said something terrible, there in the empty beach lot, the rain pounding on the roof of Kyle's shitty car. "Maybe it isn't supposed to last past the summer," he said quietly.

Kyle turned to him, looking like he'd been slapped. "What?" he asked, his voice small, any trace of flippancy or humor drained out of it.

"I don't know, Kyle. Aren't you supposed to be going to New York or something? And I have to get back to Boston. Maybe this is a sign."

Kyle balked, angry tears welling up in his eyes. "We literally just said 'I love you' to each other, like, *two hours ago.*"

Jason sat silent, feeling dark and stubborn. "Maybe I didn't mean it. Maybe I just said it because it's what you wanted to hear. We're too young to love each other. We don't know what we're talking about. We barely even know each other."

Kyle let out a caustic laugh. "You're such a fucking coward, Jason."

This stung because, of course, it was true. He was. He was being cowardly and pathetic. But he couldn't stop now; every mean thing Jason could possibly say was swarming in his head. "At least I'm not some loser who lies to everybody about a life he's never gonna have."

Kyle flinched, tears now streaking down his cheeks. "All right," he said, starting the car again. "I'm done. Get out. You have to walk the rest of the way home, don't you? So your mommy doesn't see you with me?" Jason said nothing as he opened the car door and slammed it, walking across the lot toward home as Kyle maneuvered around him and sped off, tires kicking up gravel and then splashing down the road.

That was the last time he saw Kyle. For the rest of Jason's life, that would be it. Two days of silence, and then, on Sunday night, the eve of the last day of summer, Alexa was on the phone, frantic, shrieking, saying Kyle's name in between sobs.

And then what? Jason falling back, into the void of his life before, his life to come. His sister's radioactive, repellent grief. She so clearly needed him to be there, to be present like he had been, but Jason found it impossible. He was already gone. The summer had ended and the cold had come early and he was sinking into it, far out from the shore, the glimmer of the sun dimming, everything watery and dark. It was so easy to just float away.

But not easy enough. Suddenly, Jason was pulled back to the hospital. Someone was saying his name. He turned around to see who it was and saw Morgan, eyeing him worriedly.

"Jason? Jason?"

He blinked, the lights of the waiting room seeming newly harsh and glaring. "Yeah?" he said, trying to sound alert.

"Do you mind sitting with your sister? I have to pee." He looked past Morgan and saw Alexa, not crying anymore but still curled up in her chair. He nodded at Morgan. "Yeah, of course. Of course."

Jason made his way to his sister. Kicked her chair lightly. "Hey." She looked up at him, looking almost surprised to see him there.

"Hey."

"Do you need anything?"

"No. I'm fine. I should—" She pushed herself up from the chair. "I should go talk to someone. I should ask Mary Oakes if she knows anything. She might. If they know about Kate . . ."

Jason nodded. "Yeah. She might."

Alexa straightened herself up, wiped her eyes, strode toward the nurses' station.

Jason thought about the red taillights of Kyle's car, disappearing around the bend in the road, the steady hiss of the rain as he walked the fifteen minutes home. When was the last time Jason had gone sailing? Had it been early that morning, the day of Nate Carlsson, the day of the fight? Or had he, despite everything else changing, still gone the next day? He couldn't remember anymore.

Alexa turned back to look at her brother. "What are you going to do?" she asked, probably already knowing the answer.

Jason said the only thing he knew how to say these days.

"I don't know."

Chapter Eleven

Alexa

IT WAS A regular enough night at Grey's, the night she found out, tinged as it was with end-of-summer sadness. Alexa had told her manager Nate that she would be back on weekends in the fall until Grey's closed for the season, after Columbus Day. But she and Nate both knew that probably wasn't going to happen all that often. The Cape was far, and she'd be busy with school. ("And friends!" Nate said, Alexa realizing she'd forgotten all about her paltry social life back in Boston.)

But Alexa insisted to Nate, and to herself, that this was not it. That she'd be back, that the spell was not going to lift on Monday morning. It was the only way she could make herself enjoy this last weekend.

Still, knowing this *could* be Alexa's last night at Grey's, Nate put Kyle and Laurie on with her, figuring they'd have fun, be a good team as they'd been all summer. Courtney and Davey's parents were out of the house that night, off in Woods Hole at some huge end-of-summer bash, and so the twins were having a party of their own.

The last few hours of work were fraught with anticipation. Kyle had the earlier shift, so he'd clock out and head up to the party ahead of them, and Alexa would catch a ride with Laurie after they closed down. Though, toward the end of his shift, Kyle started saying maybe he didn't want to go after all.

"You've been in a weird mood all weekend," Alexa said, when they were out back, tossing foul-smelling bags of old food and trash into the even worse-smelling dumpster. "What's going on?"

"I don't know." Kyle shrugged. "I'm fine. I'm not in a mood. I just . . ."

Alexa frowned. "What, Kyle?"

"I just had a little . . . bumpiness, with a boy. And I feel like I screwed things up, and he *definitely* screwed things up, and I want to fix them. I want to fix the things."

Alexa was surprised, a little hurt, even. "A *boy*? I didn't know you were dating anyone."

Kyle sighed. "I am. Or, I was? I don't know. I hope I am."

"Who is he? Is he anyone I know?"

He laughed, a tiny, almost imperceptible bit of breath. "I don't think so."

"Well, what happened?" Alexa pressed.

"Look, I don't really want to talk about it. I'm sorry. It's fine, I'm gonna be fine. He's going to be fine. *We're* going to be fine. It's all fine."

"O.K. It's fine."

"It is. And with that, I'm off. I'll see you and Laurie there?"

"Yes! Can't wait."

"Should be a scene. Have you ever met Davey's home friends?"

"No . . ."

"They're awful. But in a fun way? And cute! So, maybe . . ." He gave Alexa a little *wink-wink* elbow nudge, and she laughed and swatted him off. "O.K., my love, see you there."

Alexa gave him a hug. "I'll see you there." She walked back toward the store, but then heard Kyle calling her name. She turned around but could only barely make him out in the dark.

"Hey, Alexa! I was wrong. It's not going to be fine. It's going to be *great*." And then he was gone.

She and Laurie had another three hours of work, serving the last customers, an unsurprisingly long line of people wanting to cram in one last ice cream. Then the arduous cleanup, the restocking of things, counting the cash and matching it with all the receipts, entering it all on the computer in Nate's office.

But eventually, finally, they were done. Alexa was waiting out back for Laurie, who always took too long to leave, when she heard a kind of shriek or a wail coming from inside the store. Alexa ran back in, calling Laurie's name, thinking she might have seen a rat or something else that scared her. She found Laurie in the break room, one hand over her mouth, phone in the other hand, pressed to her ear. She was crying. Alexa looked at Laurie, and maybe it only felt like it now, with the hindsight of a year, but Alexa could swear she knew right then that something had happened to Kyle.

Alexa shook the memory out of her head. She couldn't mope now. Skyler's news, her happy news, had been a strange, unexpected shock, and it had sent Alexa reeling. Because Alexa had, for a second, as the little doctor with the round glasses walked toward her, let herself think that the news was for her—and that, despite the grave faces, the news was good. Less than a second, even. But it was enough to pry open some fissure in her, letting all the panic and horror of the day flood in. It sent Alexa staggering, retreating to a chair to think dark thoughts, pulled her back to Kyle's death, to the heavy grief of the past year, to her anger at Jason.

But all that was wasted energy, Alexa knew. She needed to be active, to take care of things that could be taken care of here in all this chaos. She'd find Mary Oakes, or some more helpful doctor, and she'd demand something, some kind of answer. A timeline, a theory, whatever. Someone had to know where her parents were by now. It had been hours, and as Alexa looked around the waiting room, she saw that there was only a handful of people left. Little groups huddling together, a few lone people looking frayed and shell-shocked. *These are the people who are going to get the worst news,* she thought, knowing that meant she was one of those people. So. What could she do? How could she keep her world from spinning entirely out of control?

Her family. She should call them. Her aunt Ginny in Connecticut. Maybe Ginny and her second husband, Henry, could drive up. Wouldn't Alexa and Jason need some adults around? She wondered if Ginny already knew, but then, how would she know? Someone would have to call her. Alexa would.

She'd also have to track down her mother's brother, Paul, who lived in London and didn't speak to the family anymore. There had been some big fight, years ago, back when Jason was a baby, and Linda only occasionally mentioned her brother, little memories from the house in Wellfleet from when they'd been kids. "Paul used to . . ." Like he was dead. But he wasn't. He was just across the ocean, living with his partner—Nikhil, Alexa remembered, from a Christmas card the Elsings had received one year, a photo of a tall thin man, her uncle, standing with a handsome younger man, Indian or Pakistani maybe, the Tower Bridge proud and gray behind them. Alexa would find them and they'd get on a plane and then there would be at least some semblance of family around them.

She'd need to tell school, too. Of course, they knew something. They'd seen her tear out of the building earlier that day. It was so strange that it had all been the same day. That just hours before, Alexa had been living a relatively normal life—a sad one, but still, mostly normal. And now here she was, thinking about calling another country to tell a family member she'd never spoken to that . . . what? Her parents were dead? She didn't know that for sure, there was still some bit of hope left. Maybe she should wait. Maybe it was hasty to call anyone when there wasn't any concrete news.

But the idea of waiting more made Alexa feel crazy. She needed to do *something*, to feel some sense of movement, of progress, even if it was toward a scary future.

She got her phone out, checking Twitter and e-mail for updates. To her surprise, there were already some victims named, with photos. A thirty-year-old mother of two from Saugus. A retired piano teacher and her husband. A whole family from Maine. The *Boston Globe* said the death toll was at thirty-two. How many people had Alexa seen brought into the hospital? A few dozen? More? She couldn't remember, it had been such a blur. She should have counted.

She read more. There were some high school students, from Newton, who were missing. Alexa realized that must be Scott's girlfriend and her friends. There was no news beyond that, that they were missing and thought to have been on the bridge when it snapped and crumbled. Alexa had seen the semi photo, the one Scott had shown her, and now, on Twitter, there were more pictures, posted by friends, saying "Pray for Aimee," all showing a smiling blonde, sometimes in costume from a play, one on the beach, another of a big group at a restaurant. Scott wasn't in any of them, but maybe he was the kind of guy who didn't like to pose for pictures.

Alexa felt nosy, peering in on this missing girl's life, so she closed Twitter. Poor Aimee. Poor Scott. She turned and saw him, fiddling with the strings of his hoodie, lost in thought. She went over to him, touched his shoulder. He looked up, smiled, his cheeks making big, friendly creases when he did.

"Hey!"

"Hey. You doing O.K.?"

Scott nodded. "Yeah . . . just thinking."

"Have you heard from Aimee's parents?"

"Uh, no, they're . . . on their way, I guess. I think they work kinda far away, so it takes a while to get downtown."

Alexa nodded, wanting to help Scott in some way, to distract him or comfort him—so she could distract and, maybe, comfort herself too.

"You want to go for a walk?"

Scott looked confused. "Where? Like outside?"

Alexa shrugged. "No, like, just around the hospital, I guess. I think there's a chapel somewhere. We could go find that."

Scott hesitated. "Oh, I'm not, like, religious or anything. I mean, my parents are Catholic, but only on Christmas and Easter, really."

"I'm not either. We don't have to pray there or anything. It's just a change of scenery."

So they went, asking one of the nurses where the chapel was. She nodded seriously, saying, "Of course," and pointed them in the right direction. They had to go up a few floors, the elevator slow and creaking. Standing next to them, in a surreal contrast to the despair and grimness of the waiting room, was a pregnant woman, hand on her belly, looking serene and optimistic as she watched the floors pass.

Scott and Alexa got off on the third floor, walked down a few strangely quiet hallways, and there it was, an unremarkable door with a sign saying "Chapel." Inside, the room was decorated in stained glass, the lights far dimmer than the hallway, a few rows of chairs set up. There was no cross or Star of David or any particular iconography. Just a sense of hush and peace and solemnity. It actually was calming, Alexa realized, to be in a place specifically designed for comfort and reflection.

There was only one other person in the chapel, an older man sitting in the second row of chairs, bent over, head down, possibly praying, possibly asleep. Scott and Alexa found two chairs toward the back, sat down, and stared at the big round blue stained glass window at the front of the room. They sat there without talking for a minute, some respectable observance of silence that the place seemed owed.

Alexa couldn't remember the last time she'd been in any kind of church. Maybe the Quaker-style meetings at her school counted, though they were held in the assembly hall, not some sacred space. Her parents had never taken her, except when there were weddings, though oftentimes in Theo and Linda's circle, those weddings were outdoors at country clubs or on private estates with sprawling views of some body of water. Only a couple of funerals. Churches had been rare in Alexa's life, and she realized now that they did hold some kind of soothing power, like they were a confirmation that the stakes of the world are really high and really scary, in a way that the drab fluorescent and linoleum of downstairs did not.

She let out a sigh and crossed her arms. "You know what I'm most scared of?" she said to Scott, who turned in his chair and looked at her seriously, his round brown eyes kind and expectant.

"No, what?"

"That I'm going to have to figure out who I am a lot sooner than normal. If they're gone, I mean. Like . . . I'm supposed to get a few more years before I have to do that, right? To be young and screw things up and try lots of different things. In college, or wherever. Maybe not college. Somewhere else. But now . . . I mean, if you don't have parents to, like, bounce off of, what do you do? Maybe you just have to get your shit together and be a grown-up. Just like that. I mean, it's not like Jason will. So, one of us has to."

"Why won't Jason?"

"Because he won't. Because that's not who he is. Last summer . . . Last summer, my friend died? His friend too. They were friends."

"I'm so sorry."

"Yeah, me too. But when he died . . . Jason just, like, *shut down*. Like the light went out, and he was gone. We'd gotten close again, I thought, over the summer. Something was different. It was good. But then Kyle died, and . . . I guess I was wrong. I was wrong. So today? I mean, I didn't really expect anything of him. But it makes me think about how if my parents are, y'know . . . I might just have me. I might be it."

Scott nodded. Alexa felt dumb, burdening the moment with this selfish stuff about her future, when Scott's girlfriend could be dead, with no future waiting for her whatsoever.

"Sorry," she started to say, but Scott interrupted.

"No, no, I'm sorry. I get it. I was just . . . I know what you mean. I guess for me I never really thought I'd have any of that time to figure myself out or whatever. My life feels sorta planned already. Stay in Boston for college. Work at my parents' store. Take over the store when they retire. And that's that. My family doesn't really get out. They've all stayed around here. I have cousins who live in Maryland, but it's this, like, big deal that they moved, and everyone kind of hates them for it."

Scott sat back in his chair, pulled his hood up. "With Aimee, at least it was like I was leaving my life for a little bit, every time I was with her. I knew she'd go away to college and stuff, and that we were young and probably wouldn't be together forever . . . It's just weird, y'know? To feel like someone's outgrowing you, and that they were always going to."

Alexa wasn't sure what to say, thinking how sad it was for Aimee, for her parents, for Scott, to have everything cut so short. Maybe cut short. *If* she was dead. She might not be. It was still possible that she was fine, only missing.

Alexa would never say this to Scott, of course, but something about his story, the simplicity and tragic romance of a dead girlfriend, of a great love cut short, made her feel jealous. It was so complicated with her parents. The feeling was, of course, compounded by the fact of Kyle, this inspiring—and, yes, magical—being she had known ("It's like you think I'm an *actual* fairy," he'd said to her once) until he was swiftly taken away. Maybe Kyle was like Aimee in that way: short-lived, a bright star burned out quickly.

But Alexa couldn't really find anything literary in it, not really. All this shitty sadness and hurt that had consumed her life for the past year. She'd never imagined that she, of all people, would feel so stuck, so mired in the swamp of a life that had begun to feel so heavy, so full of painful and horrible things. And she was only seventeen. She realized how exhausted she was, how she felt so little of herself anymore.

So much of her time was spent being sad about Kyle, or angry at Jason, or worrying about her parents, before the accident even. Where had she gone? She felt a little panicked, sitting there in the quiet chapel, trying to place herself, to locate the curious, ambitious, focused Alexa who had existed at some point, who had been real, she was sure of it. Her teachers seemed to have known her, this old Alexa. Her parents too. And Alexa had records of her, this person who was a *person*, who didn't just react other to people. There were journals full of that Alexa, papers and plans and all kinds of things.

And yet she felt mostly gone, as the present Alexa sat in the chapel, listening to Scott talk about his girlfriend, feeling jealous in ways she didn't want to admit to herself.

Scott was so cute—a little sloppy, a little crooked, but handsome, decent, and humble seeming. So unlike the boys that she and Jason knew, in their world, with their highborn snobbiness and their seen-it-all jadedness. Jason was one of them, wasn't he? That's all he was. He was just another one of those boys, Alexa thought, letting a laugh escape.

"What?" Scott asked eagerly, maybe wanting to laugh at something in that moment too.

Alexa shook her head. "Nothing, it's nothing. I just . . . I don't know. I sort of realized something. I had an epiphany."

Scott gestured toward the stained glass window. "Power of the chapel."

Alexa laughed again. It felt good, even if the laughter was followed by little needles of guilt. She looked at Scott, at the faint fuzz coming in on his lip and jawline, a scar near his right eye, deep and long. She pointed to it. "What's that from?"

Scott touched the scar, as if he'd forgotten it was there. "Oh. Soccer.

Got elbowed by some asshole from Needham. Blood everywhere. It was gnarly."

Alexa reached out, ran her thumb along the line of it. "Must have hurt," she said, feeling Scott lean into her hand. They looked at each other, the chapel lights dim, and Alexa let herself imagine that they were in some other world, some other dimension where nothing bad had happened and this could just be an exciting moment before a nice kiss. But there was no such place, or if there was, it was impossible to get to from where they were, power of the chapel or not. So she pulled her hand away and said, "Aimee's lucky. You're a really nice guy, Scott."

Scott, seeming to understand that the moment was over, the spell broken, sat back, nodded. "Uh, thanks. I'm the lucky one, really. She's the best."

"And she's going to be O.K."

"She's gonna be fine."

Alexa heard people behind her and turned to see an older woman and a younger woman, a mother and daughter maybe, making their way into the chapel. They'd both been crying, from the looks of it, and the mother was leaning on her daughter for support. Alexa felt nosy again, like she was seeing something she shouldn't. "Let's go," she said to Scott, feeling her anxiety welling up. "We should go back. There might be news."

They walked the hallways in silence, rode the slow elevator without speaking. They were almost back to the emergency waiting room when Scott said, "Alexa, wait." She stopped, not sure what was about to happen. He looked her in the eyes, some mix of worry and determination on his face. He opened his mouth, started to say something, but then stopped. He sighed.

"What is it, Scott?" Alexa asked.

He shifted his weight. Shrugged. "Nothing. Never mind. It's just . . . They're going to be fine too," he finally said. "Your parents."

Alexa nodded. She hadn't liked it when Jason had assured her that everything was going to be O.K., and though she wasn't mad at Scott, had no reason to be mad at him, she didn't like his saying it either. It felt almost condescending, or patronizing. Still, for the first time all day, something in her agreed with the sentiment. She smiled at him. "Thank you, Scott. I know."

They walked the rest of the way to the waiting room, and saw Morgan and Jason talking to a couple about Alexa's parents' age. They looked distraught and were still wearing their jackets, like they'd just gotten there. The woman was showing Morgan and Jason something on her phone, and they were shaking their heads.

"Hey," Alexa said, and all four turned to look at her. Scott was hanging back, but when the woman saw him, her eyes widened with what looked to be shock.

"Scott?" she said, walking quickly toward him. "What are you doing here?"

Alexa reeled around to look at Scott, who was beet red, flustered. "Mrs. Peck, I was just—"

The man had caught up to the woman now. "Scott, is everything O.K.?"

Scott just stood there, his face ashen.

Alexa waited for Scott to answer, but when he didn't, she jumped in. "He's . . . um. He's waiting for his girlfriend, Aimee."

Scott gave Alexa a panicked look, and Aimee's mother balked. "Scott, what are you—""

"Mrs. Peck, let me explain." Scott paused, gathered his thoughts. "I just wanted to make sure she's all right. I won't bother her, I won't bother you. Please just let me stay."

Alexa stared at Scott, not knowing what to think. "Scott?" she asked.

He looked her, looking pitiful and ashamed. "She's not . . . We're not . . . I still love her." He turned to Aimee's parents. "I still love her. I know we broke up, but I still love her."

Aimee's mother was crying now, turning and walking away from Scott, her husband following after her.

"I still love her," Scott whimpered, to no one, to himself. Maybe to Alexa, who suddenly felt sick.

"Alexa?" Scott said, his voice cracking. And, not knowing exactly why, all Alexa could do was laugh.

Chapter Twelve

Scott

SAM STEIN'S PARTY was a shitshow. He lived in a big Victorian at the end of a dead-end street off of Waverly, the kind of dark and rambling old house that was always drafty and chilly in the winter, even with an expensive heating system installed. The night of the party, though, the house was hot with a crush of bodies, music blaring and kids occupying almost every possible square inch. Scott and Pete took an Uber over together, Pete talking a big game about getting laid that night, Scott still stormy and sad about his fight with Aimee.

They walked in and were immediately greeted by a blitzed-looking Stein. He gave them a quizzical look, maybe not expecting these sophomores to just walk into his party. But Scott was on the team, so he was technically allowed, and Stein knew Pete through various seedy channels at school. "Yooooo," Stein said, doing a messy fist-bump, handshake thing with both boys. "Drinks are back there," he said, thumbing toward the kitchen, "and chicks are . . . everywhere." He laughed, winking— really, blinking—conspiratorially at Scott and Pete before he was dragged away by Asher Birch, another of the soccer seniors, one who was perhaps even meaner, and thus even more revered at school, than Stein was.

Pete and Scott made their way to the kitchen, a sprawling array of marble with a huge center island that was littered with bottles and Solo cups. Pete suggested they do shots, and Scott, normally not much of a drinker, obliged, wanting to wash Aimee's hurt and angry face from his memory. They did shots of what Scott was pretty sure was vodka, and then another round. Pete found them two beers and they went off to wander through the party, Pete keeping an eye out for Taissa ("Or Cara. Your girlfriend has hot friends, what can I say?") while Scott dimly hoped to see Aimee pop up somewhere, ready to make amends and leave this loud and sweaty mess together.

But he didn't see her anywhere, instead running into Nik Damilatis and Zach Arko, two sophomore guys who were still on the JV team. The rumor had been, since eighth grade, that they were secretly a couple, or at least fooling around, and they weren't doing much to dispel that suspicion at the party. They were hanging on each other, drunk and laughing with their faces very close, when they saw Scott and Pete. They made a weak effort to pull apart, and said hi.

"Fun party?" Scott asked. "We just got here."

"It's all right," Nik slurred. It was strange to see him in this context. Outside of school, Scott usually saw Nik with his family. They would sometimes come into the store to get lunch after mass at the Greek

Evangelical church they went to, just outside Newton Centre. "Birch and Stein are being dicks, as per usual, but there's tons of booze."

"And we have weed," Zach said in a bleary stage whisper, pulling a sad-looking little joint out of his shirt pocket. "You wanna spark it?"

Pete had spotted Taissa standing over by the enormous living room fireplace, talking with Cara, so he shook his head. "I have somewhere I need to be. But you ladies have fun."

Scott shrugged. "You wanna go outside?"

They walked back to sliding doors that opened up to a large deck, a few kids out there huddling against the cold, smoking and talking. It was nice to be out of the din and heat, and with these two decent guys. Scott wondered if he'd maybe be able to talk to Nik and Zach about Aimee. Pete was no good with that stuff, but weren't gay guys supposed to be more sensitive? Zach lit the joint with shivering hands, took a long pull, and handed it to Scott.

"So what's up, man?" Nik asked, coughing out smoke. "How was your break?"

"I dunno. Boring. Worked a lot."

"Oh yeah, man. My folks and I were gonna come in, but we had family in town so we just ate at home."

Scott nodded. "Cool, cool."

"Okemo was *sick*," Zach added. He and his family had a ski cabin up in Vermont. Scott had never been skiing, but it seemed terrifying, hurtling yourself down a mountain on two pieces of plastic.

Scott figured he'd try Nik and Zach out, maybe get some advice. "So, me and Aimee got in a fight tonight."

"Who's Aimee?" Nik asked, squinting as he took another hit.

"Oh, uh, my girlfriend?"

Zach's eyes widened. "You're dating Amy Lee?" He shot a glance at Nik. "I thought she was gay."

"No, no, not Amy Lee. I think she is, though. Aimee Peck? She's a junior."

"Oh, riiiiight," Nik said. "She's cute. How you guys doing?"

"Well, we just got in a fight . . ."

Zach shook his head. "Sucks, man. Fights are the worst. No fun at all."

They were not going to be any help, Scott glumly realized. But they were pleasant enough company. Maybe he could just hang out and shoot the shit with them until Pete wanted to go home. It's not like he was going to get lucky with Taissa or Cara. That was never going to happen—Aimee had told Scott as much, firmly, many times. Scott declined another hit of the joint, not wanting to get paranoid, as he had the other two times he'd ever smoked weed.

"How was JV this season?" he asked, but Nik and Zach weren't paying attention. Zach was whispering something in Nik's ear and Nik was laughing.

"Hey, uh, yo," Zach mumbled to Scott. "We have to go . . . check out a thing . . . upstairs. We'll find you later, though, cool?"

Scott nodded. "Sure, sure. Have, uh, have fun with your thing."

Nik giggled again. "We will! We will!"

And then Scott was alone, trembling in the cold. He was considering just saying fuck it, Pete be damned, and getting an Uber home right then, when he felt a tap on his shoulder. He turned around and there was Maddy Cohen, the source of it all. Or at least the girl whose birthday party had provided the opportunity for Scott and Aimee to first get together. She was a junior, like Aimee, and was on the girls' soccer team, square-shouldered and sturdy and pretty, with a big mane of curly brown hair and an amused arch to her eyebrows.

"Costas," she said, as always calling him by his last name. "I didn't expect to see you here."

Why did no one expect him to go to these things? "Well, I'm on the team," he said, trying to sound upbeat, but it coming out more grumbling and defensive.

"I know, dude. You just, like, don't come to the other ones!"

"I went to your birthday party, didn't I?"

"That you did," Maddy said. "That you did. Worked out pretty well for you, from what I can tell."

Aimee. He wanted to text Aimee. Or call Aimee, even though they so rarely talked on the phone.

"It did," he said instead. "Thanks, uh, thanks for that."

"Any time," Maddy said, giving him a hard-to-read smile. "Hey, you wanna go inside? It's fucking freezing out here."

It was. "Yeah, sure." He followed Maddy back into the party. She led him through the packed living room, through the kitchen, where she grabbed them two beers, and down a hall toward a closed door. "What's in there?" Scott asked.

"Peace and quiet," Maddy said, opening the door to reveal some kind of study, shelves crammed with books and plaques. Maddy pointed at the plaques, gold mounted on dark wood. "Those are Stein's dad's, like, judge trophies or whatever." Mr. Stein was a high-level circuit judge, a stern and imposing man who often stood on the sidelines of Sam's games barking things at his son. Maddy lowered her voice. "We are *not* supposed to be in here, but whatever. Stein won't mind. He and I go way back."

They sat on a squeaking leather sofa, Maddy pulling her long hair behind her shoulders and settling in, taking a sip of beer. "So where's Aimee?"

Scott looked down at his beer. He hadn't really spoken to Maddy one-on-one before. She ran in an intimidating crowd of junior and senior kids who were among the coolest, most popular people at North. "Uh, at home. She just got back from a college tour trip, so she's tired."

"Oh Godddd," Maddy groaned. "I guess I should be doing those too, huh?"

"I guess. I dunno. I really don't want her to leave."

"Awww! You're so sweet. Of course you don't."

"Yeah. We kinda . . . got in a fight about it tonight, actually."

"Oh no! What happened?"

"She was just going on and on about how great these schools were, in, like, Chicago and Ohio and stuff. And I got kinda pissed. Because, like, she seems so excited about leaving."

"Yeah. That's bad. I dated a senior—do you remember Chris Bender? So hot—when I was a sophomore, and it was *rough* when he was doing all that shit."

"It sucks!" Scott said, louder than he meant to. Maddy laughed.

"You're so cute. But it'll be O.K. Just, I dunno, just try to enjoy her while you have her. Aimee and I are only juniors. We're not leaving any-time soon, unfortunately!"

That was true. But it already felt like Aimee had one foot out the door. Like she'd turned away from Scott, and the present, and was only looking ahead. "I guess."

"Look," Maddy said, leaning forward and putting a hand on Scott's arm. "I'm not hitting on you, I promise. But look. She's gonna leave at some point, sure. But you guys have, like, a year and a half. So just try to enjoy it. And then you can figure out if you're staying together or what later on. Cross that goddamned bridge when you get to it, you know?" She smiled at Scott, took a swig from her bottle.

"Yeah, yeah. Thanks. You're right. What happened with you and your boyfriend? With Chris?"

"Oh, we fucking broke up, like, immediately after he graduated," Maddy said, letting out a cackle of a laugh. "Sorry, sorry. But that's the truth. And it was different. He was an asshole. *I'm* an asshole. But you and Aimee are both not assholes. You'll be fine."

"Thanks. Yeah. Thanks."

Maddy stood up. "You want a hug?"

Scott never really hugged girls who weren't Aimee, but it seemed appropriate then. "Sure."

Maddy leaned in and gave him a friendly squeeze. When she pulled back, she said, "You know, it was *my* birthday party. You were supposed to hit on *me*," and she laughed again.

Scott laughed too. "Sorry."

"Tell Aimee you're sorry, not me!" She gave him an affectionate knock on the head, and then she was out the door, back into the wilds of the party, and Scott was alone again. Not wanting to return to the noise just yet, he sat down on the couch, the leather creaking. He pulled out his phone, drafted a text:

aims. im so sorry. pls kno that ilu so much. im really sorry.

Hoping this would reopen the lines of communication, Scott hit "Send." He sat there for another minute, feeling happier, a little relieved. Maddy was right. This was going to be fine. He downed his beer and then headed out into the party. He found Pete, looking dejected by the kitchen island. "Yo."

Pete looked up, red-faced and swaying. "Heyyyy." He narrowed his eyes, more than they were already narrowed. "So, Maddy Cohen, huh?"

"Huh?" Scott said, not sure what Pete meant.

"Nothing, nothing. Anyway, dude . . . I think I gotta go home and, like, knock one out on my own, you know? Taissa was *not* biting tonight."

"Yeah, let's go," Scott said, glad to be heading home. He ordered them an Uber and they waited for it on the curb, the house still thrumming with music, the clamor of kids rising like steam into the midnight air. Things felt all right. Things felt on their way to good again.

The next morning, Scott woke up with a pounding headache and a dry staleness in his mouth. It had been a while since he'd had more than two drinks in a night, and he felt nauseated. He padded to the bathroom, filled his water bottle in the sink, and then went back to his room to check his phone, suddenly remembering that he'd texted Aimee that he was sorry the night before.

When he looked at his phone he saw that he had a missed call from

Aimee, and three text messages. *Scott? u there? we need to talk* and *call me when ur up pls. Call me.* That seemed way more ominous than Scott had expected. In fact, he'd expected an apology back, a "Sorry we fought, let's hang out after you get off work" kind of a text. But no, she wanted him to call. Taking another few gulps of water and clearing his throat, Scott pressed "Call" on Aimee's number. She picked up after one ring. She sounded tense and angry.

"Hey," she said, curt.

"Hey, what's up? Sorry I missed your texts. I'm kinda hungover."

"Oh, you are? Huh. Do you remember what happened last night?"

"What? Yeah. I mean, I went to Stein's party and, I dunno, I had some drinks with Pete. And I smoked a joint with Nik Damilatis and Zach Arko, who are definitely doing it, by the way."

"Cool. Yeah. Speaking of doing it, did you, uh, did you hook up with Maddy Cohen last night?"

Scott was blindsided. If he'd been standing up he would have actually staggered. "What?"

"Maddy Cohen. Did you hook up with Maddy Cohen last night?"

"Aimee, seriously, what the hell are you talking about?"

"Taissa was at the party, as I'm sure your little friend Pete made you well aware, and Taissa says she saw you and Maddy Cohen go into some room together and shut the door for, like, twenty minutes."

"It was more like ten minutes."

"Oh, so you did go into a room with Maddy Cohen?"

"Yes, but, like, just to talk. I was upset about you, and she was being nice."

"So this is my fault?"

"Is what your fault?"

"What I'm asking, Scott, is why did you go into a room, alone, with Maddy Cohen, leave, like, three minutes after she did—to not look suspicious—and then later that night I get a text from you saying you're so sorry, that you still love me?"

"Because! Because I talked to Maddy and she was nice and said that I shouldn't be freaking out about all this, you know, this college stuff, and so I texted you to say I was sorry about our fight. That's all. Nothing happened, I swear. I swear, Aimee. Nothing happened." Scott felt close to tears. He and Aimee had never had *this* kind of fight. Cheating was never imaginably on the table with them.

There was a silence on the line. "Hello?" Scott said after a few seconds.

"Sorry. I'm here. I'm just . . . trying to decide if I believe you. Maddy hooks up with everyone."

"C'mon, Maddy's nice."

"Maddy *is* nice. But she hooks up with everyone."

"Well, not with me. We talked about you. Seriously. That's all we did. And then I texted to say I was sorry."

"You've just been such a prick lately, like you want to break up or something. Do you want to break up?"

"No! I don't want to break up! Aimee, seriously. I don't. And nothing happened with Maddy."

Scott could hear Aimee sighing. "O.K. I'm sorry. I believe you, I guess. I believe you. Sorry."

"I'm sorry," Scott said quietly. "Seriously, Aims. I'm sorry I've been such a dick lately. It's hard for me, is all. I don't want you to leave."

"I know you don't. I . . . I don't want to leave you either."

"Sometimes it feels like you do."

Aimee was quiet on the line. "I mean . . ."

"You mean what?" Scott had a lump in his throat, and he was trembling.

"Look, you have to be at work soon, don't you? Want to talk later? I have a history project I completely fucking forgot about and my parents are freaking, so you can't come over tonight. But what if I came over there tomorrow?"

"O.K. . . ." Scott said slowly. "And I'll see you at school?"

"Yeah, yeah, of course. Of course. But, like, let's just talk about all this tomorrow night."

"O.K." Scott saw the time on his alarm clock. "Shit, I have to shower and stuff. Talk to you later."

"O.K."

"I love you."

"Yeah, you too." And then she hung up.

Scott spent his shift at work in a daze, utterly unsure what to think about his phone conversation with Aimee, that stilted and vaguely horrifying thing. At home that night, he ate dinner and went to bed early, still dragging, wanting it to be the next day so he and Aimee could talk. He'd never wanted a vacation to be over and to be back at school so badly.

The next day was busy, with teachers fighting to get their kids focused after the break, piling on homework and other assignments.

Scott and Aimee usually met up at lunch, but it was the one day of the schedule rotation when they didn't have the same lunch, so he waited by her locker after fourth period, when she typically switched out her books and they'd have a little moment to talk and furtively touch. (They'd gotten detention last September for making out in the hallway, and Aimee was intent on not repeating that embarrassment again.)

But she never showed. Maybe she got stuck in a class and didn't have time to come by her locker, or maybe she was avoiding him. Not knowing either way was agony, and Scott went into the bathroom to send her a text, the only place a teacher wouldn't see him using his phone during school hours.

hey where are u, he wrote.

She wrote back quickly. *sorry. bad day. ill see u tonite.*

Whenever Aimee came over to his house, which was rare, it was always around eight o'clock, after he and his parents had eaten dinner. (They didn't work late at the store anymore, leaving that to a manager. "We're old, we've earned it," Scott's dad said.) Scott ate hurriedly, cleared the table, and did the dishes, watching his phone vigilantly as it ticked toward eight. Then the doorbell rang, and Scott's heart leapt. Scott heard his mother open the door, say, "Aimee, honey, hello. Scott's just finishing the dishes." Aimee came back into the little kitchen and gave Scott a small, timid wave. No hug, no kiss. That was strange. Something was about to happen.

On a normal school night when Aimee came over, they would have gone to the living room to watch TV and pretend to do homework, but tonight felt different; there were apparently serious things to talk about.

It was an oddly warm night, so they decided to go out to the little back-yard, with its faded patio furniture and overgrown lawn, still a circle of half-grown grass where an ill-advised above-ground swimming pool had been, years ago.

Scott flicked on the floodlight, but it was too bright, made the whole thing seem like an interrogation. So he turned it off, and they sat in the dim light coming from the kitchen window, Scott wanting to pull Aimee close to him, to have her tell him that they were going to be fine. But he sensed something guarded about her. Something between them had shifted. So he sat in the chair next to her and waited for her to speak.

"I'm sorry about school today," she said, her voice wavering a little. "I'm sorry I missed you. And I'm sorry about yesterday. I shouldn't have accused you of that."

Scott shook his head. "It's O.K. It's O.K. It's fine."

"Maybe . . ." Aimee said, sounding unconvinced, distracted. "I just feel like so much has happened in the last couple of days. Everything feels different, you know?"

Scott did know. But he wasn't sure if his different was the same as Aimee's different. Not from the way she was looking at him, a breeze making him shiver.

"It's just . . ." Aimee continued, "we love each other. Or, like . . ."

She trailed off and started crying. How serious was this, actually? "We do love each other," Scott said, reaching out to put his hand on hers, which was resting tentatively on the table. But she pulled it back, put it between her knees. She looked down, sniffled some more.

Scott could hear cars whooshing by, the buzzing of the streetlights, a few dogs barking. Normal sounds. And yet nothing about this was normal.

"I want to break up," Aimee finally said, barely audible.

Was it possible to be both stunned and somehow not surprised at all? The way Aimee had said it, that little, terrible sentence, made it seem like they had already broken up, that her mind had long been made up and she was just now telling him. This was not any sort of negotiation.

"Aimee . . ." he started to say, but she interrupted him.

"I'm so busy with school and grades and shows and stuff. And you're going through a lot too, and I just feel like it's all a little overwhelming. This whole thing has gotten too intense or something."

"Isn't it supposed to be intense?"

"Yeah, I guess so. I mean, it is. But not like this. It's supposed to be intense in a *good* way. But you've been freaking out about me graduating, doing stuff that's not you at all, and now this whole thing with Maddy . . . I just think maybe it would be better for us if we ended things now, so we have some time to, like, enjoy high school before it's over."

"Before it's over for you, you mean," Scotty said, the words sounding more indignant than he meant them to. Maybe, anyway.

"Before it's over for me, yeah. But I dunno . . . Don't you want to, like, figure out who you are without me getting in the way?"

Scott's face felt hot, he was dizzy. "You're not in the way, Aims. You're, like, all I have!"

"See, that's what I mean!" she said, a sob cracking her voice. "That's so intense, Scotty. That's so intense for you to say, and for me to hear, and I just don't want to do it anymore. I need to not feel all this pressure to keep you happy, to, like, not be excited about what I'm doing next because it's going to make you sad."

"Aren't you sad?"

"Of course I'm sad. I'm sad all the time! But I feel like . . . It's still early enough that I have, like . . . Like maybe I can actually enjoy visiting colleges and getting excited about that, and graduating, and being with my friends and stuff, without always feeling so guilty all the time. You make it really hard, Scott. You just don't . . . get it, sometimes."

Scott was stung. "You mean, I don't get how exciting it is that you get to go away to college and live some cool life, because I'm never going to do that, because I'm going to be stuck here forever?"

Aimee let out another little sob, wiped her nose with her sleeve. "No, it's not that. I mean, maybe it's that. I don't know, Scott. I feel like you kind of think it's my fault that you're not in the same place as me."

Scott didn't know what to say. Of course it wasn't her fault. It was *his* fault. Or maybe it was no one's fault. But either way, wasn't that *his* problem? Didn't he get to decide what to do about his own shit? He wanted to fight with Aimee, to make her see that she was wrong, that she was being melodramatic, that she was overreacting. But she seemed so determined. Even though she was crying—real tears, not stage ones.

They sat without talking for a moment, Aimee sniffling, Scott trying to grapple with the utter surreality of the moment. Finally, Aimee sat up straight, wiped her eyes. "I'm sorry. I have to go."

Scott nodded. There didn't seem to be much else to say beyond "O.K.," to walk Aimee around the side of the house to her car, to let her hug him goodbye while she cried a little more, the night quiet and foggy with melting snow. Aimee said she'd talk to him soon, that they should still talk. Scott, shell-shocked, wanting to go up to his room and scream, said yup, yup, of course. Then Aimee got in her car and was gone, disappearing down Scott's narrow little street, putting her blinker on and turning right, back to her house, off to start a life without him.

Scott spent the next months dazed and grieving. He and Aimee barely spoke, Scott sending a few misguided text messages, but mostly retreating. He was quiet at school, quiet at home, going through the motions at work. He and Pete hung out, Pete trying to get him to go after other girls, saying shit like "I mean, Maddy clearly wants it, and now you're free and clear." But Scott had no interest. He wanted Aimee back so badly it was like having a disease, a massive tumor throbbing inside him.

But Aimee wasn't coming back to him. By that summer she'd started seeing another guy, Tim Tumposky, another theater kid. Scott saw this on Instagram, not sure why he still followed Aimee, or why she hadn't blocked him. Scott, meanwhile, remained in stasis. He spent his summer at the store, working long hours and helping his dad with stuff around the house. It was a lonely existence, but something about all the deafening quiet and stillness helped drown Aimee out. He still thought about calling or texting her almost every day, but he never did.

He did email her on her birthday, though, late in August. He wrote,

Happy 18th, Aims. Hope it's a great year and you get where you wanna go. Love always, Scott.

He instantly wished he could unsend it, but there it was. Sent. She wrote back a day later.

Hey Scott,

Thanks so much for your e-mail. It was a nice birthday, especially nice to hear from you. Hope you're doing well. Let's say hi to each other at school in September?

They gave each other a wave once they were back at North, after Labor Day, but that was all that really happened. Just a wave.

They were done, had been done for months by the time of the accident.

The last time Scott saw Aimee before the bridge collapse, he was leaving soccer practice and realized that Aimee, who had gotten the big part in *The Crucible* she'd been wanting since the drama department announced they were doing it, the winter before, would probably be getting out of rehearsal around the same time. Scott was driving by then, puttering around in an old Camry his dad had gotten cheap from a friend. Scott was throwing his soccer gear into the trunk when he figured that, since he was parked near the theater doors, maybe he'd wait for Aimee, thinking it might be a little private moment between them. Maybe they'd even say hi, talk a little.

But when Aimee finally did come walking out of the building, she was with a whole group of friends, laughing and oblivious to all of Scott's pain. Aimee caught sight of him, waiting there, staring at her, and her face did a sorrowful little dip. She gave him a sad smile, and he, immediately regretting his decision, waved. She waved too and then that was it. Scott, red-faced and devastated all over again, for the millionth time, got in the car and drove home.

The next day, Aimee headed up to Salem with Taissa and Cara and the rest. And Pete ran up to Scott after fifth period to say that something had happened, and now here Scott was, skipping a shift at the store to be in the waiting room, saying he was Aimee's boyfriend because it felt good to say, gave him some authority. Aimee's mother, frantic and teary, had shot Scott such a repulsed look when she heard the lie. And Alexa was laughing, a strange, high-pitched sound. Scott felt frozen, embarrassed, knocked hideously out of orbit, all over again. Everything was somehow even worse than it had been before.

Chapter Thirteen

Skyler

SKYLER FINALLY GOT through to her grandparents on her third try, standing a block down from the hospital, feeling a relief so deep she thought she might actually melt into the sidewalk. When her grandmother answered, she sounded tired and confused, and it was clear to Skyler that she hadn't heard anything about the bridge collapse in faraway Boston.

"Why are you calling?" her grandmother asked, sounding concerned, but the kind of concern one might have about something simple and everyday—was the house O.K., was there a leak in the upstairs bathroom again, had Skyler passed her French test? It was so strange to think that Skyler had lived through these hours of pure terror and her grandmother knew nothing about it. So she didn't tell her much, explained that there had been an accident, a car accident, and that Kate had been

200

involved, but that she was O.K. She had broken her legs, but the doctors said she would be fine, would walk again, it would just take some work.

Her grandmother started crying, saying she was sorry for not being there, that she and Skyler's grandfather would fly home that day. But Skyler said no, it was all right, they didn't need to, that there wasn't anything they could do right now. She just had to tell them that Kate was alive, that she was going to survive. Skyler's grandmother kept saying, "Thank God, thank God, thank God," over and over again, and Skyler could hear her grandfather's voice in the background, asking questions in Khmer, wanting to know what was going on, if Skyler and Kate were all right.

Skyler figured that her grandmother would tell him everything, so she said, "O.K., Grandma? Grandma? I have to go, I have to go see Kate again," and her grandmother said, "I love you"—not something she said all that often, but not because she didn't—and Skyler hung up, another teary wave of relief passing over her.

With the rain gone, the night felt renewed and cold, like real fall had finally set in, the city preparing itself for a long winter. But Skyler didn't mind it then, the bite of the wind as she stood on the street corner, her fingers getting numb, her legs trembling. She didn't even flinch when her phone buzzed and it was the unknown number, Danny again, sending just *wtf*.

She put the phone back in her bag, not knowing what else she would need it for that night. Unless she decided to track down her mother, but that prospect seemed exhausting and depressing, and Skyler wanted to keep feeling light and relieved.

She wasn't sure what to do with herself. The doctors had told her that Kate would probably be asleep most of the night because of the pain medication. There would be another surgery early in the morning—nothing life-threatening, the doctors had promised her—and then the long road to recovery would begin.

But it would begin. Kate was already on her way, the short-haired woman, Dr. Lobel, had said, her smile warm and comforting. They were in the room with Kate, but she was asleep. Her face was bruised and she had lots of cuts, but she was still Kate, intact and alive and already fighting. It was the happiest Skyler had ever felt, knowing that she and Kate still had time, they had so much time, that Skyler could repay her sister for all the things Kate had done for her.

Suddenly, she thought of the others in the waiting room. Alexa and her brother, Scott and Morgan. She had promised them that she'd come back. That she wouldn't go home until they all knew for sure about their loved ones. Skyler barely knew them, these scared and sad kids, but she didn't want to go home, to be alone, just yet anyway. So she walked back down the block and through the emergency room doors, seeing that there were even fewer people now, that the four people she knew were all standing together, having some sort of heated discussion. When she got closer, she realized that Alexa was yelling, pointing a finger at Scott.

"I mean, you've just been *lying* to us this whole time?" Alexa was saying incredulously to Scott, who looked stunned, his mouth slightly agape, his chin quivering.

"I wasn't lying," he said meekly. "She *was* my girlfriend. She was my girlfriend!"

Skyler stood there for a second, not sure what to say, suddenly not sure she wanted to be back in this room at all. She considered turning around and quickly leaving. But then Alexa caught sight of Skyler and strode toward her.

"He lied, Scott lied this whole time. His 'girlfriend,' Aimee? They broke up, like, months ago. Her parents," Aimee said, gesturing toward a well-dressed couple huddling close together in a corner, "they could not have been more shocked to see him here."

Jason was shaking his head, glaring at Scott. "It's pretty fucked up, man. It's pretty fucked up," seeming to enjoy someone else being at the receiving end of his sister's disapproval.

Alexa nodded vigorously. "It's really fucked up. Why lie? Here? When we're all, like, going crazy just trying to hold it together."

Scott didn't speak, only turned to Skyler, his eyes pleading—for help or rescue or something. "You're not Aimee's boyfriend?" she asked him, as calmly and objectively as she could.

"I was. For a long time. But we broke up, in February. Because I messed up. And I don't know. I guess I just put too much pressure on her."

"What do you mean, 'pressure'?" Skyler asked, hoping he wasn't going to say what she feared he would say.

Scott seemed to sense her fear, though, quickly saying, "No, no, no, not, like, that kind of pressure. Just . . . I don't know. She's graduating. And I messed up at a party."

"Messed up how?" Skyler asked, taking a step toward him, trying to put herself between him and Alexa, whose anger only seemed to be growing. And then Scott explained that people thought he'd hooked up with another girl at a party after a fight with Aimee. That when Aimee found out, she broke it off. That it happened over eight months ago, but Scott still loved her, would always love her.

"And so now you're what?"

Everyone turned, surprised to hear Morgan speaking up.

"You're here to make things better with the girl who dumped your ass? I'm sorry, but all of us"—Morgan pointed to Skyler and Alexa and Jason—"actually *belong* here. We're all here for *family*, for people we *love*. I'm not sure pathetic ex-boyfriend really counts."

It was the most Skyler had heard Morgan talk all night, and her voice was quivering with anger. Scott looked distraught, and Skyler felt an odd pang of sympathy for him, even though he'd been lying to them all day.

"What were you doing with my sister?" Jason said suddenly, as if he'd just realized something.

Scott looked confused. "What?"

"With my sister. You guys have been talking all night; you went off somewhere just now. What the hell were you doing with Alexa?"

Alexa shot a hard look at her brother. "Jason, shut up, I didn't do anything with him. That is not the point. The point is he lied and it's really shitty that he would do that for this many hours when we're all . . . when we're all *here*. I mean, Jesus." Her eyes welled up, and she turned and took a few paces away from the group to collect herself. Scott stood stock-still, his eyes cast to the ground.

Jason continued, "My parents might be dead, Morgan's dad almost died." Skyler saw something flash across Morgan's face, there and then gone. "And you're just lurking around, lying to us so you can see some girl who dumped you months ago? I mean, it's fucked up, man. It's really fucked up. They clearly want you to leave," he said, gesturing toward Aimee's parents. "So why don't you get. The fuck. Out of here."

Jason advanced on Scott as he said this, Scott bristling and standing up a little straighter, Morgan trailing after Jason. Skyler could see that things could be about to get bad, that Scott would maybe only take Jason getting in his face for so long. She thought about turning and leaving, about going for the door, about walking away from them and letting herself return to that place of relief, of good news.

But instead she found herself walking up and getting between Scott and Jason, putting a hand on Jason's chest. "Stop it, Jason," she said. "Come on. Just stop it." He backed off, throwing his hands up. But then a second later he turned back toward Scott, looking like he was going to lunge at him. Skyler stepped in front of him, using her whole body to block his advance. "Jason, stop!" She pushed him back, not hard, but enough to create some space between them. Jason staggered back. He threw up his hands again, muttering, "O.K.! O.K.!"

Skyler turned to Scott, who was pacing, his defenses up. Skyler knew what that pacing meant; she'd seen it before, of course. She reached out, put a hand on his arm. "Scott?" she said calmly. "Scott." He stopped and looked at her, chest heaving. "Look," she said. "I don't know what you did, or why you and Aimee broke up. But, yes, you could have told us. You probably should have told us."

"I just really needed to be here. Even if I didn't see her, I needed to know—"

"I know, I know. I get that," Skyler said. She felt centered, somehow, though also a little like she was watching herself, from beside or above herself. She felt a little like Kate. "But everyone's emotions are so crazy right now. You have to understand why Alexa's upset. Maybe you should go. One of us can call you or something. I'll call you. I'll wait. I said I wasn't going to leave until all you guys know, so I won't. O.K.? Maybe just go home, and I can call you."

Scott seemed to think about this for a moment. Skyler looked over to where Aimee's parents were. They were watching this scene now, Skyler trying to calm everyone down. She shot another look at Scott, who was nodding his head, working through something.

Watching Scott sort things, Skyler felt oddly sure that she could defuse this situation, like she suddenly had some kind of divine strength or something. Maybe her grandmother saying, "Thank God, thank God," on the phone had done something to Skyler, conferred some blessing upon her. Or maybe it was Kate, finally seeing her alive, touching her cheek in the hospital room. Some transference had happened. Kate always kept a cool head, or at least always seemed so confident that she knew, somehow, what to do. And now Skyler almost felt that way too.

She looked up at Scott, and he nodded one more time and said, "O.K. O.K. You're right. I'm gonna go. I should go. You're right."

Jason put up a hand, said, "Bye!" while Morgan glared. Scott turned to get his coat from one of the chairs. Alexa was staring from a slight distance away, expression hard and fixed.

Though, Skyler quickly realized, Alexa wasn't watching them, she was looking past them, at Aimee's parents, who were now talking to a doctor, a tall South Asian woman with a puff of dark hair. Where had she come from?

The doctor was saying something softly to Aimee's parents, her arms folded over her chest, Aimee's mother clutching her husband, nodding her head, and then letting out a wail—a terrible sound, like something they talked about in the ancient Greek plays Skyler had read in English class the year before—so loud that everyone in the room turned, even the nurses. Aimee's mom was crumpling to the floor while her husband tried to hold her up, looking only a little more sturdy himself. The doctor reached out a hand to put on Aimee's mother's shoulder, but she couldn't reach her. Mrs. Peck was all the way on the floor now, shrieking, "No! No! No!"

Skyler saw Morgan grab Jason, who stood frozen, watching Aimee's parents. Alexa had a hand over her mouth. Aimee's mother made a loud, guttural sound, her husband now on the floor with her, holding her, the doctor standing over them, patient and waiting.

Skyler turned and looked at Scott, holding his coat, watching this all unfold with a faraway look on his face, as if he'd just been told something he didn't understand, even though it was so horribly clear just then that Aimee was dead.

Chapter Fourteen

Alexa

IT WAS AS if the hospital, and the whole unfathomable day, suddenly snapped into focus; whatever hazy unknowability had existed was gone. Nothing had quite felt real until then, not even when Skyler got her good news.

None of it had been hard and provable and tangible, until Alexa watched Aimee's parents, the parents of this stranger she would now never meet, sob in a heap on the floor, knowing now that their daughter was gone, that whatever hope they'd had—driving to the hospital that day, or from the hospital after she was born, or any day in between—was lost, irretrievable in the wreckage of the bridge. Alexa felt heavy and out of breath, like she was being crushed. She forced herself to tear her eyes away from Aimee's parents, and retreated to a far corner of the room, to catch her breath and try to stop the room from spinning.

Why was she so upset? Of course it was sad that someone was dead, someone so young especially. But she didn't know Aimee. She'd only learned of her existence a couple of hours before, in a photo from a school dance. It was just so strange to think that that smiling girl, happy and dressed up, was now dead. It was hard to even understand what that word really *meant*, the finality and severity of it. Alexa found a chair and fell into it, stunned and tired and reeling with ideas about her parents, about how they might be gone too—over, ended, no more life.

Of course, Alexa had known this feeling before, the suddenness and boggling, staggering vastness of it.

An image of Kyle flickered in her head, him at the ice cream store one night, showing her some little choreographed dance he'd made up to a local car dealership's ad jingle, the two of them laughing like crazy at this stupid thing, Kyle waving a washcloth over his head as he swiveled his hips.

When had that been? June? July? Alexa couldn't remember anymore. It had just been some silly night, the two of them punchy at the end of a long day. Kyle had probably driven her home, as he did on a lot of nights when they closed together. Maybe they'd listened to some music in the car, maybe they'd talked. Probably they had, speculating about life after summer, after school, after whatever came after that.

Sitting now on the hard chair in the waiting room—Aimee's parents had been scooped up and led off somewhere deeper into the hospital—Alexa felt an acute and burning pain, missing Kyle so much just then. How could he be gone? How can anyone just . . . go away and never come back?

It had been over a year since Kyle died, and yet it all still felt so raw. Yes, Alexa's grief had evolved—hardening, focusing itself, lodging somewhere permanently in her. It was once new, almost a surprise, a shock of sadness. But now it was just a fact of her life, mingling terribly with her feelings about Jason, her sorrow and dismay over his regression to the way he was before the Elsings' summer of happiness and, eventually, doom.

Two months after Kyle's death, another dark Boston fall setting in, Alexa and Jason had barely spoken about what happened. All Alexa knew was that Jason seemed allergic to her grief. Kyle died, and Alexa's reaction was too much for Jason, so he backed away, as if the summer and their closeness had never happened. But of course they still had to exist in the same house together, and one night in October, alone in the basement kitchen together, Alexa felt a burning need to say something to her brother, to coax something out of him, some acknowledgment of where they were, and where they had been.

"It's two months next Tuesday."

Jason looked up from his cereal, his preferred dinner when Linda and Theo were out, confused. "Huh?"

"It's two months, to the day. Next Tuesday. Since Kyle . . ."

Her brother's face slackened and seemed to lose its color. "Oh."

He returned to his cereal, chewing loudly for a few seconds before looking back up at this sister. "Why would you tell me that?"

"Because I can't get it out of my head, Jason. Because you knew him too, and you liked him, and he was a part of our lives and now he's gone and I just want to talk to someone about it."

"Talk to Mom and Dad, then. Or talk to a therapist. I . . . don't want to talk about that stuff. I can't talk about it. I mean, what's the point anyway?"

"The point is to, like, share what you're going through with someone else, because it helps? Are you even sad that Kyle died?"

Jason stood up and practically threw his cereal bowl into the sink. "Jesus, Alexa."

"Are you? Because it's been two months—almost two months—and you've barely . . . I'm sorry if I'm, like, too much for you or whatever, but I'm here, and I'm hurting, and a little support from you would—"

"Would what, Alexa? Would bring him back? Would make you not sad anymore? This is so pointless. You can't change anything. What happened happened, and we— You just have to deal with it and move on. That's it."

Alexa was stung, as if Jason was saying that everything she was feeling was pointless. But maybe he was right. Maybe all this was doing was pushing Jason further from her, not helping her get through a difficult time. Maybe she did need to be more like her brother, detached and unmoved, guarded and self-preserving.

But try as Alexa did throughout the year, she couldn't shake her feelings. She gradually gave up on Jason, the brother she knew that one summer becoming a memory, a fond one tainted with bitterness and hurt. But she kept Kyle active and present in her mind. She approached school less intensely—not because she was checked out but because she was focused on something else. Alexa held on to everything she'd shared with Kyle, everything she had let herself hope for her life. It took a year—a hard and punishing one, one affected as much by Jason's absence as it was by Kyle's—but Alexa finally worked up the courage to tell her parents that she was going to put off college, that she had a different life in mind.

And then the world fell apart.

Alexa was startled out of these thoughts by the sound of a voice, calm and quiet as it was. She looked up and there was Morgan, a concerned, nervous look on her face. "Hey. Alexa? You O.K.?"

Alexa's mouth was dry, her eyes felt itchy. "Yeah. Thanks. I'm fine. How's . . ." She looked around the room but didn't see Scott.

"Oh. He went to the bathroom. I think he's throwing up."

"I don't blame him," Alexa murmured.

Morgan sat down next to her, pulled her sleeves over her hands. "I shouldn't have said that to him. About not deserving to be here. That was . . ."

"You didn't know. And I was mad too. He lied to us."

"Yeah."

They sat in conflicted silence—guilty, sad, scared, exhausted—for a minute. Morgan kept picking at the safety pins on her sweatshirt.

"He's hurting, you know," Morgan finally said.

"Of course he is. His girlfriend—his ex-girlfriend, whatever—just died."

"Scott, yeah, but I mean your brother. Jason. He's . . . hurting."

Alexa was confused. Why was Morgan telling her this? How did she know anything about Jason?

"What?"

Likely hearing the pointedness in Alexa's voice, Morgan stuttered out an explanation. "I just mean, he's worried about your parents, obviously. But also . . . I don't know. You should talk to him. I think he's pretty messed up."

The sadness and tiredness Alexa had been feeling suddenly drained and all she felt was an anger, a raging, roiling kind of anger that propelled her out of her seat.

"I'm sorry, what?" she yelped at Morgan, who jumped back in her chair, maybe not expecting this from Alexa, at least not in this moment of grief and shock. "*I* should talk to *him*? Do you have any idea—no, of course you don't. We just met you. I have no idea who you are. What did he tell you? What did he say to you?"

Morgan stammered, "I just meant, I didn't—"

Alexa wasn't really listening to her. It didn't matter what she said, it wasn't Morgan's fault. She was just trying to help. But watching Aimee's parents, and remembering Kyle's mother, how sad, on a bone-deep level, she'd been at the memorial service, how it was clear her life would never recover, and then to have Morgan say that Alexa should talk to *Jason*, after he'd essentially gone mute when Kyle died, too scared to deal with Alexa's emotions, to help her in any way, to be the brother she needed and, fuck it, *deserved*, was enough to send Alexa over the edge.

She scanned the room for her brother, spotting him by the little water bubbler, handing a cup to Skyler, then taking a sip of his own, slow like he was drugged, face so annoyingly expressionless despite everything happening around him.

Alexa strode toward him, running high on the fuel of her shock at what Morgan had said. When Jason saw her coming, he lowered his water cup. Skyler gave her a small wave, her face falling as she saw that Alexa was clearly in some sort of rage.

"What did you say to Morgan?" Alexa demanded of her brother. He blinked, confused. "What?"

"To Morgan. What have you been telling her about your poor, sad life?"

"Alexa, I—" Jason started. But he stopped himself, frowning in resignation. "I don't know. I don't know."

"Because she seems to be under the impression that you're in some great pain that I need to talk to you about. That I need to, like, give you therapy or something. Which is weird, don't you think? Considering you haven't really done a single thing to be there for me, to help *me*, today, or for, I don't know, the past fucking year."

Jason gave her the same blank look, the zooming out in his eyes, the unmoored, indifferent detachment that had broken her heart so many times, confused her so much, since Kyle died. But now it was making her furious, desperate to shake her brother awake and make him be her brother again.

"I mean, Jason, do you even understand what is happening here? What happened today? Do you understand that that girl is dead, that Mom and Dad are probably dead? Because I have been walking around with this alone, Jason. *Alone.* And I am so tired of it. I am so tired of wanting you back, and hating you, and wanting you back, and hating you."

Her brother was trembling now. He brushed a piece of hair from his eyes. "I'm here. I mean, I'm here, right now."

"No you're not!" Alexa screamed. "No you're not. You haven't been here in a long, long time, Jason. And I just want to know why. That's all I want you to tell me. I just want to know why you've been ignoring me, why you refuse to acknowledge that something really shitty happened to me last summer. That something really bad is happening to us right now. You're my older brother. You're supposed to help me. You're supposed to . . ."

"I'm supposed to what, Alexa? Magically make you feel better? I can't do that. How many times do I have to tell you that? I don't know what you want from me!"

"I want you to be a fucking human being for once! You're like a robot. Do you feel *anything*? Aren't you scared? Aren't you sad? This stranger," Alexa yelled, pointing to Morgan and immediately feeling bad for doing it, "tells me that you're all 'messed up.' What does that even mean? Who are you, Jason? Honestly, who *are* you? You know, Kyle always thought that—"

"Don't tell me what Kyle thought," Jason spat back, surprising his sister. His eyes were watery but angry, and he had the beginnings of a mean sneer on his face. "You don't know a fucking thing about what Kyle thought."

"What the hell are you talking about, Jason?" Alexa cried. "He was my friend, *my* friend, remember?"

"You didn't know anything about him!" Jason roared back, people in the waiting room turning to look at these two screaming kids. "That's the most pathetic part! You think you and Kyle had some great thing, some great friend affair last summer. But you didn't even know who he was. Or who he was with most of the time . . ."

What was Jason saying? What did he mean, who Kyle was with? Then, looking at her brother, trembling and teary (when was the last time she saw Jason cry?), it suddenly hit her, like an electric shock, her world inverting, the past warping. And then her brother confirmed what she'd just realized.

"He was with *me*, Alexa," Jason yelped, his voice croaking. "He was with me! Kyle loved *me*, he was *mine*. Not yours. So don't tell me what he thought, or what he said, or who he was. Because you have no idea. You had no idea. Kyle was mine. He loved me. And I loved him. And it's my fault that he's gone."

Chapter Fifteen

Jason

THE FIRST TIME Kyle left a voice mail for Jason, the day after their first kiss, Jason was surprised, but overjoyed. He listened to it over and over again. There was nothing remarkable about it, just Kyle's voice rambling about some customer at work, then followed by a little pause, a sigh, and then Kyle saying, "I don't know. I just wanted to talk to you, I guess."

The next time they saw each other, their first time alone together, carefully orchestrated around Alexa's work schedule, Jason made fun of Kyle for the voice mail.

"I mean, who leaves voice mails? It's 2016."

"I leave voice mails. Don't you want to hear my beautiful voice?"

Jason blushed. They were sitting far down the beach from Jason's house, watching the afternoon dog walkers throw tennis balls into the ocean, black labs and golden retrievers bounding after them.

"Of course I want to hear your voice. It's just funny! I dunno."

"Well, I'm not gonna stop. Voice mails are my thing."

"I thought moving to New York was your thing. I thought theater was your thing."

"I can have multiple things."

Jason laughed, a juvenile, embarrassing, knee-jerk response to the word "thing." Kyle seemed to catch what Jason was laughing about and raised an eyebrow.

"Only one thing on your mind, huh . . ."

Jason blushed again. This was flirting, huh? Here Jason was, on a beach, with a boy, and they were flirting. He watched a cocker spaniel go running into the water and he wanted to chase after it, to tell it the good news. But he also wanted to stay right where he was.

"Well, fine then. Leave me voice mails. I promise I'll get around to listening to them eventually."

Kyle nodded his head. "Good," he said. "Good." He turned to Jason, looked him in the eye. "You wanna kiss again?"

Jason nodded, and they did.

Kyle did indeed keep leaving voice mails. One from a party in Provincetown that Jason had been scared to go to. He left another while driving home to Bourne to see his mom. Another from the freezer at work, whispering. Another from his car just after sneaking out of Jason's bedroom, a particularly sexy message that Jason listened to a lot on nights when he and Kyle couldn't be together.

It was a little tradition they established over their short time together, half joking, half sincere. Jason relished getting them, and sometimes thought about leaving one for Kyle, but felt weird about it, like he wouldn't know what to say, that he wouldn't be cute and clever like Kyle was. So it remained one-sided, like so much in Jason's life, people giving him stuff and Jason just gobbling it down and giving nothing in return.

So it was fitting, then, in some tragic way, that the last time Kyle ever spoke to Jason was over voice mail. That Sunday night, the night he died. They hadn't spoken for two days—unprecedented since they'd first kissed—and with the summer over, essentially, the next day, Jason had fallen into a consuming gloom, convinced that he and Kyle were done forever, that they'd never be together again.

Jason's parents were off to the end-of-summer dinner dance at the club, and Alexa was at work. There was a big party that some of the Grey's employees, the twins, Dave and Courtney, were having, and earlier Kyle had tried to persuade Jason to come. But Jason said he wanted the two of them to spend the night alone together.

"We'll have the place to ourselves . . . a whole house! With, like, beds," Jason said, trying to sound coy and enticing.

But Kyle kicked at Jason from the other side of the backseat of his car, where they'd just hooked up, as they often did. "What's wrong with this?" he said, gesturing to the barely functioning car. "Come onnn. It'll be fun. I want to end the summer with a bang!"

"But we could!" Jason joked.

Kyle rolled his eyes, leaned across the car, and kissed Jason, softly. "Pleeeease."

Jason said he'd think about it. But then it was Kyle's birthday, real or made-up, and the disaster in Provincetown happened, and the fight, and all of a sudden it was Sunday and there were no plans either way.

Kyle hadn't called or texted, and Jason felt too stubborn to contact Kyle. So, once Jason's parents were off to their dinner, and Alexa went to work, Jason—feeling reckless and sorry for himself, like he hadn't since before the summer—dug into his parents' liquor cabinet, finding a mostly full bottle of vodka and going to sit out on the porch, smoking a joint and wallowing in his misery. He scrolled through Kyle's photos on Instagram, always so fascinated by the ones from before they'd gotten together, the life Kyle had lived before Jason, both mysterious and plain.

He kept drinking until he passed out, maybe around nine, he wasn't sure. All Jason knew was that he was awoken around midnight by his phone ringing, his sister on the other end, screaming and crying. Jason, groggy and still drunk, tried to comprehend what she was saying.

"Alexa, Alexa, slow down, what are you saying? Alexa?"

"Kyle!" she said. "Kyle! He was in a car accident! He crashed his car!"

Jason felt sick, like he was going to throw up. "Is—is he O.K.?"

He heard his sister break down into sobs, and he knew then that Kyle wasn't O.K. But he needed to hear his sister say it. He needed someone to say it, if it was real.

"He's dead, Jason. He's dead. Kyle's dead. Oh my God. Oh my God."

Jason threw up, vomit splattering on the porch as he dropped the phone. He couldn't remember if he screamed or cried or anything. All Jason saw when he tried to remember the finer details of that night was a wall of blackness descending, separating his life before and the life after.

It was only hours later, when Alexa and their parents were home,

Jason sitting numb on the couch while his sister wailed and Linda and Theo tried to comfort her, that Jason felt his phone buzz, a little reminder that he had a message. He looked at it, his eyes bleary and unfocused. It was a message from Kyle. From the night before. From 9:07 P.M. Hands shaking, Jason pressed "Play" and put the phone to his ear.

"Hey, babe. I'm leaving work, wanted to talk to you all day. I've been thinking about it, and maybe you're right. Maybe there's time. Maybe all that stuff can wait. I know why you're not picking up, but maybe you'll listen to this after I leave it, so here's me telling you that I'm just gonna drive over there and wait like a creep outside your house for a few minutes. If you want to come outside and talk or make out or yell at me some more or just sit next to me and not say anything, I'd really like that. I'd like that a lot. But I gotta hang up now because I'm driving. So, see you in like fifteen minutes. I hope."

Kyle had driven to the house that night. To make up with Jason, to fix things, to set things right so they could figure out the future together. But Jason had been passed out drunk. He didn't hear his phone, and Kyle had waited and waited outside. He was *right there*. All Jason had to do was run outside, tell Kyle he was sorry, and they could have gone to the party together. Or stayed in and talked and had sex, like the rest of the once-perfect summer.

But when Jason didn't come outside, didn't call back or text or do anything, Kyle went to the party alone, upset probably. He drank more than he normally did, making the careless, fatal decision to drive himself home. Or, even worse, maybe he was headed back to Jason's. To try one more time. And then he died. Because Jason was asleep on the fucking porch. Because Jason couldn't keep his shit together for a few hours, because he'd fallen right back into his stupid, destructive old self the minute he felt Kyle pulling away from him. Because Jason was too stubborn to apologize in time. Because he was too cowardly to just tell Nate Carlsson, "Yeah, I'm gay, and this is my boyfriend." Because Jason had done everything wrong, the whole time he and Kyle were together. He knew that now. That this was all his fault.

He should have known that Kyle would call. He should have called Kyle. He should have driven to Grey's and, who cared what his sister saw, apologized to Kyle and told him he loved him and everything would be O.K. Kyle would be alive, if Jason had just had two or three fewer drinks, hadn't gotten stoned, hadn't been so consumed with his own sadness and self-loathing that he'd forgotten there was another person, someone else on the other end of the line, waiting for him to say something too.

Jason had listened to that message probably hundreds of times in the last year. Torturing himself, agonizing over it. Sometimes he let himself slip into fantasies about what could have been, about the life he'd have now if he'd only heard his phone, run outside, grabbed Kyle and never let go. But most days he just buried himself deeper. He drank more, scored pills, stumbled in a haze through school, disconnected, speaking to no one, feeling empty and worthless.

And of course he had let Alexa grieve for her friend alone, not knowing that Jason was ruined inside too, that he wanted to scream and cry at his funeral, cling to Kyle's mother, Sheila, and beg her to forgive him. But he couldn't do that, because then people would know, and he would have to hear himself say it. That he failed Kyle. That he let him die when all he had to do was stay present, to keep being the person Kyle loved for a little while longer. It was the last night of summer. They'd almost made it. But Jason had, at the very end, managed to destroy everything.

"Oh my God, oh my God, oh my God." Alexa kept saying it, over and over again. She had her hands on her head, her eyes wild and frantic.

Jason wasn't sure what to say next. He'd let it all pour out, telling Alexa everything, about him and Kyle, about how they'd been in love, or at least they'd said they were and it had felt that way. That he was supposed to see Kyle that night. That the accident was his fault. That he got drunk. That he could have saved Kyle, but he failed. He was out of words, so he stood there dumbly while Alexa reeled.

Finally, she ran her hands over her face and stared her brother in the eyes. "How could you not tell me? How could you do that to me, Jason?"

"I wanted to tell you . . ." Jason started, but Alexa cut him off.

"No you didn't. That's a lie. You had a year. You had more than a year. How could you do this? Oh my God, Jason. Oh my God. I'm such a fucking idiot. You must think I'm so stupid."

"I don't think you're stupid, Alexa."

"Yes you do! And so did he. Oh my God, Kyle."

"He didn't think you were stupid!"

"No, you were right. I didn't know him at all. I had no *idea* who he was. That whole time! That whole time, you two were sneaking off and . . . So who was I? Just a cover? So Kyle could come over for dinner and you guys could get stoned on the beach and be so in love together?

Jesus Christ, Jason. This is so much worse. This is so much worse than anything I could have imagined. Here I am this whole year, this whole miserable year, thinking that I'm too sad, that I'm too needy, that I pushed you away because I was asking for too much. And the whole time, the real truth is . . . it wasn't about me at all. It's never really about me, is it? It's always you. Somehow, it's always you."

Jason had never heard his sister talk like this. All Jason wanted then was to make Alexa feel better. He wanted to say the right thing. But he had no idea what that was. It all felt so much bigger than anything he knew how to handle.

Alexa turned away from Jason and paced across the room, trying to collect herself. But then she spun around, angry about something new. She strode back toward Jason. "I asked you."

"What?"

"That summer. I asked you if you were seeing someone. I know I did. And you just straight-up lied to me. Kyle lied to me too. God. Do you realize how *cruel* that was? Do you know how lonely and tricked and just . . . tossed aside this makes me feel?"

"We would have told you, at some point . . ."

"Ha! At some point. Well, thank God that point has finally arrived, now that Kyle's been dead for a year and Mom and Dad are probably about to join him."

"Jesus, Alexa."

"No. You don't get to do that, act like I'm overreacting. Not about this."

Jason just stood there, feeling utterly stuck. The more his sister said it out loud, the more he realized how mean it had been, to lie to Alexa like that for so long. But he couldn't fix the lies, and he couldn't take back what he'd admitted to her today, tarnishing her memory of Kyle in the process. He should have told her back then, but he should not have told her now. No matter which way he turned, Jason was met with his own fuck-ups, yet again.

"And now you're disappearing," Alexa said, shaking her head, looking at her brother, eyes wide with shock. "You're getting that druggy look. Do you know you haven't even said 'sorry' yet? Did it even occur to you to apologize to me? Or do I not deserve that, am I just some nobody to you?"

"I'm sorry!" Jason yelled, immediately feeling stupid for hoping that saying it might fix things. "I'm sorry," he repeated, more sincerely, more pleadingly.

Alexa shook her head again. "I can't believe you're telling me this now. Today. This is surreal." She threw up her hands in disbelief and walked to the other end of the room, collapsing into a chair, putting her head down, to cool off or cry. Jason watched after her, feeling like he might cry himself. Talking about Kyle like this, the definitiveness of his death, of his absence, made Jason ache all the more acutely. He turned and looked at Morgan, who was teary too.

"I'm sorry," she said in a small voice. "This was my fault. I shouldn't have said anything."

"No." Jason sighed. "It's my fault. It's always been my fault."

Morgan wasn't listening. "I shouldn't even be here. I should have gone home. I just made things worse for you, and I shouldn't even *be* here." She looked over to the exit, clearly planning an escape of sorts.

"Of course you should be here," Jason said. "You're here for your dad."

Morgan's eyes darted to Jason, some strange mix of sadness and panic in them. "I was," she said, her face suddenly crumpling. "But . . . not anymore."

"What do you mean?"

"He's dead. My dad died this morning. Before any of you even got here."

Chapter Sixteen

Morgan

WHEN MORGAN'S MOTHER got sick, as Morgan's dad called it, he did his best to shield Morgan from the worst of it, the late-night fights, the days and weeks she'd disappear without word, the lying and the bargaining and the manipulation. Of course, it was impossible to protect Morgan from all of it: She saw her mother fade away, replaced by some hungry, barely human thing, saw her father lose his grip on her, the change in his bearing, from hope to tired resignation to a determined drive to keep his daughter as apart from the ugliness as he could.

When her mother had finally left—disappeared, really—a strange sense of peace had descended on the little house in Dorchester. Beneath all the fear, and sadness, and utter disbelief at how quickly Morgan's mother had crumbled and blown away, there was a feeling that things could, at least, get better for Morgan and her father, that they'd lost a big fight, and would hurt for a long time, but were still alive, able now to try to pick up and move on as best as they could.

And life hadn't been all that bad, somehow. Morgan's father, a retired Boston police officer, had old friends from the force who checked in on Morgan like doting uncles and aunts, occasionally filling the house with laughter and happiness, a warmth it hadn't known in a long time. Morgan liked to think that her dad and his friends, and what she'd experienced with her mother, made her tough. She saw Dorchester changing, hordes of young people with college degrees moving into her neighborhood, fancy restaurants and stores opening up on corner after corner, so she clung to her scrappy, native Boston roots, wore her hardness with pride. She always felt on the defensive, but she got through most of her days, and indeed even a couple of years, without breaking down or otherwise losing it. Her father, often distant but amiable in a beery fog, stumbled on in his way too, the two of them a weather-beaten little team, pressing on as they slowly healed.

But then, that spring, her father started getting tired, all the time, and had a pain radiating throughout his lower back, one that went from bad to debilitating. Morgan finally convinced her stubborn, doctor-phobic father to get some tests done, and when the results came in and the office told him they'd like to discuss them in person, Morgan insisted on coming with him.

The office, way out in Wellesley by the side of Route 9, was drab and menacing in its attempts to be soothing. Smooth wooden chairs with stiff cushioning, soft-colored paintings of seashores and birch trees hanging forlornly on the walls. Right up until they were brought into the doctor's little office—Dr. Koskinen telling them to please have a seat, the calm in her voice edged with something hard, like she was bracing the room for a difficult conversation—Morgan had convinced herself that everything was going to be fine. But then she knew. It was bad news.

And indeed it was.

"This here is where you've been feeling the most pain, Mr. Boyce," Dr. Koskinen said, turning the monitor to face Morgan and her dad. She pointed at a dark mass, looking like one of those ink tests for crazy people. "That is your pancreas," Dr. Koskinen said. "Which I'm afraid is very bad place to get cancer."

"What does 'very bad' mean?" Morgan's father asked, giving a nervous glance toward his daughter.

"Well, in certain cases we would begin chemotherapy immediately. But I'm afraid that because we found this so late—the cancer is in stage four—there isn't much we can do."

Morgan's throat felt tight. She felt irrationally angry at the doctor, her pointy glasses and her snaggletooth, her tight bun and measured way of talking. She wanted to slap her.

"I see. So, what are we talking about here? Months? Years?" Morgan's dad asked.

"That's hard to say," Dr. Koskinen said, turning the monitor away from Morgan and her father. "Sometimes in cases like this a patient can go a year. Sometimes only a few months. It depends on many factors, including, well, luck."

He nodded, but said nothing. So, the doctor pressed on.

"The best course of action in these situations is usually some kind of in-patient palliative care. Among other things, we find it takes a great deal of the burden of daily care off the family," the doctor said, looking sadly in Morgan's direction.

"You mean like a hospice," Morgan's dad said, his tone hollow and faraway.

"Yes, like a hospice. There are many options in the city. Your policy from the BPD will cover a great deal of the cost, I'd imagine. I'd be happy to discuss any and all options with you and, of course, with your daughter," the doctor said, once again zeroing in on Morgan, who felt small and utterly overwhelmed, like she'd just noticed a tidal wave coming and didn't have time to flee.

Morgan's father shook his head, either in resignation or disbelief, Morgan couldn't quite tell. He grabbed Morgan's hand and squeezed it. "I'm so sorry," he said, tears welling in his eyes. "I'm so, so sorry."

Morgan said nothing, too shocked to cry. They said thank you to the doctor and left, walking out into the parking garage, getting in the car, and driving home.

She watched him fade. Another parent, all over again. He was weak, didn't leave the house much. The hospice discussion never went beyond the doctor's office, because even with the department pension a decent place was, in fact, too expensive—"Even dying costs money," Morgan's father said to her with a sigh, the two of them sitting at the little table in the kitchen—and because Morgan wanted him there, in the house with her. Even though it was horrible to watch, her once strong father withering and graying.

There was still laughter, sometimes, still a steady enough stream of friends and well-wishers, bringing food (that he couldn't keep down), sometimes cigarettes ("Can't hurt you now!" one of Morgan's father's friends said, with a gravelly laugh). But many times, summer nights when the house was hot and quiet, it was just the two of them, Morgan's father dozing in his recliner while something played on the television—a cooking show that he liked, or a Red Sox game, the cheers of the crowd and the announcers' voices a soft drone as Morgan sat reading on the couch, one eye on her father, sometimes going over and leaning in close to make sure he was still breathing. A relief, mixed with something else, when she determined he was.

And then, suddenly, late in the summer, he was better. A little, anyway. The doctor told them, after they called her, elated and hopeful, that this might happen. A swell of energy, a dulling of the pain. But it did not mean her father was getting less sick.

"We're not always sure why it happens," she said, over the hum of the phone line. "But you should try to enjoy it."

So, they did. They went to a game at Fenway, Morgan's father taking the stairs to their seats very slowly, but staying awake for all nine innings. It was a perfect August night, warm and breezy, a round moon hanging high and serene in the sky, the stadium lights bright and reassuring.

Morgan drove them up to the beach in Nahant, where her father had gone swimming when he was a kid. They sat in beach chairs, two towels over her father's legs to keep him warm in the wind. He drank a couple of cans of Coors, told Morgan a few rambling stories about his "salad days." About meeting Morgan's mother on that very beach, years ago, Morgan hearing a kindness toward her she had not heard in a long time.

His resurgence, his swan song, whatever it was, lasted longer than the doctors said it would. By October he was still mostly alert, still somewhat mobile. Morgan set him up in a chair on the sidewalk so he could supervise her decorating the house for Halloween, a tradition he held dear, doing the little house up in new and elaborate ways every year. It was strange to be hanging cobwebs and skeletons, all these symbols of mustiness and death, but it seemed to make him happy, so Morgan did her best to make the house look good.

"That'll scare 'em," her father said when Morgan was done, giving her a pat on the behind, like he used to when she was little and had done well at something—a hit in softball, a good grade, a nice homemade present for her mother.

They had a few more weeks together, Morgan coming straight home from school every day, making sure her father was comfortable, that he was warm enough, seeing if he was hungry, if he needed anything. He would wave her away, say, "Do your homework," and they'd spend the rest of the evening in the living room, Morgan trying to focus on whatever work was in front of her, some math problem or impenetrable Shakespeare speech, but mostly worrying about her father, about how long they had left.

She did not want him to go, she was not ready for it, but she also hated not knowing, every day, if she would come home to find him dead, her hands trembling as she turned the key in the lock every afternoon, walking hesitantly into each room until she found him. "You snuck up on me!" he'd say sometimes when she discovered him, but usually he was asleep, looking small and frail in his Patriots sweatshirt, lightly snoring, the house smelling strange and sour.

The night before the bridge collapsed, Morgan brought her father dinner, setting up the TV tray so he could stay in his chair, and he ate a few spoonfuls of soup before he said, "Listen, kiddo, we have to talk."

Morgan didn't want to talk, not about what he wanted to, anyway. She knew a conversation like this was coming—one about funeral arrangements and what she would do after he was gone—but she was not ready for it. She would never be ready for it. But she knew they had to have the conversation someday, because she would have no idea what to do otherwise. So she nodded, said, "O.K."

But then her father said something she hadn't expected.

"I'm gonna do the hospice thing. You're just a kid. You shouldn't have to see this, to take care of me like this every day. Not after what you went through with your mother. It's not right."

Morgan shook her head. "No. If you go to one of those places, I'll be alone! Is that even legal? Wouldn't the state take me away or something? Put me in foster care?

"Only if they find out," her father said with a shrug. "It's gonna happen eventually anyway," he added, giving her a little smile, its corners creased with sorrow.

Morgan stayed firm. "Well, all I know is unless you want to drive yourself there or take a cab, you're staying here."

He tensed up, shook his head, said, "No, no, Morgan. This is my decision, this is up to me, come on now. I want to do this. It's the best thing. It's what's right."

Morgan could see that he wouldn't let it drop. He may have been physically weak, but he was still stubborn, was still her father. "All right," she said, a heaviness rising in her throat. "I guess we can look into it tomorrow."

He nodded, satisfied, and they continued eating, he more pretending to eat, really.

They watched a movie, *Casino*, one of her father's favorites, and he fell asleep before Sharon Stone had her freak-out on the lawn, Morgan covering him with a blanket and turning out the light. She always wondered if she should kiss him on the forehead or something, just in case, but it was just not something they did, Morgan and her dad. There was love there, a quiet abundance of it, but it mostly went unsaid, undemonstrated. Morgan knew her father knew. And that was enough. So she went upstairs and went to bed, lying awake thinking about the next day until she drifted off into a restless sleep.

And then, the morning.

Morgan came downstairs and saw her father's chair empty. Which wasn't all that unusual, but he wasn't in the bathroom either, or in the kitchen, or out on the little back porch smoking a cigarette. Morgan didn't think he'd have gone upstairs, wasn't sure he could even have made it upstairs, but she checked up there just in case.

His bedroom was still and empty. He wasn't in the bathroom. And he obviously wasn't in her room. Panicked now, Morgan raced downstairs and out the front door, the decorations from Halloween still there, damp from rain, fake cobwebs billowing in the cold morning air. The car was gone. Her father had driven somewhere, even though he could barely stay awake for a half hour at a time.

She went back inside, figuring she'd call one of her father's friends who was still on the force. They'd be able to find him, track him down, get him back home safely. But before she could get her phone, the land-line in the kitchen rang, a loud, jarring sound that froze Morgan in place. That was the bad-news phone. Morgan's dad's friends never called, they just showed up. The phone really only rang when it was telemarketers, or, back when Morgan's mother was still living with them, a new minor disaster had happened—it was usually some police station, giving Morgan's father information about his wife's whereabouts. Morgan hesitated, not wanting to know who or what was on the other end.

She answered on the fifth ring, her voice shaky as she said, "Hello?" There was a fuzz, the crackle of a not-great connection. And then she heard the familiar voice of Mike Murray, her father's childhood friend, a police sergeant in Lynn, where her father had grown up. "Hey, Morgan, honey, it's Uncle Mike. Listen, I need you to head up to the hospital. They've got your dad here. He's . . ." The rest of what Mike said was blurry, Morgan saying, "Thank you, thank you, I'll be right there." She called a cab and waited out on the front stoop, her mind oddly blank. Her father had done something. Somewhere he knew she wouldn't be the first one to find him.

When she got to the hospital, running into the emergency room in leggings and a hoodie she'd dug out of her closet (laundry had gone by the wayside in recent weeks), the one she'd stuck safety pins through during a long-gone punk phase, she saw Mike waiting for her, talking to her mom's old co-worker, Mary Oakes. Mary had been more than a co-worker, really, she'd been a friend of the family. But when Morgan's mom started stealing pills from the hospital, Mary had been the one to report her, saying it was for her own good. "A real stickler for the rules," Morgan's father had called her.

Mike gave Morgan a hug, looking weary and sad. "Where is he?" Morgan asked, pulling away from Mike and knowing from the expression on his face, before he said it, that her father was gone.

"He took some of his pain pills, honey. Drove up to Nahant, must have been early this morning, parked by the water. Trooper found him about an hour ago. They tried to get him back in the ambulance, but he was already gone. There was nothing they could do, honey, there was nothing they could do."

Mary nodded, her eyes glistening. "They tried, Morgan. I promise they tried."

"I know, I know," Morgan said, instinctively giving Mary a hug, to reassure her as much as herself. "I know, I know." She said it over and over again, not knowing what else to do.

"I don't . . ." she started. She had no idea what came next. Were there arrangements? Had her father left any instructions?

"There was this," Mike said, reaching into his coat pocket and pulling out an envelope, legal-sized, most likely from the desk in the corner of her dad's bedroom, largely untouched since Morgan's mother left. Mike handed the envelope to Morgan. Her name was written on the front in her father's wobbly script. She wondered when he'd written it. How long he'd planned on doing this. If the discussion about the hospice the night before was just a test, to see if she'd agree to send him on his way. She was angry at her father, that he left without saying goodbye. But she also, in a way she didn't quite understand, felt glad for him. Or, at least, relieved.

She hated the thought of him dead in his car, but it was good at least that he'd been somewhere he loved when it happened, looking out at the water, hearing the seagulls, smelling the salty air. It was peaceful, in a way that dying in the house maybe wasn't. And now it was done. He'd decided it for both of them, the final thing he could do for Morgan. She hadn't been the one to find him, as she had so often feared. She put the envelope in her bag, unsure when she would, or could, read it.

"I don't . . ." Morgan said again. Mike put an arm around her. "I'll help you with all the paperwork. And then, we'll, well, we'll figure the rest out when we can."

Morgan said thank you. She turned to Mary. "Can I see him?"

Mary looked to Mike, then back at Morgan. She gave her a quick nod. "Of course. He's . . . he's downstairs. I'll take you." Mike gave her another hug, and Morgan turned to follow Mary further into the hospital.

Mary led her downstairs and into a small room, where Morgan's father, a sheet covering most of his body, was lying on a table. Morgan found herself worrying that he was cold and almost asked for a blanket. She walked up to the table, stared down at her father. It was his familiar face, but there was something different about it. A distance, a dimness. He was gone.

She began to cry. "Oh, Dad . . ." she said, her voice cracking, the sobs now coming in big heaves. She felt a hand on her back, and there was Mary, giving her a sympathetic look. Morgan turned and hugged her, crying into her blazer, Mary stroking her hair, saying, "I'm so sorry. I'm so, so sorry."

They stood like that for a moment, hugging in that cold and finite room, until Mary's phone buzzed in her trouser pocket.

"I'm sorry," Mary said, pulling away from Morgan. "I have to take this." She answered the phone, said a few quick yeses, and then hung up. "I have to go back upstairs. But you can stay here for a little while if you want. I'll tell them not to bother you."

Morgan nodded. "Thanks. Yeah. I'll be just a little bit."

Mary put a hand on her shoulder. "Just come upstairs and find me when you're ready. And we'll go through everything. Do you have anyone you want us to call?"

Morgan thought of her mother, dying or already dead somewhere. She shook her head. "No. I'm it. It's just me." Mary gave her a tight smile, nodded, turned, and left.

There was a chair in a corner of the room. Morgan pulled it closer to the table and sat down, staring at her father. Time drifted.

When she was finally ready to leave him, to go back upstairs and do whatever needed to be done, Morgan looked at her phone and saw that not only had hours passed, but she'd missed five phone calls, three from friends, and two from a 617 number she was pretty sure was her school. She'd forgotten to tell them she wouldn't be in that day.

Morgan made her way upstairs, back toward the doors to the emergency room, and saw that the place had exploded into activity. Mike was gone. Nurses were running around, phones ringing everywhere. She found Mary, who looked startled to see her.

"Morgan! I thought you'd gone home. Something's happened. There's been an accident."

And there was the day, rushing away from Morgan and her dad, from this small, private pain, into something much bigger, something far beyond the new and lonely life Morgan suddenly lived.

Chapter Seventeen

Skyler

MORGAN WAS CRYING. It was strange to watch, as she'd been so quiet, so composed and watchful, all day. She told them that her father had died that morning, something about cancer, about a car. It was hard to put it together while Morgan wept, Jason looking at her, face frozen in shock. Everything seemed to be happening at once.

"He wasn't on the bridge?" Skyler asked, not sure why it mattered. Morgan shook her head.

"I didn't know where else to go. I had nowhere else to go. I have nowhere to go."

Morgan seemed to be spinning out, and Skyler impulsively grabbed her and pulled her into a hug. Morgan was much taller than Skyler, so it must have looked silly, this small girl clutching to this crying girl's midsection. But Morgan returned the hug, her sobs softening into watery hiccups.

Skyler said, "Let's go sit down," and Morgan nodded, Skyler walking her over to some chairs and easing her into one. Morgan wiped her eyes and nose with her sleeve, took some deep breaths, said, "Sorry, sorry" a few times, then "I'm O.K., I'm O.K."

Skyler sat there, not sure what to say, wanting to offer Morgan some words of comfort, to say something about how she'd be all right. Skyler had lost her parents too, in a way. But she knew it was different—much, much different—from what Morgan had experienced that morning. Skyler thought about her grandparents, about what she would do if—when, really—they died. She couldn't imagine it, the feeling of being un-looked after, unwatched, untethered. Being alone in the world.

But, of course, she had Kate. After a terrible scare, Kate was still with her. That was something. That was enough. And in the coming months, Kate would need *her* help, while she recovered. Physically, yes, but Skyler knew there would be some emotional fallout too. She thought about her grandfather, about the things he had likely seen before fleeing Cambodia, the way he was so clammed up about his trauma. She hoped that Kate wouldn't experience the same thing. She hoped Kate didn't remember it. But if she did, if she was haunted or terrorized by memories of it, Skyler would have to be there to help her through it. She wanted to be there. What good was having people to help you if you couldn't, in whatever way possible, help them too?

Morgan was mostly quiet now, sniffling a little, head down and rocking gently back and forth.

"What was his name?" Skyler asked Morgan. "Your dad."

Morgan looked up, gave Skyler the faintest of smiles. "Daniel," she said, with a little laugh. "Danny. Everyone called him Danny."

Skyler thought she might wince, hearing that name, but instead what flashed in her mind just then wasn't her Danny, not the controlling, angry boy who had scared her into timidity so many times, but some vaguely defined dad, ruddy and cheerful, like so many men she'd known growing up in Boston. "That's a nice name," Skyler said, and Morgan smiled again.

"Yeah. It is. The only problem is, our last name's Boyce. So he's Danny Boyce. Like 'Danny Boy'? He hates that song. He hated that song. Which is a problem, if you live here."

Skyler laughed a little, not sure how lightly to treat the moment. But she could see that just getting Morgan talking was making her more relaxed, her face already brighter.

"He was really sick," Morgan said. "I mean, he'd been feeling better the past couple of months, but the doctor said that didn't mean anything. He probably only had a little while left. So I get it. I get why he did it. This way he could decide. I get that."

"Yeah," Skyler said softly. "I get that too."

"You're lucky." Morgan sighed. "You got good news today."

"I know. I'm really lucky."

"Maybe I'll be lucky someday too."

"I'm sure you will be."

Morgan sighed again. "I don't know what to do with myself. I don't know if I should go home or what." She picked at the safety pins on her sweatshirt. Skyler thought that maybe Morgan shouldn't be alone now, not just yet. Though this was not exactly a happy, stress-free place to be. But still. Maybe it was something. A distraction.

"Well," Skyler said, pointing to Jason and Alexa, who were watching to see if Morgan was O.K., seeming to not want to return to the fraught conversation they'd just been having with each other. "I'm going to stay until they hear about their parents. Do you want to stay with me?"

Morgan nodded. "Yeah. That sounds . . . I was going to say 'good,' but none of this is good. It sounds right, though, I guess."

"O.K.," Skyler said. "Good."

"Thanks." Morgan sniffled, pulling her sleeves over her hands. "I'm gonna go get something to drink. Do you want something? They give me free sodas and stuff here."

Skyler shook her head. "No, I'm good. Thank you, though."

Morgan stood up, looked around the waiting room, this small space where so much happened, every day. She turned to Skyler. "You should talk to them," she said, gesturing to Jason and Alexa. "You're, like, calming or something." She gave Skyler another smile and walked off, Skyler a little amused, or was it amazed, at the idea that she could calm anyone down. But it had seemed to work on Morgan.

So she got out of her chair and went over to Alexa. "Hey," she said, raising her eyebrows a little, as if to say *How crazy, how strange.*

"Hey," Alexa said, arms crossed over her chest, looking rattled and on edge.

"You O.K.?"

"I don't know," Alexa said, her mouth crinkling into a frown. "I really don't know."

"Who was Kyle?" Skyler asked, noticing Jason, who was now wandering in a little circle near them, bristle. Skyler turned to him. "He was your boyfriend?"

Jason nodded. A little dip of his head, and then a bigger one, his eyes wet with tears. "Yeah. Yes. He was."

"And he was my best friend," Alexa added. "Or at least I thought so."

"He was," Jason said, turning to his sister, a pleading sound in his voice. "He was," he repeated, more quietly this time.

"What happened to him?" Skyler asked, hoping she wasn't pressing too much, but thinking that maybe, if Jason and Alexa just talked about it together, it would help somehow.

"He was in a car accident, last summer," Jason said, eyes on his sister. "He died. I was supposed to be with him that night, but . . ."

Jason trailed off, looked at the ground, the three of them falling into silence. Skyler wasn't sure if she should ask anything else. But before she could, Alexa turned to her brother.

"It wasn't your fault," Alexa said to Jason, softly, but seeming to mean it. "You didn't make him drink. You didn't make him drive. That was him. He did something really stupid. And he did it on his own."

"But if I'd just been with him!" Jason was getting worked up again, his eyes wide and pained. "If I had just answered the phone and been with him. It wouldn't have happened. And he'd be alive. He'd have New York. He'd have his five houses. And maybe you wouldn't hate me."

"I don't hate you," Alexa said. "I just didn't know. I didn't know you were so sad when he died. I thought you were just ignoring me. I thought you didn't care about me. It hurt. I didn't hate you. I don't hate you. I was just . . . it hurt." She was teary now too, her arms pulled tight against her chest, trying to keep herself together.

"I didn't tell my sister a lot," Skyler interjected. "I mean, we're close, but there was a lot . . . happening in my life that I didn't tell her." She paused, thinking she should stop talking, but Jason and Alexa were both looking at her, waiting to hear what she had to say.

"Because I was scared to. Because I was embarrassed. Because I thought it might change her opinion of me. She figured out what was going on, eventually, but I wish I'd told her sooner. When I thought she might be dead today, I felt so lost, like the only other person in the world who speaks this . . . whole *language* was gone, and I'd never get to speak it again. That no one would ever understand me in the same way, for the rest of my life. I'm so lucky that she's alive. I feel so, so lucky. That I get to talk to her again. That I get to tell her things."

Skyler felt silly, a little embarrassed, a little cruel, for talking about life and the future when everything around her was death and ruin. "Sorry."

Jason snorted. "No. That was good. It was good. But Alexa and I don't exactly speak some secret sibling language."

"But you have Kyle, right?" Skyler said. "To remember, I mean. That's something you both have in common. Someone you loved."

"Maybe," Alexa muttered, arms still crossed, looking sad and wary, wounded.

"I don't know." Skyler sighed. "I don't know you guys. I don't mean to butt in. It's just, if something happens to your par—"

She caught herself, but too late. Jason and Alexa both flinched. "I'm sorry," she stammered, "I just meant . . ."

"It's O.K." Jason shook his head. "It's fine. You're right." He looked at his sister, who wasn't meeting his gaze. "I'm sorry," he said. "Alexa, I'm sorry. I'm sorry I didn't tell you. I'm sorry I shut down after. I just . . . I didn't know how to be in my head. So I ran from . . . all of it, I guess."

Alexa ran a hand through her hair. Let out a deep breath. "I mean, I can't imagine what that must have felt like for you. I just wish . . ." She fell silent.

Jason nodded. "Yeah. Me too."

Skyler was sure she was intruding now and was about to excuse herself, but then she felt a tap on her shoulder and turned around. There was Dr. Lobel, her gray hair spiking off in different directions.

"Ms. Vong?" she asked. Skyler felt a sudden surge of fear. What if something had happened, what if they'd been wrong earlier, what if Kate wasn't O.K.?

But Dr. Lobel put a hand on Skyler's arm and gave it a squeeze. "Your sister is awake," she said. "She asked for you." Skyler's heart lifted back up. "Normally we wouldn't do this, but would you like to go back and see her before we have to prep her for surgery?"

Skyler looked to Jason and Alexa, who both gave her small, encouraging smiles. She waved to them, not sure if it was goodbye or what, and followed Dr. Lobel through the swinging doors and into the hallways of the hospital.

She felt strangely scared. What if things with Kate were different? They were both altered now, weren't they? What if they couldn't connect with one another anymore? What if they had nothing to say? Skyler thought about her grandparents, so far away, probably panicking, trying to get back to Boston as quickly as they could. Even though Skyler had told them to stay put, she couldn't wait for them to get there, for her little family to be back together. For everyone to be in the house again, same as it had been for years.

She thought about her mother, wondered where she might be at that moment. Skyler wondered if maybe her mother had felt something, when Kate was in the accident. People said that parents have an extra sense like that. Maybe Lucy had been in the middle of some desert in California, or on a rocky, lonely beach, and had felt a sudden stab of panic and dread and had missed her daughters just then. Had worried about them. But maybe it didn't matter, either way. Maybe what Skyler had, what she and Kate had, was enough.

Dr. Lobel guided Skyler around a corner and into a small room. "Kate," she said, "you have a visitor." Skyler walked in and saw her sister, bruised and bandaged and surrounded by beeping machines. She had so long to go before she was better. Still, as she walked in, she saw that Kate was smiling, looking happy and relieved to see Skyler, to see someone she could count on. To see her sister, crying and scared and grateful all at the same time, there in the room with her, ready to help her through.

Chapter Eighteen

Jason

JASON WATCHED SKYLER leave with the doctor and felt a prickliness, the knowledge that he and Alexa were now alone, and that he'd have to face her again, would have to live with all of his secrets out in the open, the ones he'd held so long and so bitterly. So intensely.

Ambulances were arriving more slowly now, the local anchors on the TV saying that most of the injured victims had been removed from the scene and were at or were on their way to area hospitals. Investigations were under way, the mayor promising that a cause would be determined and if there were parties responsible—he kept saying "negligence"—they would be brought to justice. But still no word on Jason's parents, if they were just bodies in the rubble or if they were on their way, injured but alive. He and Alexa were among the few people left, waiting for news, for closure, for some bloom of hope.

He looked at Alexa, her eyes still fixed on the door where Skyler had disappeared. She had a lot to think about, he figured. A lot to process. He had hoped he would feel lighter after he told his sister everything, but the space between them only felt heavier, more charged with hurt and confusion. Maybe he had made everything worse, as he always seemed to do, eventually. He and Alexa hadn't said a word since Skyler left, Alexa staring at the door like she was trying to see through it to something else, Jason watching his sister and trying to figure out what she might do next.

Jason never would have guessed that Alexa would turn to him, her voice even and familiar, and ask, "Do you have any cigarettes?"

Jason blinked at her, not sure he'd heard her right. "Any what?"

"I know you smoke sometimes. Do you have any?"

"I—you don't smoke."

"You don't know everything about me. Sometimes I do."

"Oh. Well . . . Um, I don't. Morgan had one of those e-cigarette things. But she's . . . I don't know where she went."

"Maybe she's outside. Let's go outside."

Alexa started walking for the door, and Jason followed her, not sure what had suddenly taken hold in her, but happy that she was talking to him. If she did blame him for Kyle, if she was angry that he'd lied to her for so long, kept his distance and shut her out, at least she wasn't going to shut him out in return. Alexa was walking quickly, and Jason raced to catch up.

Seeing Alexa move swiftly through the hospital, Jason chasing after her, brought him back to a summer ago, like pretty much everything did these days. They were always with him, those seismic few months. And yet how far away they felt too. Jason thought of a day in early August, just before the heavy dog-days heat set in. Alexa must have noticed that Jason had been using his bike a lot that summer, revisiting that childhood joy, and she suggested that maybe they could go for a ride together. She had an hour before she had to be at work, more than enough time to take a longer route to Grey's. Jason, happy to be out on the road, and to maybe catch a glimpse of Kyle at work, had agreed, and they set out, brother and sister, like they used to when they were young.

Their route was green and quiet, the occasional car whooshing by, but it was early on a Saturday morning, so for the most part, all Jason heard was the sound of the wind, the pleasing tick of his bicycle wheels, summer cicadas, and songbirds. Alexa rode fast, always more competitive and more athletic than Jason was. On Old Orchard Road, she zoomed around a corner, and when Jason eventually rounded it he couldn't see her anywhere, though the road ahead was straight and unobstructed. He slowed down, suddenly nervous. He pedaled a little more, then pulled over to the side of the road.

"Alexa?" he called out, unable to hide the panic in his voice. "Alexa?" And then, there she was, jumping out from behind the entrance of the Eastham recycling station. She laughed. "You sounded so worried!"

"Jesus," Jason said, but he was laughing too. He took a long sigh, made an audible "Whew," before they hopped on their bikes and pressed on, disappearing down the road.

The little memory stung him, as he made his way out into the cold night. It was sad to think of a time when he and Alexa had been partners. They were only a year apart, and had been, when they were kids, best friends and confidants, with a close, almost telepathic understanding. "You're so lucky that they're such pals," Linda's friends were always saying to her, as if Jason and Alexa weren't standing right there, brought around to amuse party guests before they were excused and could go get lost in one of their elaborate, made-up games.

And now Jason was chasing after his sister, whom he may have lost forever, but hoping that something outside, away from the oppressive light of the waiting room, would bring them back together. Now that the truth was out, now that his guilt was laid bare and she could see him for who he really was.

Alexa walked to the end of the driveway and stopped at the curb. She closed her eyes and took a deep breath, Jason realizing that she probably hadn't left the building in hours. He walked up next to her, reveling in the whirling, utterly alive sounds of the city. Boston was always nicest on nights after it rained, he thought, lonely and cozy all at once. It was windy, though, and a chill quickly seeped in through Jason's clothes. He shivered.

"It's cold."

Alexa didn't look at him, her eyes pointed straight ahead, at the apartment buildings across the street, some windows lit up, making a pattern, an uneven checkerboard of life, little boxes of light each representing people—a family, a couple in love, someone alone. All probably watching the news, to see what the latest word was on this disaster. Jason realized it had likely gripped the city, maybe even the country, this terrifying story. How strange, then, to be there at the middle of it, the story still ongoing, his parents somewhere, still lost in uncertainty.

"Do you think they're O.K.?" Jason asked her quietly.

She shook her head, stuffed her hands in her pockets. "I don't know. I don't know."

They stood in silence, watching the lights of the apartments, seeing silhouettes moving around, people preparing a late dinner, or putting their kids to bed, or maybe just wandering their homes, unsure what to do with themselves.

"Are we going to be O.K.?"

Alexa finally turned to look at him, brushing a strand of hair from her face as she did. She shrugged. "I don't know. I don't know that either. Do you want us to be O.K.?"

"Of course. I never meant to—"

"You know what the worst part of it is, besides Kyle being dead, I mean? Besides the lie? It's that we could have been there for each other, you know? If I had just known. If you had just told me. All this time. This whole year. It could have been so much different, Jason. It could have been so much easier. Or less hard. Or something. I just wish you'd told me. I wish I'd known. Do you have any idea what that feels like? To find out something like this? It's like the whole world just changed, Jason. Even more than it already had today. I don't . . . I don't know where I am anymore."

"I wanted to tell you. All year. But I thought you'd blame me . . ."

"I wouldn't have blamed you. It wasn't your fault. I know you think it was. And I wish you had been with him. Maybe he wouldn't have . . . But maybe you would have, too. You could be dead too. Did you ever think of that?"

Jason had, more than a few times. At his lowest points, he thought that maybe that wouldn't have been so bad. If they'd just gone out together. At least then he wouldn't miss him so much, wouldn't feel so guilty all the time. It wasn't quite being suicidal, he didn't think. It was just wishing that Kyle had taken Jason with him. Wherever he was going. Wherever he went.

"I guess I didn't," he lied to Alexa, not wanting to burden her with more of his darkness. "I guess that's true."

"It is true," Alexa said. "It is." She took her hands out of her pockets, crossed her arms over her chest, her familiar pose, indicating that she was thinking through something. She took a deep breath, exhaled. Looked back at the apartments. "It was my fault, today. Sort of, anyway. They were driving to Northrup. I had a meeting with them and my guidance counselor. I was going to tell them that I don't want to go to college. Not right away, anyway. So it was my fault that they were on the bridge. They were coming to see me for some stupid thing."

She looked like she might cry, but she took another deep breath, catching herself. Jason shook his head. "No. No. That's not your fault. Jesus, Alexa. Is that what you've been thinking all day?"

"It's some of what I've been thinking."

"Well, you shouldn't. So you had a meeting at school. They had to go to like a million meetings at my school. At my *schools*. That's normal. That's what parents do."

"I guess." Alexa sighed, a watery little sound.

"You should have told me," Jason said, and Alexa laughed.

"That's my line."

"So we're both just . . . not telling each other things, huh."

"I guess so."

Jason laughed too, more out of tiredness than anything else. He felt emptied. He'd poured all of himself out and now there was nothing left.

Alexa sighed again, put her hands over her eyes. "Oh Godddd . . . I just need this to be over. I need to know. I need to know." She ran her hands over her hair, clasping them behind her neck. Jason wasn't sure what to say, not wanting to disturb the uneasy peace between them.

Alexa bit her lip, looking like she was deciding to say something.

"What did you like about him?"

"What?"

"Kyle. What did you like about him?"

Jason didn't know why she was asking this, if it was some test or if she was genuinely curious. The only thing he could do now, though, was tell her the truth.

"Everything, I guess. He was smart. And weird. And funny. And really . . . himself, you know? I liked that. A lot. I guess I was more myself when I was with him. Which is corny. But it's true. He made me feel like me, you know? And he made me do things I was scared to do. But that were still, like, *me*, I think. He felt like . . . the future."

"He felt like the future . . ." Alexa repeated. "Yeah. He did. He did."

"Plus," Jason added, trying something out, "he was really cute."

Alexa barked, a yelping laugh. "Sorry. That's just . . . weird. I've never heard you say that about anyone."

"Well, he was."

"Yeah."

Jason sighed. "I miss him, Alexa. I really, really miss him."

"Me too," Alexa said, blinking back tears. "Me too."

Without thinking, Jason reached out and put his arms around his sister, hugging her tight while she cried, and he cried. "I'm so sorry, I'm so sorry," he whispered, apologizing for everything, for all of it. For lying, for running away from her, for Kyle, for their parents, wherever they were. "I'm so, so sorry."

As Jason hugged his sister, he heard an airplane passing overhead, looked up and saw the lights on its wings blinking as it descended toward Logan. Watching it pass, he was filled suddenly with a happy memory, from the summer of Kyle.

A night in July when the three of them had gone down to the beach with some sparklers left over from Theo and Linda's big Fourth party. They smoked a joint and lit the sparklers and ran around on the beach like idiots, Alexa laughing so hard she said she was going to pass out. Nothing had been particularly funny, but still, Alexa was laughing. Thinking about that night now, after so much had happened, Jason thought he finally knew why.

Alexa was laughing because it was ridiculous, wasn't it? To be as happy and lucky and dumb as the three of them were that night, young and together, awash in limitless summer. To be tearing around clutching little sparklers, under a vault of billions of stars. It was silly to not feel small, to not feel afraid, to miss the big and frightening world for a beach. But they had. That night, at least, those many perfect nights together, they had. And that was why Alexa was laughing. Because what else could anyone have done just then but laugh? What else could you ever do?

Jason closed his eyes and saw Kyle, wading into the water, heard himself and Alexa yelling, "Come back! Come back!" the light of Kyle's sparkler dimming as it burned out. But Kyle kept splashing off into the water, the two of them watching him go, feet stuck in the cool sand.

Alexa had hooked her arm around her brother's and rested her head on his shoulder, the wind making her hair dance. She gave Jason's arm a little squeeze and then said, "Let's go," and made a break for the water, Jason chasing after her, both of them running to find their friend. Kyle out ahead of them, just past where they could see. Kyle waiting, gone but not lost, out there somewhere in the night.

Chapter Nineteen

Alexa

IT FELT GOOD, and strange, to hug her brother. Just as it felt good, and strange, to hear him talk about Kyle, some glimpse into a life they had had together that she knew nothing about. She thought it would make her feel sad, or at least left out, to hear Jason talk about Kyle like that, but it didn't, not really.

It gave the past year some much-needed clarity, it lent some new shape to the brief summer when everything had seemed to click into place. Part of her wished she'd known then that Kyle and her brother were falling in love, were *in* love. But she also thought, standing there with her brother outside the hospital, that maybe it would have changed things. Even though the summer had ended so terribly, what had come before was the happiest she'd ever been, just as it was. And she didn't want to change that for anything.

Alexa pulled away from her brother, who gave her an awkward smile.

"Do we hug now? Is that a thing we do?"

"That can be a one-time thing if you want," Alexa said, sniffling and shivering. "It's cold. We should go back inside." She gave one last look to the glowing apartments, not knowing when she'd be outside next, and then headed back in, into the familiar and sallow waiting room, all the nurses looking haggard and frayed, though probably not more than she and Jason did. Jason had bags under his eyes, and his hair was in tangles. Though, Alexa supposed, that wasn't exactly anything new.

When they walked into the waiting room, it was almost empty. She figured Morgan and Scott had left. There wasn't really any reason for them to still be at the hospital. But then she saw Scott's jacket, crumpled on a chair, and heard someone's throat clearing behind her. She turned, and there was Scott, eyeing Jason warily, looking pale and guilty, his eyes round and dewy. He was like a pitiful cartoon, or one of those big-eyes paintings her aunt Ginny loved so much.

"Hey," Scott said. "Any word?"

Alexa shook her head. "Nope." She paused, not knowing if she even wanted to talk to him. "Where are Aimee's parents?"

"Uh . . . I don't know, actually. I mean, they went back there, and I haven't seen them since. But I was, like, not here for a little bit."

"Where'd you go?"

"To throw up."

"I'm so sorry about Aimee. Before, I shouldn't have—"

"It's O.K. I get it. I . . ." Scott shot a quick glance at Jason, looked back at Alexa. "You want to, uh, go talk somewhere?"

Jason threw up his hands. "I'm actually going to go find Morgan, if she's still around. See if she's O.K. So, it's all yours," he said, gesturing to the waiting room. He turned and walked off.

"I just want to say again that I'm sorry," Scott started once they were alone. "I shouldn't have lied. I guess, just, in my head, or something, it *wasn't* a lie, you know? We were together for a long time, so I just thought . . ."

"It's O.K., Scott. Really. It doesn't matter now. You love her. I get why you came. I would have done the same thing."

Scott's shoulders dropped, suddenly less tense. "Thanks. I mean, thanks for saying that."

"So what will you do now?"

He shrugged, frowned. "I don't know. Go home, I guess. My parents are probably freaking out. They know where I am, but . . . I should go home. They really liked Aimee."

Alexa nodded sadly. "Yeah."

Scott burst into tears. He put his hands over his eyes. "I'm sorry, I'm sorry. I just . . . I missed her so much, for so long, and now . . . Now I have to miss her forever. And I don't know what to do, I don't know what to do."

Alexa reached out and gave him a tight hug, Scott falling into her arms while he sobbed. "I don't know what to do, I don't know what to do," he repeated.

"It's O.K., Scott, it's O.K. It's O.K."

He hugged her until his body stopped shaking with sobs. He pulled away, looking very young, very lost. "I can't believe any of this happened."

"I don't think anyone can."

"What am I going to do?"

"I don't know," Alexa said. And that was true.

"You know," Scott said, sniffling, "a while ago, when I was feeling sad about Aimee, a friend told me that I just had to, like, be in the present and deal with things and, y'know, cross bridges when I got to them." He realized immediately what he'd just said. "Jesus," he whimpered, the tears coming again.

"Your friend was right, though," Alexa said.

"But how do we know when it's going to feel better?" Scott asked, pleadingly. "Will it ever feel better?"

Alexa shrugged sadly. She wished she knew for sure. "It has to eventually, right? The longer we keep living, the more time passes. I think it has to get easier at some point. For now, I guess all we can do is wait."

"You're right." Scott sighed. He shifted, gave Alexa another doleful look. "I wish we could have met, like, some other time, y'know? In some other life or something."

Alexa knew what he meant, or thought she did. She wished none of this had happened too. That the alternate dimension was out there somewhere, that she could just slip into it, where everything was better and easier. Where, sure, maybe she'd meet Scott, or some version of Scott, and things would be different. But that place felt even further away than it had in the chapel.

And the more she thought about it, the more she realized she didn't want to go searching for that other place. She wanted to stay where she was, as shitty and awful as it was just then. And she certainly didn't want to follow Scott into some what-if fantasy.

She smiled at Scott, did a little *what can you do?* with her hands. She took a step toward him, gave him another hug. He hugged her back, grateful for the comfort. "I'm so sorry about Aimee," Alexa said. Scott had lost someone today, someone very important to him. That was something big. Something Alexa knew too much about. "You'll be O.K.," she whispered—to him, to herself. "You'll be O.K."

"Thanks," Scott said. He hugged her for another second and then let go, wiping his eyes with his palms. "Thanks."

"If you need anything . . ." Alexa started to say, but Scott shook his head.

"No, I'll be fine. I'll be fine." He smiled at her. Alexa turned around and grabbed his coat from the chair and handed it to him.

"Thanks," Scott said again. "Thank you." He hesitated for a second. Then waved. "Well. I'm gonna go. Bye, Alexa."

She waved back. "Bye, Scott."

"Your parents are gonna be O.K."

"Yeah. I know."

Scott turned to leave, got halfway toward the door, then turned back to Alexa. "Oh, and tell your brother bye for me."

"I will."

And then Scott was gone, walking through the sliding doors as he pulled on his coat. Alexa was all but alone in the waiting room then, feeling a swell of sadness rise up in her. She looked at her phone. It was ten thirty. Nine hours since the accident, almost ten. She'd know something soon, she was convinced. Either way.

She got out her phone, opened Twitter, and scrolled through. She stopped when she saw a picture of Aimee. The *Globe* had tweeted out a story: "Eighteen-Year-Old Killed in Tobin Collapse Was Promising Drama Student." Alexa considered clicking on it, but thought better of it and put her phone back in her pocket.

She thought about Kyle's headline, from two days after he died: "Bourne Teenager Dead in Drunk Driving Accident."

It said nothing about who he was, about what—or whom—he'd loved, about where he had wanted to go in life. Alexa's parents, if they died, would have long obituaries. At least her mother would. But Kyle had just gotten the standard paragraph write-up, with information about the memorial service at the Elsings' and the private family service in Bourne, plus one follow-up article about the police cracking down on holiday weekend DUIs and underage drinking. She worried that was all Kyle would be remembered as, as time went on. That kid who died one summer. A sad cautionary tale whose name would slowly fade.

Alexa worried that the older she got and the more places her life took her, she'd forget about Kyle, a boy she knew once, when she was very young, who had died when he was very young too. The thought of that made her want to stay rooted in place forever, to preserve Kyle in her mind.

Kyle had helped open up the whole experience of that now faraway summer—guiding Alexa toward a heady sense of independence, a sense of being removed from the cloistered and ordered and intense life she lived back in Boston. It made her feel like she was growing up, evolving at an almost dizzying pace. But a good kind of dizzying. Roller coaster dizzying.

She felt it when she talked to Kyle, she felt it when her brother would join them in hanging out. And she felt it when she was with the other kids from Grey's.

Laurie was cool and easygoing and a little wild. On a few nights throughout the summer, Laurie invited people back to the place she shared with her cousin, Jacqui. Alexa had been too nervous to go the first time, shyly lying that she had to be home for a family thing. But the next time Laurie had a party, a week or so after the Fourth of July, Alexa felt emboldened enough by her new self that she agreed to go. Kyle had a closing shift that night, so he said he'd see her there after, meaning Alexa would have to go alone. Which scared her, but some new part of her knew that she could do it.

She got a ride with Davey and Courtney, a short drive to the little bungalow that Laurie and Jacqui had rented for the summer, a rundown kind of a thing on Governor Prence Road, already a half dozen cars parked outside. There was a fuzzy thump of music coming from the house, and Alexa found herself wondering how soon it would be before the neighbors complained. But she tried to push that anxious, scolding thought out of her head as she entered the house, immediately greeted by a billow of weed smell and a shrieking Laurie, who said, "Oh my God, you caaaaaame!"

Pretty much everyone there was from work. Amelia was even there, perking up when she saw Alexa, maybe thinking she had brought Jason with her. Maybe Alexa should have, but it hadn't occurred to her, in all the rush of excitement of even deciding to go, to invite him. Her manager Nate gave her a wave from across the living room, looking a little sheepish to be at a party with his younger employees, but also glazed and happy from beer and, probably, more.

"You wanna draaaank?" Laurie yelled in her scratchy, robust Laurie way.

"Sure," Alexa said. "Whatever you got."

"O.K., I'm gonna make you this rum thing, it's really good, I promise, and it's *strong*."

And indeed it was strong. Laurie reappeared from the little back kitchen a minute or two later with a red Solo cup, full to the top. Alexa took a sip and it burned, but not in a bad way.

"Oh my God, cheeeers!" Laurie said, sloshing her cup into Alexa's and wrapping an arm around her. "This is fun. We're gonna have fun."

Laurie was right. After downing about one and a half of Laurie's rum concoctions, Alexa felt loose, expansive. Like she was in love with everyone at Grey's, in love with everyone that summer. She found herself at one point sitting on the big, enveloping living room couch, talking to Davey—kind, dopey Davey—about his plans for the navy: where he hoped to sail to, what he hoped to see.

"You know, I think it's really cool," Alexa said, realizing she might be a little slurry but figuring everyone else probably was too. "That you're just, like, doing your own thing. You know? You're just gonna go out into the world and figure it out."

Davey shrugged. "I mean, I'd probably rather be partying at college, but, y'know, money."

Alexa nodded. "Yeah, yeah. Money. Ugh."

Davey smiled. "Easy to hate it when you have it!"

Alexa laughed. "Yeah, I guess so. Sorry. I must sound like such a brat all the time."

Davey gave her a little bump with his shoulder. "Nah. Everyone here likes you."

Alexa wanted to hug him. "Oh, good! That makes me happy. I love everyone. This is, like, the best summer of my life. It's crazy to think that life could be like this all the time, you know? Just working and hanging out and not, like, always trying to get toward something bigger and better." She caught herself. "Not that you're, like, not trying to better your lives or whatever. I just mean . . ."

Davey smiled, nodded. "I know what you mean. It's a fun job. Summer jobs are fun."

Alexa rested her head on his shoulder. "I hope you'll be safe, in the navy."

"Not a lot of naval battles happening these days."

"That's true," Alexa said, suddenly feeling the room begin to spin, just a little. "Hey, I'm gonna go outside, get some fresh air. You wanna come?"

"Nah," Davey said, eying Laurie's cousin, Jacqui, sitting across the room. "I'm gonna stay inside."

Alexa said O.K. and gave Davey a quick kiss on the check, then stood up and wobbled out to the scraggly little backyard, where some kids were smoking, Courtney Price telling some story that had everyone in stitches.

"Hey, Alexa," Courtney said evenly, but not in an unfriendly way.

"Hey, guys," Alexa said, feeling a little less spinny now that she was outside, but suddenly nervous about an interaction with scary Courtney and these other kids, who didn't work at Grey's and seemed a little older, Nate's age maybe.

"I was just telling them about Kyle and that bitchy lady last week."

"Oh God, the one with the declined credit card?"

"Yeah."

"What a nightmare. But Kyle handled it so well. He shut her down!" Courtney laughed. "Shut. Her. *Down*."

The other kids all seemed to grow bored with hearing a story about somewhere they didn't work, for a second time, so they drifted off, making their way back inside to get more drinks. Which left Alexa and Courtney alone in the yard together.

"Kyle's great . . ." Alexa said, mostly just trying to fill the silence.

"Yeah," Courtney agreed. "I really hope he actually comes to New York with me."

Alexa was surprised. "I thought he was for sure gonna go?"

"I don't know," Courtney said, running a hand through her long, silky hair. "Kyle likes to talk big, but it's tough, with his mom. I think it would be hard to leave her behind."

Alexa had gotten vague intimations, from Kyle and others, that Kyle's mom was not always well, maybe a drug thing, maybe a mental illness thing, maybe both. She nodded. "Yeah. I bet that would be hard."

"You're lucky," Courtney said, turning to face Alexa.

Alexa was taken aback. Courtney Price, cool and gorgeous and New York–bound Courtney Price, was telling Alexa that *she* was lucky? "What do you mean?" was all she could muster in response.

"Because. You can do anything," Courtney said matter-of-factly. "Your family isn't crazy, they have money, you're smart, you're clearly, like, a good person. You'll be fine wherever. You're lucky."

Alexa had never felt lucky, or unlucky, really. She'd always just felt like her one-track self, until that summer, anyway, when new and unexpected possibilities had begun to glimmer on the horizon.

"Take advantage of that," Courtney said, dumping out the remainder of her probably warm beer in the grass. "I know Kyle's jealous of you."

"Kyle is jealous of *me*?"

Courtney shrugged. "Maybe not *jealous*. But if he had everything you had going for you? He'd do a whole hell of a lot. Anyway . . ." she said, turning back toward the house. "I'm going to grab a fresh drink. You want something?"

Alexa shook her head, lost in thought about what Courtney had just said. "No, I'm . . . I'll be in in a second."

Courtney sauntered off and Alexa stood in the backyard, thinking about Kyle, about herself, about possibility. Courtney was right, of course. Between Alexa and Kyle, he was the one who would really seize on opportunity. Like the kind of opportunity that Alexa had, just because of what she was born into.

Maybe that was when Alexa had really decided. It had taken a year, and a great tragedy, to summon up the courage to actually act on it, to begin telling her parents, but maybe that was the turning point, standing there on that little patch of crabgrass, the warm and rocking hug of alcohol making Alexa's mind loop and wander.

Remembering that night in Laurie Gomes's backyard, that charged and revealing moment, Alexa felt a swell of something urgent, demanding rise up in her. She knew that if Kyle was watching her from somewhere, he would be mad if she didn't make good on at least some of the promises they'd made together. Maybe she wouldn't own five houses. But she'd go to all those places. For Kyle. For herself. Maybe that's what Kyle would gradually become: some part of her, an inner voice pushing her, encouraging her along. Eventually she might not be able to tell the difference between his voice and hers, but maybe that was O.K. Maybe that was how you kept moving, day after day, year after year.

Alexa wished she could hug Kyle just one more time, muss his hair and coo "You're so prettyyyy" in a fake gushy tone. (He'd pretend to blush, but then say "I know.") She missed her friend. But she also felt herself, there in the hospital, waiting on news of her parents, saying goodbye to him, letting him go. She closed her eyes and pictured him, a year or two older, happy and excited, walking up the stairs from Penn Station. Taking in the city, and then, with one of his satisfied smiles, disappearing into the crowd.

Then Alexa heard her brother, calling her name.

"Alexa! Alexa!"

She opened her eyes and saw Jason by the doors. Two stretchers were being wheeled inside behind him. It was them. She knew, instantly, that it was them. She ran to her brother as the stretchers were swarmed with nurses and doctors.

"Finally got them out of their car thirty minutes ago!" an EMT was saying. "Male has a skull fracture, female has a collapsed lung. Both have internal hemorrhaging."

"Oh my God," Alexa said, as she tried to move toward the stretchers but was pushed away by a nurse. Theo and Linda were whisked past Jason and Alexa, a doctor yelling to get them into separate ORs. Alexa managed to catch a glimpse of her mother's face, her eyelids fluttering, her head in a brace. She saw her father's feet, only one shoe on, the other foot caked in blood and dust.

The sight was horrific, but they were *alive*. At least right then, they were alive. Jason gave Alexa a panicked look. She shook her head, said, "They're going to be fine," and grabbed his hand. They stood there, the Elsing kids, holding on to each other, as they watched their parents disappear down the hallway, trailed by nurses and doctors. "I'm here," Alexa kept saying. "I'm here, I'm here, I'm here."

And then Jason was saying it too, clutching his sister's hand.

"I'm here. I'm here. Alexa, I'm here."

Epilogue

Morgan

MORGAN DIDN'T WANT to say goodbye. To have the others tell her they were so sorry again, to have them give her the same look Dr. Koskinen had given her when her father first got his diagnosis. The one that said she was some sad orphan. So she told Skyler she was going to get a soda and left the waiting room, walking down the hallway and then slipping out the door, out into the night, into a new world where her father didn't exist.

She walked aimlessly for a while, just wanting to put some distance between her and the hospital. She never wanted to go back there again. Never wanted to be reminded of her mother, working there in a happier life, of her father lying on that table.

She thought about going home, but couldn't face that quite yet. So she walked south, through Beacon Hill, past the Public Garden, into the theater district. The rest of the city seemed to be carrying on like normal, though the streets were emptier than they might have been on a regular night.

There were some people sitting in bars, a group of foreigners, speaking in some Russian-sounding language, stumbling drunkenly down Tremont Street. As she turned down Kneeland Street, Morgan realized that she was near a diner her father used to take her to when things with her mom were bad at home, one of the few twenty-four-hour places in Boston. He and his cop buddies used to get coffee there at late hours, shooting the breeze after patrol, telling war stories. Her father had seemed to know all the waitresses, flirting with them a little, even though they were all mostly old and crabby. Maybe that's why he did it.

Morgan figured she could go there, sit for a while. Maybe one of the waitresses would remember her. When she got there, a little corner place by South Station, it was mostly empty, a few loners sitting at the counter. Morgan settled into a booth and ordered a coffee, the waitress casting her a suspicious eye, wondering what this teenager was doing there by herself on a school night. But she didn't ask any questions, so Morgan sat there quietly, sipping her coffee, trying to imagine what her next move might be. She'd been walking for a while, and it was almost midnight. The T would be shutting down soon, and she didn't have the money for a cab home. Maybe she'd just wait it out at the diner.

She sat there, looking out the window, watching cars rattle by, on their way to South Station to drop someone off for a late bus or a late train, or to pick someone up. It was nice to imagine that there were still people coming and going, the city forever expanding and contracting, even as it was rocked by yet another terrible thing.

When the Marathon bombing happened, Morgan had watched Boston become something she'd never seen, not even when the Red Sox won the World Series: It was communal, bonded, forged together. She thought that whole "Boston Strong" thing was corny, but there was something true about it too. She felt a deep, aching affection for the city just then, even though there was maybe nothing left in it for her. Not her dad's friends even, not Mike and Pat and the rest of them. They all had their own lives, their own kids and grandkids. Morgan hated the idea of being a burden, so she would probably not ask for their help.

She sat at the diner for hours, doing nothing but drinking coffee and looking out the window. She dozed off a few times before being woken by the waitress, asking, in an annoyed voice, if she needed anything else. Morgan shook her head no each time. "Just some more coffee, please."

At four A.M., the city still and quiet, Morgan decided to leave, saying thank you to the waitress, and walking, both buzzing and tired, out into the night. She retraced her steps, back past the Majestic, past the Common, through the narrow, pretty streets of Beacon Hill. When she got to the other side of the hill, instead of turning toward the hospital, Morgan walked toward the river, finding the Longfellow Bridge and crossing it, over the Charles, into Cambridge, which was even quieter than Boston. She walked quickly, to stay warm and to evade anyone who might be lurking. She crossed the MIT campus, and then down Mass Ave, all the way to Harvard Square.

The square was empty, the traffic signals blinking and changing for no one but her. There was something hushed and dreamlike about it, being the only person walking around this normally bustling place. She walked past Harvard Yard, past the newsstand, and then into the pit by the Red Line entrance. She sat on a step and crouched into a little ball to keep out the cold. It was almost six then, and some light was starting to bleed into the sky. The T would be running again soon, and Morgan finally felt tired enough to go home. She'd get on the Red Line and ride it all the way to Ashmont, and then she'd be there, back where this surreal and terrible day had started.

She looked up and saw a light flickering on in the newsstand across the way. A man was outside stacking up the day's newspapers. Morgan got up and walked over, wanting to see the front pages of the *Globe* and the *Herald.* Of course it was all coverage of the bridge, huge photos of the gaping yawn where the Tobin used to be, headlines saying 46 dead, 125 injured. She wondered where Alexa and Jason's parents fit in those numbers.

Some part of her hoped to see something about her father, but of course he would never merit the front page, even on a completely uneventful day. The bridge would have to stand in for him. The bigger tragedy representing Morgan's own relatively small one, somehow. Morgan scanned all the headlines and then walked back to the T, which was open now, early commuters riding the escalator down.

Standing on the platform, Morgan suddenly remembered something she'd forgotten in all the chaos of the hospital. How had she forgotten the envelope, the one with her father's note inside? She dug around in her bag and found it, a little crumpled, her name scrawled in her father's familiar handwriting. She looked at it, but did not open it. She was not ready just yet. She felt the tunnel wind of the train approaching and stepped back from the edge, the T coming whining into the station.

Once on board, still holding the unopened envelope, Morgan put her head against the glass of the window and watched as stops went by, people entering and leaving the car. There were so many people in Boston. She wasn't sure she'd ever really noticed them all before—how many tired moms, how many college kids looking like they were waiting for something, how many solitary men staring into space as they thought about who knows what. Maybe no one was alone, she thought, as long as there were all these people.

The train rattled out of Kendall and then out onto the bridge, and there was the skyline, the Hancock and the Prudential, the slow drone of Storrow Drive. It was such a pretty place, ugly as it was for Morgan just then.

She closed her eyes and imagined what it would be like to go home, to put her key in the lock and open the door and find no one there. Of course she would be put somewhere, maybe with Aunt Jill in Nashua, maybe somewhere else. But that morning, for those minutes or hours, Morgan would be alone in the only house she'd ever known.

Morgan sat on the train and tried to imagine that bit of time, and then tried to imagine life past it. As much as she felt sad, as much as the world felt dark and closed around her, she couldn't help but also feel infinitely curious. About what might be coming, about where her life could possibly take her. She was so devastated; how heavy that felt as the train rumbled out into the thin early morning light. But she was also relieved, in some deep part of herself, lying under the ruins, that she was still alive.

Everything would be different now. Everything would be strange. But she was still herself, still Morgan, still the girl with bitten nails and purple hair, still in her body, in her skin, still young. Life can end, suddenly. But it can also stretch on and on and on. And there, on the bridge, Morgan felt her future reaching out very far. She would someday beat this sadness, she'd find the end of it and then pass on into something else.

The train arced over the river, and Morgan wished the best for all of them. For Jason and Alexa. For their parents. For Scott. For Skyler and her sister. Morgan doubted that they'd ever see each other again. She had the feeling that morning that she might not be in Boston for much longer, that there was somewhere else she was supposed to be. The adventure would be in finding out just where that was, and what roads and sturdy bridges could take her there. Morgan opened her eyes and there was the sun, beginning to dance on the Charles, the train wheels whistling as they carried her toward whatever was next. Whatever might happen after all of this.

Acknowledgments

Many thanks to the eminently capable and supportive team at Razorbill, particularly Marissa Grossman for her level-headed faith, encouragement, and insight; to Brianne Johnson at Writers House for facilitating with compassionate expertise; to family and friends who have been generous readers, sounding boards, and hand-holders over the past two years; and to Crystal Gomes, whose guiding spirit was felt throughout, as it will be always.